The Black Cat Murders

Karen Baugh MENUHIN

Published by Little Cat Publishing

Copyright © 2019 by Karen Baugh Menuhin

Front cover: National Trust Images/Arnhel de Serra. View through the Topiary Garden to the east front at Chastleton House, Oxfordshire.

First paperback and ebook edition March 2019

ISBN: 979-8-3792350-9-3

For Jonathan,
Scarlett & Hugo
Baugh.
With Love

CHAPTER 1

Spring 1921

'Rather an unlikely murder weapon,' I remarked. 'A soprano.'

'Well, yes, yes, Lennox,' I heard Cyril Fletcher bluster, despite the crackles on the telephone line, 'the circumstances were peculiar. Actually, the whole damn event was peculiar — although earls are like that.'

I had sympathy with the sentiment, but Cyril Fletcher, our family doctor since before I saw the light of day, wasn't making any sense at all.

'Why were you there, Cyril?' I asked, not unreasonably. 'You hate opera as much as I do.'

'Invited, of course.' His voice rose in indignation as he recounted the incident. 'Virtually ordered to go by the Earl. Forced to sit through three hours of Tosca, with all the bells and whistles. Then just as the soprano burst into some sort of tortured lament over Crispin Gibbons, the trap-door collapsed under their combined weight and they vanished from sight with an ear-shattering shriek.

And it had already been uncommonly ear-shattering up to that point, let me tell you.'

'Well, at least it put an end to the whole palaver,' I said.

'If only it had! There was the usual call for a doctor in the house and everybody immediately looked at me, so I had to go and officiate. The lady had landed on Crispin and was only shaken. He, on the other hand, was flattened and quite dead.'

'I assume said soprano is built on traditional lines, then?'

'Dame Gabriel Forsyth – and yes, very much so. Crispin was no beanpole either. Rotund sort of chap, bit like an overgrown cherub actually,' Cyril replied.

'But what on earth makes you think this could be anything other than an accident?'

'Because they'd been prancing about on the stage all week, having rehearsals and dressing up and what have you. The full show was put on in the evening for invited guests, me included, and it was only at the very end of the whole rigmarole that the trap-door failed. At first I took it for a simple misfortune and told the police so in no uncertain terms, but now I'm having second thoughts…' His voice trailed off in doubt.

'Well, it probably failed *because* they'd been bouncing around on it, Cyril.'

'Yes, that's what everyone says, and I'd agree with you if it wasn't for the strange commotion with the cat just before it all happened. And I was the one who picked up the body.' He let out an exasperated sigh.

'What cat?'

'Black cat. It rushed on stage, then raced off across the orchestra. At the time I thought nothing of it. After the accident, the police tried to persuade me that there was malicious intent, which I argued was poppycock. But now I am not so sure. It's been troubling me.' He paused. 'Lennox, I think there's mischief afoot.'

'But Cyril, the chances are too random.' I mused over the run of events. 'The lady could have landed first and he'd have just bounced off.'

'Exactly! So nobody would know who was to be killed,' Cyril exclaimed – as if this were somehow rational. 'You have to go, you know, Lennox.'

'Cyril, I am most certainly not going to gatecrash the Earl's country pile and snoop on his guests. Particularly based on such a hare-brained notion as you've just told me.'

'Lennox, don't you ever read your correspondence?' Cyril retorted snappily. 'You were invited ages ago – it's Caroline's marriage.'

'Good Lord, really?' I'd heard some vague rumours about Caroline, but I had better things to do than listen to tattle about weddings and whatnot.

'The nuptials are next weekend and the Earl has laid on another full-blown production on the eve of the ceremony.'

'What? It sounds appalling. Why the devil is he inflicting opera on people?'

'Because he's determined to hand over his only daughter in style – and the bridegroom is obsessed with opera.'

That raised my eyebrows. 'Nonsense. I can't imagine Caroline marrying someone who even *likes* opera.'

'Well, there you are. No accounting for the tender heart, is there?' Cyril said.

'Doesn't happen to have a lot of money, does he, this groom?' I suggested.

'Of course he does, and the Earl needs every penny of it. Now get a move on, Lennox, you should be there already. I'm surprised you haven't been reminded – you know what the old man is like. Not to mention Caroline.'

I knew exactly what they were like. Lord Neville, Earl of Bloxford, known to the commonality as 'His Lordship', Brigadier Bloxford had never really left Army life behind him. His only daughter, Lady Caroline, was a no-nonsense country girl whom I had known virtually since the cradle. Neither of them beat about bushes.

'Oh very well, I'll go if I must, and you had better be there to point the way, Cyril, because your idea of murder by opera singer sounds absurd,' I warned him.

'Ha, not a chance. I've got better things to do than have my ears scourged by any more caterwauling. I've already passed my regrets to the wedding party – I'm off to Tuscany. See you after Easter. Good luck, old chap.' He rang off.

I placed the receiver back on its candlestick stand and stood, irresolute, with my hand to my chin. Doctor Cyril Fletcher had been our family physician since before I was born and I'd just passed my thirtieth year. He'd done his best to prevent my lamented parents from falling off their respective twigs – although in the end, they'd both succumbed. Nevertheless, I considered it entirely infra dig to call me up and demand that I go off and detect a murder, especially since no one thought it was a murder, and then declare he was shoving off to Italy.

It's not that I wasn't keen on detecting – quite the reverse, actually. I'd developed a certain taste for sleuthing last Christmas when I'd been accused of murder by Chief Inspector Swift – a man whose path I hope never to cross again – and had to track the murderer myself. That had taught me the rudiments, and I'd invested in a couple more volumes of Sherlock Holmes to expand my knowledge. But I had no desire to go anywhere near a society wedding – even if the bride was a childhood friend.

It had been a long cold winter but spring had finally sprung and I wanted to make the most of the bright sunny days fishing and shooting here at my home, the Manor, near Ashton Steeple. I'd already been out every day for almost a week shooting pigeon in the woods with my dog, Mr Fogg. I admit, I may have been rather slow to pick up my correspondence and might have overlooked the odd missive, but I really did have more interesting things to do.

I stuck my hands in my pockets, and, with my thoughts perturbed, went off to my library. It was looking particularly spruce today as the maids had been spring cleaning and all the leather-bound books gleamed; they smelt of lanolin and neats-foot oil, and I could barely make out the usual whiff of damp, mould and must. The grate had been swept out, the fire set but not yet lit, for in spring we only had fires in the evening. I rifled through the pile of papers the maids had stacked in a wicker basket on my desk and found a telegram that must have arrived a few days ago.

To Major Heathcliff Lennox. STOP. Where are you? STOP. Come immediately. STOP. Brigadier Bloxford. Bloxford Hall. STOP.

Must say, it was hardly the sort of invitation you'd expect to a wedding.

Just as I was quietly contemplating the turn of events, my aged retainer walked in with the dinner gong. He bonged it three times, then turned to leave. He'd taken to doing that of late and it was becoming quite annoying.

'Greggs, will you stop that and come back here,' I called after him.

He returned slowly and stood in the doorway – straight-backed, paunch to the fore, togged in his usual butlering outfit of black tails, dickie, starched shirt and collar, with an expression of weary patience, as though I were being entirely unreasonable.

'Why don't you just announce the meal as usual?' I asked.

'I am saving my voice, sir. For the singing,' he intoned.

'What singing?'

'Gilbert and Sullivan, sir. I have joined a group. I am a tenor,' he said with some pride.

'Good God, not you too, Greggs? What is this passion for opera?'

'Operetta, sir. It is amusing, sir.'

'Unlike the real thing?'

'Quite, sir.'

'Greggs?'

'Sir?'

'Seems I should be at some wedding beano. Didn't happen to see an invitation, did you?'

He looked meaningfully at the mantelpiece, where a fancy gold-lettered envelope rested against the clock. 'I placed it in plain sight, sir.'

'That clock hasn't worked for decades, Greggs, what's the point in putting it there?'

'Because you never look at the papers on your desk, sir.'

'Right, well, never mind that.' I snatched the invitation up and tore it open, muttering to myself. 'Brigadier Bloxford invites Major Heathcliff Lennox ... Wedding ... Lady Caroline ... Mister Hiram Chisholm....What sort of name is Hiram? I mean, *is* it a name?'

'American, sir?'

'I suppose it must be,' I ran my hands through my hair. 'Right: packing required, Greggs. Load up the old trunk with the stiff rig would you, old chap, it's going to be top hat and tails. And I'm told there may be some detecting involved, so I'm going to need jam jars, tweezers and a magnifying glass.'

'Certainly, sir. May I remind you that your dinner is waiting to be served.'

He turned and left as I looked after him. His lack of curiosity was out of character, and his usual hangdog demeanour held a hint of quiet amusement – he was hiding something. I followed briskly in his footsteps to the dining room, where he had raised the domed lid from a plate of roast spatchcock pigeon and waited for me to sit. Which I did, because it was the pigeon I had shot that very morning and it smelled delicious.

'Wouldn't you like to know why?' I quizzed him as he spooned boiled sprouts onto my plate.

'Would it be concerning the death of Sir Crispin Gibbons?'

'How the devil did you know about that?' I spluttered. 'Were you listening in on the telephone again, Greggs?'

'No, sir, I have received certain information. Excuse me, sir, I will commence with your trunk now.'

He departed the room as he said this, leaving me to mull over his insinuation. I hastened through my dinner, excellent though it was, and skipped pudding to track him down to my bedroom, where he was inspecting the contents of the open wardrobe.

'What information, Greggs?'

He placed a couple of formal shirts into my packing case and straightened up to brush a few flecks of dust from his waistcoat.

'My nephew, Richard Dicks, is the head footman at Bloxford Hall, sir,' he intoned.

'Is he indeed. Excellent! What did young Dicks say?'

Ha! I thought: this could help me slay the doubts of the doctor before I'd even left the Manor.

'I couldn't possibly say, sir.'

'Yes, you can, Greggs. Come on, spit it out.'

'The information was given in confidence, sir.'

'Nonsense. If I do have to carry out any detecting, I'll need all the help I can get.'

'I'm sure you will, sir.' Greggs carried on emptying drawers and folding shirts.

'This is about that bottle of Jameson, isn't it?'

I received no reply. He slid my indoor shoes into a canvas sack, then wedged them tightly in the bottom of the trunk as he held me to ransom.

'Damn it, man. That whiskey was a gift from my Uncle Charles,' I argued. 'I was saving it for the grouse season.'

Nothing – not even a sniff of disdain. He carried on gathering up the small stuff and whatnots and stowing it in the side pockets of the trunk. We'd been through the Great War together, Greggs and I; he'd been my batman while I'd flown aeroplanes into battle against the Boche. We'd had spells on the front line too, which had gouged deep scars in our hearts and minds. It was mostly thoughts of this old place and the quiet country life here that had kept us going. We'd returned at the war's end, two years ago, wearied and troubled. I had immersed myself in country pursuits and Greggs had taken a liking to good Irish whiskey – and I knew he'd had his eye on my bottle of Jameson.

'I haven't even taken a sniff of it yet,' I objected, and sank onto the edge of my four-poster bed. Once he had something in his sights, Greggs could be as dogged as a bloodhound. And he'd probably help himself to the stuff once I was out of the door anyway.

'Oh, very well, Greggs, it's yours. Spill the beans – and it had better be good.'

He stopped folding handkerchiefs and drew up his paunch in a dignified manner.

'Sir Crispin was the head of the Noble House of Opera singers – an amateur group who perform renditions for gentlefolk at homes of distinction.'

'You mean they troop around the country singing for their supper at upper-crust shindigs.'

'Only in the Cotswolds, sir. There are sufficient estates surrounding Oxford to keep them fully engaged.'

'Very true,' I agreed, knowing full well the place was awash with toffs.

'The unhappy event happened during the recital the night before last. The trap-door gave way.'

'Yes, Cyril Fletcher already told me. That bottle is not going to be forthcoming unless you've got something more enlightening, Greggs.'

'There is more, sir. The staff were of the opinion that there was something peculiar about Sir Crispin.' Greggs paused as he spoke, clothes-brush in hand, then recommenced carefully whisking dust from my best grey tailcoat.

'Is that it?' I asked.

'If only it were, sir. There is lurid talk.'

'Really? Lurid, eh.'

'Sir Crispin had a habit of *dressing up*, sir, and not just for the opera. He was known to attire himself in frocks. Ladies' frocks.' He nodded for emphasis.

'Good Lord. And this wasn't connected to the opera?'

'It was not.'

'Why on earth would he want to dress in frocks?'

'He had a penchant for such things, sir. The opera singers are currently housed on Brigadier Bloxford's estate. Apparently, Sir Crispin would dress himself up, apply maquillage and rouge, and depart surreptitiously from one of the rear gates. Then later in the evening he would come back again. He was observed a number of times by the staff, sir.'

Well, this did add another complexion to the story: perhaps he was murdered after all – most likely by someone who didn't like men in frocks. Although it did seem rather extreme – a quiet word in the ear would probably have done the trick.

'This investigation could be a touch on the racy side, Greggs.'

'Indeed, sir. Will you be requiring a hat?' he asked, reaching to the top shelf of the wardrobe.

'Yes, the topper and fedora.'

'Not a deerstalker, sir?'

'Very amusing, Greggs,' I retorted, and strode off in the direction of my dog.

Mr Fogg was curled up in the kitchen where he'd retired after our long day out. Fogg had an aversion to anything dead so I'd had to pick up my own birds while he gambolled in the green sprung woods. An undersized golden spaniel, Fogg led a dog's life of treats, walks and sleep and was my closest companion. I knelt beside him, gave him a half biscuit I'd saved, patted his head and ruffled his fur. He gazed at me with chocolate-brown eyes full of affection, and wagged his stump of a tail. It didn't take much to persuade him to leave the comfort of his basket and join me for an evening stroll in the calm of my overgrown gardens, where strange puzzles, such as fellows in frocks and mischief and murder, are best contemplated.

CHAPTER 2

I'd exhausted my funds last year on a gleaming black three-litre Bentley tourer, a machine of beauty, power and indifferent reliability. It was stabled in the old coach house, a place of cold and damp, so starting the car required a great deal of cranking, bruised knuckles and quiet cursing to coax it into life.

I motored around under bright sunshine to the front of the house and set the servants to work. Actually, it was the boot-boy, Tommy Jenkins, and I who loaded the paraphernalia, as Greggs was suffering a bad back as usual. But once packed with trunk, dog and various essential what-have-yous such as Fogg's basket, balls, bowls and blanket, I set off for the hills and vales of the deepest Cotswolds.

The Bentley ate the miles as I raced down highways and through country lanes. I wore my customary goggles, gloves, scarf and flying cap against the early spring chill. No doubt, I reflected, Greggs would be looking forward to my bottle of Jameson, though he'd have a task on his hands – I'd locked it in the tantalus and the key was snug and safe in my waistcoat pocket. It would take him hours to pick the lock.

The sun petered out as I sped up-country, and a persistent drizzle set in to drench me and the car. I had to stop to close the roof as Fogg had become increasingly sodden and had been eyeing me with baleful looks.

Some time later, as the rain gave way to fitful sunshine, I pulled up outside Bloxford Hall's handsome Elizabethan facade. The enormous front door slowly opened to reveal a small man wearing a butler's uniform that looked at least two sizes too large for him. It would have fitted him once, but little changed at Bloxford and a diminishing butler was seen as no reason to renew an outfit.

'Greetings, Benson.' I trotted damply up the worn stone steps to the huge columned portico and hailed the ancient retainer.

'Ah, Major Lennox, sir. We were expecting you some days ago,' his voice quavered. 'We have opera …' He trailed off, then wound back up. 'Singers for the wedding, you know …' He puttered to a halt; I didn't know if it was through age or lack of enthusiasm for the subject.

'Yes, yes, excellent, Benson.' My goggles had started to steam up as I entered the interior so I whipped them off and peeled away my soggy outerwear onto a footman in the green and black house livery. He held them at arm's length as they dripped on the black and white chequered tiles.

'Boot room, old chap' I advised him.

He looked at me with hound-dog eyes in a long face, framed by lank brown hair falling each side of a middle parting.

'They're all wet,' he complained.

'Yes, I know. Would you hang them up to dry, please.'

He didn't move; he stood there looking at me.

'Name?' I asked.

'Dawkins, I am. Just a dogsbody. Dogsbody Dawkins. Do this, do that. Never a minutes peace. Always running about, no thanks nor nothin'…' he whinged, then finally trailed off, dripping, in the direction of the boot room.

Good Lord, the service round here certainly hadn't improved.

Foggy was racing around the old butler's bandy legs.

'Don't give the car a thought, Benson,' I told him as the poor fellow bent at the knees trying to stroke the excited dog. 'I'm sure some of the other chaps will unload it.'

A young man, also wearing the green and black house uniform, came from the nether regions to stand smartly in front of me. I dropped the keys into his extended, white-gloved hand.

'Good morning, sir,' he greeted me. 'I'm Dicks, sir,' he said with a little bow. 'Head footman.'

'Nephew of Greggs, I take it.'

'Indeed, sir.' He didn't look at all like Greggs, which was of great benefit to the fellow. Upright, slim, ginger hair and brows, freckles and an air of earnestness in a young face untouched by the worries of the world.

'Excellent! Greetings, Dicks.'

'Erm, you have some dog hairs on your jacket, sir. I could brush them off. Won't take a minute,' Dicks reached into his topcoat pocket and withdrew a small brush.

'No, thank you.' I took a step back and swept my arm across the old tweed shooting jacket I habitually wore. 'Not necessary, Dicks. Just have the car unloaded, will you.'

'Certainly, sir. I'll call some of the staff. Won't take a minute, sir.' He nodded enthusiastically. 'Mister Benson will show you to your rooms, sir.'

We both turned to watch the old man totter into the expanse of the hall, his white hair a frizzled crown – he looked as though he'd recently been struck by lightning, and moved as if he had, too. He doddered to the grand staircase with Fogg cavorting around him and they both set off to the upper reaches together. A line of Dicks and footmen laden with trunk, basket, dog bowls and whatnots from the car came through and slowly followed old Benson up the stairs at a stately pace.

My rooms were at the front and rather nice they were, too – nothing like an earl's pile for a touch of luxury, although this particular pile had seen better days – actually, it had seen better centuries. The gilded wallpaper, gaily painted with red and blue parrots cavorting on tropical greenery, was curled at the edges and held in place by rusty drawing pins. The varnish on the flaking wood panelling was crackled with age and the Persian rugs were as moth-eaten as the blue velvet curtains.

I wandered about my quarters while Dicks organised the servants unpacking my gear and stashing it away in a dressing room the size of my drawing room at home. The bedroom was even larger, and Fogg ferreted about under the massive four-poster bed in the hope of startling the mice while I noted the depth of the club chairs set before the marble fireplace. Fine hunting prints hung on the walls and I perused them before testing the eccentricities of the electric light fittings, which mostly didn't work. There was a handsome desk and leather captain's chair stationed in the window embrasure overlooking the long drive. I admired the view – ancient trees lined the carriageway, greening woodland in the distance, an adjoining deer park and horse paddocks beyond neatly trimmed lawns. If I hadn't known that the whole house was in danger of crumbling into woodworm-eaten dust I'd have been terribly impressed.

'Would you like a tray, sir? Coffee and sandwiches, perhaps?' Dicks asked as he smoothed the bed linen, then shook out the hangings, sneezing with the dust.

'Umm, yes, good idea, Dicks. And a treat from the kitchens for Mr Fogg.'

'Certainly, sir.' Dicks grinned and left, the other chaps following behind. I must say, Greggs's young nephew might be the saving of this place. Benson had wandered off – probably forgotten where he was going.

'Lennox, about time too! Where have you been?' Lady Caroline Bloxford blew in. Fogg raced over to her, yelped, then flaked to the floor on his back for a tummy-rub. She knelt to give him a hearty ruffle and he remained there in happy abandon as she came and kissed me on the cheek.

'Greetings, old girl. I believe congratulations are in order.' I pecked her in return.

'Don't change the subject,' she retorted sharply, looking up at me – she'd always been bossy, and a dose of the tender emotions didn't appear to have softened her up very much. 'You were supposed to be here days ago,' she declared. 'We called you. No one *ever* answers your telephone. We sent telegrams, too.'

'Greggs is not allowed to answer the telephone, it just confuses things. And he's saving his voice,' I explained. 'Anyway, why drag me into this? It's not as though you can't get married without me.'

'Daddy's been fretting, he's been asking for you. And Hiram's family are so utterly nice,' she said with a slight frown. 'I'm so glad you're here.' Caroline regarded me with intelligent green eyes in a matter-of-fact face, her straight brown hair held back by an Alice band. She was dressed in the usual country style – sensible brown shoes, tweed jacket and skirt, faded green jersey with a simple pearl necklace.

'What's wrong with being nice? Damn sight better than having a bunch of curmudgeons knocking around the place,' I remarked with a smile – despite the ticking off, I was very pleased to see her again.

'Because *I* have to be nice too and it's driving me doolally.' She plumped herself down on the bed, looked at me dryly then suddenly grinned as we dropped back into our old childhood rapport.

I laughed, then took on a serious note because I'd been rather surprised by the speed of the romance. 'You're not selling out, are you, old stick? I mean, I know things are a bit tricky for the Brigadier, but leaping into matrimony for the money isn't going to make anyone happy in the long run.'

It was her turn to laugh and her face lit up. 'No, nothing like that. We're quite dotty about each other, actually. But his family *does* have oodles of money — they're from Texas. Hiram's a rancher at heart – happiest riding a horse and rounding up cows. He's learning to be an English gentleman – it's a hoot! But I need a dose of reality, Lennox. I need you and your stupid obsession with tying fly lures and shooting and walking your brainless dog. You understand why things are funny, even when they're not.'

I went over and gave her a hug, poor girl. A wedding on this scale, even if it was going to take place at the house, was pretty tense and she had no mother or sisters to give her support.

'Dicks seems a useful addition.'

'Yes, he is. Poor Benson is entirely decrepit. We've tried to persuade him to retire, but he won't, he just totters around the place like a clockwork toy slowly running out of whizz.'

I smiled and turned to the topic uppermost in my mind. 'Cyril Fletcher told me your fiancé was mad keen on opera,' I said, wondering how a Texan cowboy could have acquired a taste for highbrow warbling.

'No, what nonsense,' she laughed. 'Hiram's parents asked father if they could arrange the entertainment as part of the wedding celebrations. Hiram's mother, Ruth, has highbrow tastes and is a patron of the arts in Texas. I tried to convince her that we are simple country folk, but she won't listen. She has a dreadful man who advises her on all things cultural, and he's not even English, he's German! It's all quite ridiculous.'

'But why opera, for heaven's sake?'

'The old theatre in the grounds – you remember: we used to play dressing-up there when we were children. Hiram's mother saw it when they stayed with us last year and declared it to be charming. Then their German chap said he knew an opera troupe and persuaded them to let him organise the show, and that was that. We had our fait accompli'ed!'

'I do remember the theatre,' I said, 'and it was rickety then. No wonder Crispin fell through the floor, I'm surprised the whole lot of them didn't fall through it!'

'For heaven's sake, Lennox, we are not complete fools. There have been workmen in there for months putting it in order – that's one of the reasons we've had to wait until now to tie the knot!' Lady Caroline retorted. 'And who told you about the accident?' She fixed me with a steely eye.

'Cyril Fletcher,' I replied, not intimidated in the slightest.

'Lennox, you know very well Cyril is a terrible gossip. He may be a marvellous doctor but he will recount a tale in the most convoluted manner and get half of it muddled up.'

'But the opera singer did die, didn't he! He got that right,' I retorted.

'Yes, but it was an accident. How could it be anything else?' She suddenly looked at me narrowly. 'Someone told me you were sleuthing last Christmas – something about your uncle and a scheming countess at Melrose Court. You haven't come here to *detect*, have you, Lennox? Because I don't want anything to spoil my wedding, and –'

We were interrupted by a sharp rap on the door and I shouted 'Enter' with a touch of relief. Caroline was a good sport but she could become quite waspish if things didn't go her way.

Dicks came in with a large silver tray heaped with teapot, coffeepot, cups and dainties.

'I brought enough for two, my lady and sir,' he said, and put it down to spread a white linen cloth upon the oval reading table in front of the fire.

'And for Fogg?' I asked.

'Liver and steak leftovers, sir.' He lifted the lid on a bowl of titbits and placed it under Fogg's nose.

Caroline turned to him. 'Dicks, did you bring Major Lennox's gift?'

'I have it prepared,' he replied while carefully stationing teapot, cake stands and dainties in serried order on the table. He even measured the distance between items with his gloved finger. 'I was awaiting the order, my lady.'

'Well, you have it,' she said.

'Yes, my lady.' He bowed and went out as we sat down and tucked in.

'What gift?' I asked warily.

She grinned mischievously but said nothing, just bit into a triangular sandwich.

Dicks returned with a wicker basket.

'Caroline, please don't tell me …'

He placed the basket carefully on a chair next to me. There was a blue ribbon tied to the lid to keep it in place – a small black paw was trying to pry through the gap and play with it. A sigh escaped me.

'Well, if Fogg eats it, on your own head be it.' Fogg jumped onto my lap for a better view. I lifted the lid and a very small black kitten stared at me with wide blue eyes. Fogg took a quick sniff, licked it around the ears and looked up at me with an expression of pure besottedness. I sighed in defeat – it seemed we had a kitten.

'The mother's vanished,' Caroline said by way of excuse. 'There are five of them ...' She glanced at me. 'Don't look like that, Lennox, you're an absolute pushover and you know it.'

Dicks bowed and left with a grin. I turned to Caroline, who was pouring cream into a saucer on the table for the kitten. It didn't seem sure what to do with it.

'Cyril told me there was a commotion with a cat,' I remarked while watching the kitten place a tentative paw in the cream, then licking it.

'Well, at least he got that right,' she laughed. 'Yes, I found the litter under the stage after the accident, and as the mother still hadn't returned this morning I decided they needed new homes. You can have two if you like.' She looked at me hopefully.

'Absolutely not,' I replied sternly, quashing any more attempts to trespass on my good nature. 'Look, if Cyril got things mixed up, you need to tell me the tale, old girl – and stick to the facts, will you.'

'Oh, very well.' She looked at me squarely and put her cup down. 'Two nights ago the opera group gave their first proper performance. All our chums and neighbours from round and about had been invited to puff up the numbers. Father and I, and Hiram and his parents, sat through three of the longest hours you just cannot imagine. Then, as the opera *finally* crawled to an end, there was a howling screech from somewhere in the theatre and a thin black cat erupted from behind the stage or under it, I didn't see where, and then onto the stage itself. It stopped, all its hair on end; the soprano shrieked, the cat shrieked, someone threw a bunch of flowers at the poor thing, and then it scrambled across the orchestra, leaping from violin to oboe to harp as it went. That caused even more chaos, and then the poor cat disappeared from sight. That was the highlight of the evening, of course, and we thought they'd end it there and then. But the troupe were determined to battle on, so we settled down in our seats again. Sir Crispin was shot.' Caroline paused to laugh at me as I raised my brows. 'Not really, it was part of the opera. So he lay flat on the floor and the soprano entered from the wings and warbled over to him, then they suddenly vanished from sight, with a sort of shriek. We all applauded, thinking it was some sort of novel finale, but then the lady screamed in earnest, and we realised it wasn't. Mayhem followed, as you can imagine. Half the audience seemed to head for the pit, so I decided to go in search of the cat, but failed entirely. You know the rest.' She smiled at me.

I mused on the story. 'Bit of a coincidence, the cat suddenly erupting like that.'

'I agree, but the plank below the trap-door gave way. I saw it when they heaved the soprano onto a stretcher. Perhaps it had already started to crack and the noise frightened the cat.' She looked at me speculatively. 'I mean, even if there were deliberate intent, it would be impossible to predict whether either singer would be killed at all, or which of them,' she declared as she finished her tea. 'It doesn't add up to anything other than an accident, Lennox.'

'What did the police say about it?' I asked.

'The police arrived just after Cyril pronounced Sir Crispin dead. They tramped about the place asking ridiculous questions, demanding statements, which they didn't get, and upsetting everyone. The inspector's name was Watson, from the local station in Bloxford; he examined the body and wanted to declare the theatre a crime scene and make everybody stay where they were until heaven knows what hour. Cyril told him he was an ass and insisted the body be sent to the mortuary. There was a lot of shouting and nonsense and Daddy lost patience with it and threw them all out.' She finished her tea as she said this.

'Hum.' There was much here to think about. Caroline hadn't mentioned Crispin's fancy for frocks, and had she known she would surely have had a word or two to say about it. I decided a spot of solitary fresh air would help untangle the mind. 'I'll take Foggy and have a look. Theatre's behind the east wing, isn't it?'

'Yes, it is, and don't you dare make a murder out of this, Lennox.' Caroline's eyes flashed.

'No, no,' I reassured her. 'Just going to allay the curiosity, old stick.'

She mellowed suddenly, which should have put me on the alert. 'By the way, Florence is arriving today. She's my bridesmaid. Do you remember her? Florence Braeburn?'

'No, not in the slightest,' I shook my head. 'Should I?'

'Not necessarily. Rather hoped you might hit it off, that's all. She's a terrific sport. Quite perfect for you, actually.' And with that declaration of meddlesome intent, she got up and left before I had time to remonstrate.

CHAPTER 3

Fogg refused to come. Long ears drooping, he sat on my chair by the table and watched with intense devotion as the kitten attempted to lap more cream from the saucer. It was a tiny thing, probably only six or seven weeks old. When it finished I picked it up carefully and took it to the dog basket in front of the unlit hearth. Fogg followed, monitoring every movement. The kitten made inexpert attempts to clean its ears, whiskers and face. Dicks had supplied a cardboard box of fresh soil, and, ablutions complete, the kitten tottered over to it, dug a delicate hole, peed, filled in said hole and skipped back to Fogg's basket to curl up in the blanket. Fogg glanced at me with a hint of apology in his limpid brown eyes, wagged his tail, and then returned to his vigil over the little cat. I sighed, left them to it and set off.

Turning a corner of the long corridor on the upper floor I spied an unknown chap fingering slicked-back hair into place in front of a mirror. I halted on the spot, not being too keen on the look of the oily specimen — a dandy if ever I saw one. I could see he was handsome, to a lady's eye, anyway. He was tall, dark, elegantly dressed in a smartly tailored suit with a silk tie and stacked heels. He finished his preening, extracted the bunch of roses from the vase on the table in front of the mirror, and with an expert flourish flicked away the water clinging to the stems. Then he tucked them under his arm and went off in the other direction, humming an operatic aria. Now there was a slick coxcomb and a damn thief besides, that I could take an instant dislike to. I frowned after him before continuing on my way.

Alone, I crossed the expanse of the hall, an echoing chamber equipped with suits of armour, a monumental fireplace and long refectory tables set against high white walls hung with dark portraits of ancestral soldiers. There were a few dimpled women looking coy, and some paintings of dogs and horses in between, which were my favourite sort of pictures, although I noticed a few were missing, their pale outlines etched in cobwebs and dust.

Sounds of a kerfuffle reached me and I diverted towards it out of curiosity.

'You cannot prevent me, damn it.' A voice rose in anger from just beyond the front door. 'I am the law,' the man declared, for all the good it did him.

The voice was familiar to me and entirely unwelcome. It was Chief Inspector Swift. He and I had crossed paths last Christmas at my uncle's home, Melrose Court, where Swift had been intent on having me hanged for murder. Had I not unmasked the culprit, Swift would even now be testing the strength of the knotted noose. I cannot say our relationship had warmed as a result.

The high words were caused by Dawkins, the idiot footman.

'Don't matter. I don't have no orders. Can't lets you in without orders. Mister Benson nor nobody didn't give me no orders.'

'Swift.' I greeted him unenthusiastically as I stepped outside into sunshine streaming across the broad stones of the portico.

'Lennox, I might have known you'd be here. This is ridiculous!' he snapped, as though I were somehow responsible. Tall and lean with high cheekbones, dark swept-back hair and a permanent frown between sharp eyes, Swift looked more hawkish every time I saw him. He tugged the belt of his trench coat tighter and glowered at me.

'And a good day to you, too, Inspector,' I replied.

'I am here on behalf of Scotland Yard to investigate Sir Crispin's death, and I will not take no for an answer.'

The footman was trying to shut the door.

'Dawkins,' I snapped at him.

'Mister Benson didn't give no orders. The Brigadier 'as said no police. So's unless someone tells me he's allowed in, he's not allowed in.'

I stepped forward. 'Let him in, Dawkins,' I told him.

'But the Brigadier –'

'I'll deal with the Brigadier,' I replied.

'But, I –' Dawkins started again.

'Major Lennox, to you.' I may have raised my voice.

'Yes, Major Lennox, sir,' he grumbled. 'Just doing my job, I am. No thanks for it, just a telling off, an do this, do that …' He sloped off, grousing as he went.

I nodded at Swift to follow, turned briskly and walked back across the hall. He had to move quickly to catch me, but by the time I'd swung into the corridor leading to the east wing he was close on my heels.

Swift demanded, 'Are you here because of Sir Crispin's death?'

'No, I'm here for the wedding,' I replied as we stepped through the French windows and into the formal gardens behind the house.

He stopped suddenly. 'You're not the *groom*, are you? I thought she was marrying a yank.'

'Good God, no!' I said, stopping in my tracks to face him, horrified at the thought. 'Lady Caroline's marrying a Texan.'

He nodded, looking dubious. 'So – where are we going? I thought you said something about seeing the Brigadier.'

'No. Best not disturb the old man, not unless we have to – touch temperamental. We're going to the theatre: scene of the accident, actually,' I informed him.

'So you *are* here about the death,' he accused me.

He was annoyingly persistent. 'Why is Scotland Yard taking an interest?' I eyed him.

He stared back, saying nothing.

Typical of Swift, I thought: tight-lipped as usual. I

turned and walked off toward the theatre, crunching gravel as I went. He came after me at a trot.

'Major Lennox,' he called, but I carried on until I reached the ornate wrought-iron gates set into the high walls surrounding the formal gardens.

The theatre had started life as an observatory, then been further aggrandised by the addition of a long, stone-pillared arcade leading into the domed auditorium. During one of the family's more fashionable periods, the building had been converted into a playhouse complete with stage, small orchestral pit, seating and two boxes.

'Humph,' Swift uttered as he followed me in.

We both stopped at the entrance to the auditorium proper, looking down at the rows of gilded chairs newly upholstered in rich red velvet. More gilding gleamed from the boxes set each side of the stage, their bow-shaped fronts depicting frolicking cherubs playing violins and lutes. Heavy red and gold curtains framed the stage, which was bordered by small lamps fastened in a row to the edge of the platform. The whole was illuminated by an electrical chandelier hung high above the auditorium.

'Is this for the sole use of the family?' Swift asked, looking around.

'Their friends, too,' I replied. I understood the hint of resentment in his voice. It wasn't only the enormous extravagance, it was the withholding of a small but beautiful jewel from public view. But then, that was what wealth often meant: the hoarding of treasure; and I might not condone it, but without the wealth the theatre wouldn't have existed anyway. 'And they used to invite all the villagers until it fell into disrepair during the war. The old man hasn't had the funds to keep it up since,' I added.

'But he has now?' Swift queried. 'Or is he in hock until the nuptials? I heard there was money in it.'

'I have no idea,' I replied sharply, although I suspected he was right.

'You be some of the opery singers, then?' A stocky man wearing a leather apron and overalls came from the back of the stage, brushing sawdust from his hands.

'Certainly not,' I told him as we walked down the red carpet covering the centre aisle. 'We're looking into the accident. This is Chief Inspector Swift and I'm helping him with his enquiries.'

'Well, part of that statement is true,' Swift remarked dryly.

The man looked from one to the other of us, sawdust drifting from his thick brown hair and beard. He wore round glasses and rather reminded me of a bespectacled bear. 'I been fixing the trap-door on His Lordship's orders. He don't want no more accidents, so I fixed it good an' proper.' He nodded for emphasis, shedding more sawdust.

'Good chap,' I said. 'I assume you are one of the estate carpenters?'

'I be the only one.' He may have been smiling beneath the beard and moustache but it was hard to tell. 'T'were me as mended it afore, you know.'

'Well, you didn't make much of a job of it, did you,' Swift retorted.

'He's from Scotland Yard,' I explained by way of excuse. I lead the way down the stage-floor staircase, half hidden behind the curtain. 'I'm Major Lennox, I didn't catch your name, old chap.'

'Clegg,' he replied, glancing nervously at Swift.

My heart sank as we walked into the area below the stage. Clegg had built a large wooden tower beneath the trap-door to secure it. In fact it was so secure that if we ever had another war it would make a very effective bomb shelter. I heard Swift curse beneath his breath as he too realised there was no evidence left to examine.

A long ladder was fixed to the ceiling beam leading up to the trap-door. Beside it was a workbench awash with tools, wood shavings and off-cuts of timber. There were oil lamps hanging from hooks skewered into the joists above giving sufficient illumination, although I drew out my flashlight anyway. It was battery-operated, and I was very keen to make use of it, it being one of the most modern pieces of technology I owned. I ran the beam across the rafters and boards that made up the underside of the stage floor, judging it to be about twelve foot from floor to ceiling.

'Why is the under-stage so deep?' I asked, looking up.

'It were the mechanicals.' Clegg's eyes followed the dot of light made by my torch, then turned to me. 'A telescope what looked at the stars. They were down here, and when all the mechanicals was given to some place in the city, it were left like this.'

'By "the city" I take it you mean Oxford?' Swift queried.

'Ay, Oxford,' Clegg frowned. 'Den of iniquity that place is – *Oxford*.'

'Um, yes,' I said, not too sure why he'd think it was iniquitous. 'So you replaced all the woodwork in here, Clegg?' I returned to the questions in mind.

'That I did, sir.' He nodded enthusiastically. 'Got two big lads in from t'village to help with sawing and hewing.'

'And how do you explain the trap-door collapsing?' I asked.

His whiskered face fell, mortified. 'It don't make no sense, sir. I replaced that plank with a good solid piece of pitch pine. You don't get worm in pitch pine, there be too much resin. Saddest thing I ever saw – that gent fallin' and the lady tumblin' after him. I knew straight off the plank had broke.' He took off his glasses and wiped his sleeve across his eyes.

'You were here? On the night?' Swift asked, as surprised as I was.

'Oh, I were, sirs.' Clegg's face brightened. 'I sneaked in the back when they was singing that night, I did. Brought a three-legged stool with me and sat all the way through. It were heaven.' He had become quite soppy. 'An' that lady what sings, she be the most beautiful lady I ever did see – like that lass on the golden harp.'

I looked at him more closely – I'd heard that certain wood resins can create delusions; but other than his predilection for opera he seemed quite sane. 'I think you mean *at* the harp, Clegg,' I corrected him.

'Oh no, sir –'

Swift broke in. 'What was it like before you did all this?' He indicated the wooden tower. 'Was it only one plank holding the trap-door shut?'

'Ay, it were,' Clegg's enthusiasm drained and was replaced by a furrow of worry.

'What held the plank in place?' I asked.

'Big iron brackets, and hinges, too; they all still be there.' Clegg pointed up.

'Yes, I see,' I encouraged him, shining the torchlight onto them. 'Blacksmith made, by the look of them.'

'Ay, that's right, sir, and a latch to secure the door. Brackets was holding the plank in place below the trap. It were the wood as gave way, not the ironwork. It broke in two, but I can't understand it. No reason to happen – and I can't be finding it, not nowhere.' He shook his head sadly, shedding more sawdust to form a haze around his head.

'You've hidden it, haven't you!' Swift was quick to accuse. 'This so called "accident" was caused by your poor workmanship and you won't admit it.' I noticed the dark rings under the Inspector's eyes; he looked to be under strain. I'd heard about his recent promotion to Scotland Yard – perhaps his ambition was pushing him beyond his capabilities.

Clegg's eyes widened, dismay in his voice. 'No, sirs, I swear I didn't. Last I saw of it, it were under that gent what died. I came down here, I did, just as the ambulance-men were carrying the lady out on a stretcher. Poor dear lady, she was all rumpled and crying. But the gent, he were dead. Puce he was. I saw the broken bits of plank lying under him. I couldn't get close enough to have a proper look because the doctor and police was arguing and shouting right next to him. I come back early next morning to find it. Like I told you, it weren't here. I reckoned them police of yourn as taken it.' He turned toward Swift.

'No, I called in at the local station this morning. They have a few items from the deceased, but not the broken plank.' His eyes remained fixed on Clegg. 'I was expecting to find it here.'

'If it's not at the station, it will be around somewhere,' I said, waving my torch into the dark distance. The trampled dirt floor was littered with sawdust and smelled earthy. The outer structure of the stage was supported by arched stone walls. I walked over to the farthest of them and discovered old boxes of mouldering costumes, some gaudy stage furnishings, a coiled rope and whatnots, but no broken pieces of plank. Swift unhooked a lamp and started searching, too. We both stopped at a green-painted arched door in the stonework.

'Where does that go?' I asked.

'Outside, back o' the theatre,' Clegg said.

I tried the handle but it was locked. 'Where's the key?'

'In my apron here.' He pulled it out and held it up: a large old black iron key.

'Is there another?' I asked.

'Ay, outside on a hook.'

The door looked sound and in good order; I could see it had been opened recently. 'I assume you bring your timber and tools through here?'

'I do,' Clegg answered. 'There's a path leads out to my workshop.'

We turned from the door and explored more of the area but found nothing of interest and came back to the workbench empty-handed.

'Have you searched the auditorium?' I asked Clegg.

'You're wasting time here, Lennox,' Swift broke in. 'The man's hidden it.'

'I haven't done nowt o' the sort,' Clegg protested. 'I've told you more times than is needed, I fossicked everywhere. You ain't listening.'

'Where's the wood store?' I asked him. 'The scrap wood for lighting fires, not carpentry.'

'You think it might be there?' Clegg asked.

Swift looked at me narrowly, then nodded. 'Reasonable thought,' he muttered.

Clegg led the way upstairs and back outside through the theatre itself. He turned away from the high stone wall surrounding the gardens and down a muddy path through a small copse of trees and shrubs. Birds were singing as we went, there were bluebells and yellow primroses beneath the budding boughs – the world smelt fragrant and fresh, just as spring ought to. There were quite a lot of pigeons around, too, I noted.

The woodshed wasn't strictly a shed, it was a roof on stilts, and gave shelter to a huge pile of broken and scrap wood in various stages of decomposition. There was much evidence of rats amongst other creatures – it was a shame Fogg had refused to accompany me, he'd have liked it here.

'There be sommat like,' Clegg shouted out, heading toward a half hidden plank of wood. 'Ee, I'm impressed, I am. That be some clever thinking. Bet you're glad you've got Major Lennox helping you, Inspector. You be in need of all the help you can get.' He pulled the piece from under a heap of rotten wood and laid it on the green grass in the sunshine.

The wood had snapped in the middle and the reason was patently obvious: it was riddled with woodworm and had virtually no structural strength at all.

'But this ain't right.' Clegg stared down at the dark, damp-looking piece. 'This is the old plank, the one I replaced. It's not the new un.'

Swift turned to accuse him. 'You've been lying to us.'

'No, I ain't, you got to stop making that up. It were the first job I did – replacing it, dangerous rotten, it were. I put the new plank in and this un got left down below. I never gave it a thought till now.'

'Maybe someone cleaned up and tossed it here. One of your lads, perhaps?' I suggested.

'No, they wasn't tidy lads at all, wouldn't have thought to clear away after the'selves.'

'But there must have been a lot of other people working in the theatre?' I suggested. 'The chairs and curtains are new.'

'Ay, the place has been all a-bother since we started. Getting in my way, painting the walls and fussing with rolls of cloth and doings. And half the house coming round, servants and gentry alike, making comments, ordering folk about. Like a blooming circus some days, it were,' he grumbled.

'So you're saying anyone could have moved this plank?' Swift said.

'Ay, but why would they?' Clegg replied. 'It's a worm-eaten bit of old wood. An' it weren't bust like this, neither. Look. This be elm, not pitch pine, you can see it clear.'

Swift and I duly looked, but it was so rotted that I can't say we were any the wiser.

'Be a good chap and look for the other half, would you, Clegg,' I told him.

He went off, still shaking his head.

I turned to Swift. 'Someone exchanged the planks.'

'Possibly.' He eyed me narrowly.

'They could have used the ladder and climbed up to switch them over. It would only take a minute.'

'Wouldn't the trap-door have dropped open when the new plank was removed?' he suggested.

'No, the latch would have held it shut. It looked strong enough to hold up if there wasn't any weight on it,' I said slowly, trying to think through the sequence.

'So why bother putting the rotten plank there at all? As you said, the latch would have given way under the weight. Sir Crispin would have fallen without the effort of exchanging the planks?'

'Agreed, but if no plank had been found, it would have instantly raised suspicion. Whoever did it wanted it to look like an accident.'

Swift regarded me, then nodded slowly. 'And that person would have to know their opera – assuming Sir Crispin was the intended victim.'

'Yes,' I agreed, my mind turning over. 'They'd have to know the exact moment he was supposed to be on the trap-door. And it explains the cat. They probably trod on the cat while moving about in the dark. Which is why it shot out when it did,' I added.

'Um, I heard about that,' Swift agreed.

'Cyril Fletcher said there was mischief here. I think he was right.'

'Who's Cyril Fletcher?' Swift asked.

'The doctor who attended the victims. Old family friend.'

'Well, it wasn't exactly mischief,' Swift stated.

'Why do you say that?' I asked, brows raised.

'I came here because the post-mortem results revealed that Sir Crispin suffered from haemophilia. Any such trauma would have killed him.'

'Ah, that rather does add a different complexion to it,' I mused.

'Exactly. It wasn't mischief, it was murder,' Swift said.

CHAPTER 4

Clegg returned with the other half of the plank. It didn't tell us any more than we already knew.

'It weren't me, Inspector.' He regarded us earnestly through his round spectacles. I felt rather sorry for the poor chap.

'That remains to be seen.' Swift said coldly.

'Thank you for your help, Clegg.' I tried my best reassuring tone, though I doubt it did much to allay the poor man's fears. 'And keep this to yourself, there's a good fellow.'

'Have them taken to my car,' Swift told him.

'Ay, sir.' Clegg left with a heavy tread as another figure approached us.

'Sir, sir …' Dicks came running over.

'What?'

'His Lordship, the Brigadier requests your presence, sirs,' he said anxiously.

'Ah, he does, does he. Someone told him the Inspector is here?' I enquired.

'I'm afraid there's a bit of a hullaballoo going on, Major

Lennox, sir. The Brigadier is demanding an explanation.' He stopped and eyed me closely, then withdrew a small brush from his inside pocket. 'Um, you have some specks of sawdust on your garments, sir. May I?'

Before I could object, he started brushing me off.

'Dicks, will you stop doing that.' I took a step backwards.

'Sorry, sir. You have some in your hair too. I have a spare comb, sir.' He reached into his inside pocket.

'No! No combs, Dicks, and no brushes.' I ran a hand through my unruly hair. 'Right, Inspector Swift and I will go and see the Brigadier now.'

Dicks insisted on accompanying us. I hadn't mentioned Sir Crispin's frocks to Swift, but as the source of said information was now dogging our footsteps it seemed like a good opportunity.

'Dicks.' I stopped and he almost ran into me.

'Sir?' He looked flustered. 'Um, I believe his Lordship to be quite agitated, sir. We should hurry.'

'Yes, well, never mind that. Tell Inspector Swift about Sir Crispin's extra-curricular activities, would you.'

He looked aghast. 'I couldn't possibly, sir. That was strictly between Uncle Greggs and myself.'

'Too late, I'm afraid. Cat's out of the bag. Just tell him.'

Swift was now eyeing Dicks. 'Tell me what?' he demanded.

Dicks had no choice but to spill the beans, which he did succinctly, although it brought a flush to his pale cheeks. Swift didn't bat an eyelid – but he was from

Scotland Yard, and I've no doubt this sort of thing goes on all the time in the Great Metropolis.

'Does anyone know where Sir Crispin went when he dressed in drag?' Swift demanded.

'There's talk of a venue in Oxford, sir,' Dicks replied.

'There are any number of venues in Oxford,' I remarked. 'Sir Crispin may have been dressing up for a pantomime or a play or some such.'

'No, sir. The name of the establishment is the Black Cat Club. I believe it is a place of ill repute.' Dicks had turned quite pink.

'Really,' I mused. I had been at Oxford, where sporting activities had taken up my time and the racier side of life had quite eluded me.

'Have you been there?' Swift asked.

'Certainly not, sir.' Dicks took a step back.

'Does anyone else from the house or opera group go there?' Swift continued.

'I have no idea, sir.'

'Where *are* the opera singers, by the way?' I asked.

'They are installed in the Dower House, sir. At the far end of the formal gardens,' Dicks said.

'What is a "Dower House"? Swift asked.

'Residence for outdated matriarchs,' I told him. 'When an earl shuffles off, his widow gets dispatched to the Dower House to clear the way for the heir and his wife. Keeps the peace and the old lady at the bottom of a very large garden. Rather a good idea, I've always thought.'

'Humph.' Swift turned over the information. 'Need to interview these opera singers.'

'Bit late in the day, Swift,' I told him.

'Um, I really think we should be going, sirs,' Dicks tried again to hurry us.

'Yes, very well.' I turned and we made our way back to the French windows and then climbed the stairs to the upper reaches.

'He's almost deaf,' I warned Swift. 'Just take him as it comes and don't speak more than you have to.'

'I'm perfectly capable of comporting myself in front of earls, thank you, Lennox,' Swift snapped. 'I don't need etiquette lessons.'

'That wasn't what I meant,' I retorted. Swift's socialist tendencies coloured his attitude, to my mind, and he was too quick to take offence.

Brigadier Bloxford belonged to another century and still lived there most of the time. I wasn't sure if he was fighting the Boche or the Boers – I doubt if he knew either. Tall, lean and looking older than I remembered, his hair now entirely white. He wore his old Army uniform complete with service revolver — his back stiff and shoulders squared, leather and brass gleaming. He stood in front of a blazing fire and glared at us from under bristling brows.

'*Lennox*,' Brigadier Bloxford bellowed at me. 'You here? You're late, man! Did you fly in? Who's winning?'

'We are, sir,' I yelled back. 'Almost over.'

Swift looked speculatively from one of us to the other, then gazed around the large room, stuffed with furniture from around the Empire. The walls were hung with paintings of battle scenes and hand-drawn maps from old campaigns. A scarred ebony table was strewn with books and papers. African shields and spears stood in one corner, a tattered Union Jack in another. A huge Scottish broadsword was propped against a bookcase, the blade glinting in the spring sunshine slanting into the room through mullioned windows filling most of the south-facing wall. The Brigadier's rooms occupied the central section of the house overlooking the front, and gave onto a broad panorama of the hills and valleys of the Cotswold countryside. At one time it would all have belonged to his family.

'Good day, Brigadier,' Swift shouted.

'Stand down, men,' Bloxford continued at volume, and sat down in a large carved chair. We perched on an antique sofa opposite him in front of the flickering hearth. Bloxford's valet was a Gurkha; he'd been a stalwart presence at the Brigadier's side since I'd known the family. He came in silently to place a rug across the old man's knees and then stationed himself behind his master's chair.

The Gurkha hardly seemed to have changed since I'd first encounter him when I was a boy. He was swarthy, with a deeply lined face, and lean as a whip. Eyes dark under the shadow of his brow, he wore a sort of turban, and a knee-length tunic belted at the waist over slim trousers and shoes like slippers. I'd heard of the fearsome knives the Gurkhas carried – the *kukri* – but I had never seen either blade nor sheath on the man.

'Do you recall Sir Crispin Gibbons?' Swift asked the Brigadier loudly.

'No,' he yelled back. 'Never heard of him.'

'The opera, sir. Gibbons was the opera singer,' I added.

'Complete arse,' Bloxford snapped back. 'Popular with the men, but no brains. Sent him to HQ out of harm's way. Tea?'

'Um, no, thank you, sir,' I replied for both of us. 'Crispin Gibbons died in the theatre the other night … You were there, sir.'

'There were police,' Bloxford said loudly, then growled. 'Not having them. Upsets the girl. Wedding, you know.'

'Yes, sir,' I replied. 'Chief Inspector Swift is here. He is known to me. He needs to look into the incident.'

'Is he sound?' Bloxford questioned.

'Yes, I will vouch for him, sir.' I replied.

The Brigadier suddenly glared at Swift, who held firm. 'You Swift?'

'Yes, sir,' Swift responded loudly.

'Need to Investigate, do you?' the Brigadier shouted.

'I do, sir,' Swift replied.

'Tread carefully. I will not allow a pack of MPs on the base. You and only you.' He stabbed a leather gloved finger at Swift. 'Understood?' the Brigadier barked.

'Yes, sir,' Swift nodded.

'I was there,' Brigadier Bloxford continued. 'Show put on for the troops. Damn racket. Fellow was killed. What was it, accident or mischief?'

'Mischief, sir,' I replied. 'Or worse.'

He glared. 'Find the miscreant – give him a good flogging. Not an officer, though. If it's an officer, bit of a slap, then send him to the front.' The Brigadier wasn't actually looking at us but some point behind us, or possibly somewhere a long way in the past.

'Yes, sir,' I answered.

'Major Lennox, take your aeroplane to Lille, they're waiting on dispatch. Dismissed.'

I stood and saluted – it seemed the thing to do; then we turned about smartly and left the old man staring into the distance.

The Gurkha was at the door and gave a short bow as he opened it, then closed it silently behind us.

'He's mad,' Swift said as we trotted down the stairs toward the hall.

'No, he's not,' I replied. 'He may not live in the same time period as we do, but he's perfectly rational. And he knows about the wedding, and he knows who you are. Don't make the mistake of underestimating him, Swift.'

He looked at me, intelligence in his dark eyes, mulling over the encounter and my warning words.

'Who was the manservant?'

'A Gurkha – had him since before I can recall. I don't know where the Brigadier found him. He's called Kalo Biralo.'

'Does he speak?' Swift asked.

'Yes, but not English, or not as far as I know. He and the Brigadier speak Nepalese between themselves.'

I had answered brusquely and felt a pang of guilt for my short temper, but I was disturbed by the encounter with the Brigadier. I wanted to find my dog and walk in the woods and meadows to think.

Swift seemed to have had enough, too. He tightened the belt on his trench coat. 'Right, reports to write up. I'll be back in the morning.'

As he spoke, Benson pulled open the front door and something extraordinary happened: a vision appeared, bathed in a glowing light and wreathed in the most extraordinary scent of flowers. My mouth may have fallen open. The vision glided toward us, smiling, and regarded us with blue-grey eyes in an exquisite face framed by pale blonde hair caught up in a simple knot.

'Hello,' the vision said over an armful of pink roses. 'Oh, I can't quite see where I'm going! Oh dear, what an utter idiot I am.' She bumped into Swift.

'Please, let me help,' he said with a rare smile.

'If you could open the door to the morning room I'd be terribly grateful,' the vision told him.

I received another glancing smile and may have closed my mouth, but then it fell open again and nothing came out. I was aware that Swift had moved away and was in fact now helping the vision by holding a door open and then following her. He was talking.

'Anything to oblige, Miss – erm ...?

'Florence. Florence Braeburn. I'm an old friend of Caroline's. Actually, I'm one of her bridesmaids.' Florence Braeburn laughed, a delightful musical laugh.

'I'm Swift, Jonathan Swift…'

Their voices faded into the distance. I awoke from my trance and realised that the bloody man had stolen a march on me.

CHAPTER 5

Florence Braeburn. I cudgelled my mind for any recollection of her, but came up with nothing more than a hazy memory of a skinny girl in overalls clambering in the hayloft with Caroline, myself and my cousin Edgar. She hadn't appeared to remember me either.

I returned to my rooms to persuade Fogg to come walking with me, but he refused. I remonstrated with him, but that achieved nothing so I picked up the kitten, who was full of cream, and sleepy. It had long whiskers and soft paws which I tickled though it didn't seem to appreciate it, so I tried its chin, which resulted in a loud purr. I gave it back to Fogg, who had now moved into his basket with the kitten and had been watching me anxiously. I slipped on my shooting jacket and emptied the pockets of the shotgun cartridges I habitually carried, which left more than enough room for one small cat. Once I had dropped it gently into my pocket, the kitten and I set off for a contemplative ramble with Fogg following closely behind.

The old man was dying. I'd seen the signs before, on my father's face as he'd neared the end. A haze of broken veins across lean cheekbones, more purple than red. The blue glaze around the irises, the pale grey hue of the skin and the slight rasp of the breath. I was surprised Caroline hadn't noticed, although she saw him every day and the changes were so very slow, so fractional, that they crept up before anyone realised. His heart was giving out and I suspected he knew it. Cyril Fletcher would, too, but he wasn't allowed to share his secrets, and besides, the Brigadier had a physician of his own.

I walked through meadow grass, bright and glossy and dotted with daisies, following a path worn down to dirt by the hooves of horses and deer. It grieved me to see the great man nearing his end – and he had been great: his military record was one of extraordinary bravery and achievement. He was a modest man, his accolades and medals secreted away and his exploits almost forgotten in the aftermath of a brutal war we all preferred to leave behind.

Fogg chased rabbits, barking as he scattered them; then he spotted squirrels and I called him to come away. The woods were cooler, shaded. Buds were greening on dark boughs, catkins hung yellow and soft, a lark in a distant meadow struck a trilling song. I stopped to listen, soaking in the scents and sounds of spring, and sent a silent word of thanks to the Man Upstairs. Then, with a deep breath of crisp fresh air, I turned back to the house and the mystery of Crispin's murder.

The kitten woke up and began fidgeting in my jacket, so I extended my stride and reached the front door just as Benson once again pulled it slowly open, this time to reveal Caroline and Florence exiting.

'Heathcliff Lennox!' Florence exclaimed at once. 'I hadn't realised it was you, you're so *tall* now.' She laughed, her lovely face alight.

I straightened my back and forced a smile — not that I hadn't wanted to smile, but I'd again frozen to the spot.

'Just Lennox. Never liked Heathcliff,' I responded. My mother had been of a romantic tilt and named me after some damn hero from a book. I have fought resolutely against it ever since.

'Oh, yes, of course.' Florence blushed. 'I'm terribly sorry.'

'Don't be a curmudgeon, Lennox,' Caroline retorted.

'I didn't … I mean … it's that … well …' I was about to start babbling, a bad habit when I'm nervous, so I shut my mouth to stop myself. I realised the kitten had started trying to climb out of my pocket so I shoved my hand in to keep it in place. That didn't work because it climbed inside my sleeve instead.

'I *will* remember – Lennox – and it is very nice to see you again.' Florence attempted another smile. 'I met your friend Jonathan Swift.'

'He's not my friend, he's a detective,' I replied, then realised my mistake.

'Lennox,' Caroline instantly snapped back. 'What are you doing letting the police in here? Daddy was quite clear, and I told you, 'absolutely no detecting'. You total rotter!'

'Now look, Caroline.' Damn it, the kitten was working its way up my arm now. 'I've squared it with the Brigadier, and Swift is sound. Well, mostly,' I added, not wanting to give him any more of an advantage with Florence. 'Anyway, I will see you at dinner.'

I raced inside leaving them on the doorstep looking after me – I don't think the encounter went too well, actually. Damn it, I never know what to say to ladies. Fortunately I spotted Dicks near the staircase.

'Dicks, I need a hand,' I told him. 'Upstairs.'

'I'm on bell service, sir. I'm not supposed to move unless someone rings a bell.'

'Nonsense, I'll ring a bell if you insist.'

'But sir ...'

'Right, fine,' I manoeuvred a hand up my sleeve, extracted the kitten, handed it to him and raced off to the nearest bell – which happened to be in the boot room – rang it, and came back. 'Upstairs, *now*,' I ordered him.

He didn't move, just stood in the same spot looking at the kitten in his hands, which was wide awake and staring back.

'Dicks!' That livened him up. He followed me and we decanted the kitten into its litter box, where it made a careful toilette before jumping back out and mewing at us.

'Dicks, you are now on dog-and-kitten duty, and don't look at me like that.'

His shoulders slumped. 'Yes, sir.'

'Fogg needs breakfast and supper – scraps of beef, steak

and liver are his favourites. The kitten needs milk and some sort of food.'

'What sort of food, sir?'

'Haven't a clue. Don't you know?

'No, sir.' He looked at me. 'I can discuss it with Cook, she's known to be fond of cats, sir.' He started tidying up, taking up the blanket from the basket and making it into a little bed. Then he withdrew the brush from his inner pocket and swept up dog hairs from around the basket. He was just moving toward my desk when I remonstrated:

'Dicks!'

'Yes, sir?'

'Will you stop doing that.'

'Sorry, sir. I have a neat streak. Uncle Greggs often remarked it.' He glanced at the clock on the mantelpiece. 'The dinner gong will be sounding shortly, sir.'

'Oh, hell. Yes, right. You go and get the food for Fogg and the kitten while I dress.'

He left while I changed. I'd no sooner spruced up and tried to lick my hair into order with a wet comb than I heard the gong. I dashed out onto the rear garden terrace, where people were dressed in country smarts and clutching glasses of champagne. A footman handed one to me as a shaft of evening sun washed pale pink light across the scene.

'Ah, you are the gallant Major?'

It was that damn coxcomb who'd stolen the roses from the house; and he spoke with a German accent.

'And you're a bloody Prussian,' I replied.

'Ja, but the war is over, Major Lennox.' He smiled at me, looking even more handsome, if that were possible. 'Come, come, old fellow, ve do not fight now. Ve are all good friends and I was on the side of Blighty in the war, you know. I am Count Gustav von Graf.' He broadened the smile, held out a manicured hand and clicked his heels.

'I don't give a damn which side you were on. If I'd come across you a few years ago I'd have shot you on sight,' I told him.

'But … but …' he spluttered. 'This is outrageous!'

I was about to deliver a few more outrages on the bloody Prussian oil slick when Caroline came over with a chap who was more mountain than man. He was dressed in a brand-new tweed jacket and trousers, a chequered shirt and tie. He fingered the collar as if everything were a touch too tight. I fixed a smile on my phiz as I watched the Prussian sidle off from out of the corner of my eye.

'Lennox.' Caroline gave me a wide, happy smile. 'This is Hiram.'

I had to look up at him. I fall in at six three, and he was taller than me, and broader. Black hair, dark blue eyes, an amiable face, square jaw, and a tanned skin that spoke of a man who lived more outdoors than in. As grooms go, Caroline could have done a great deal worse. I extended my hand to his larger one.

'Greetings, old man.' I smiled as he crushed my fingers.

'Howdy,' he returned.

'What?'

'He means "hello",' Caroline giggled.

'Ah, excellent.'

'Ah'm trying to teach you guys some American. We say "howdy" in Texas.' He spoke slowly, extending his vowels into a drawl. Not unpleasant or particularly difficult to decipher once one got used to it.

'Yes, well, "Howdy", old "guy",' I replied.

'And these here are ma folks –' he held an arm out to an older couple just behind him and Caroline '– Ford and Ruth Chisholm.'

A tall, thin lady, severely upright in a purplish frock and wearing an expression as though she'd swallowed a wasp, stepped forward. Her husband was an older version of Hiram and wore a very rum get-up – a blue serge suit of a casual cut with a white shirt and a thin black cord in place of a tie. I looked at his boots and words failed me: the leather came from the skin of something brown, shiny and exotic; they reached to mid-calf and ended in pointed toes.

'Howdy, I believe you're Major Lennox?' he drawled as he shook my hand. 'This here's ma wife, Lady Ruth. She's a high-born lady from Scotland and she don't never let me forgit it.' He smiled broadly, his eyes crinkled in a deeply tanned face, setting off extraordinarily white teeth - they must have marvellous dentists in America.

'Good evening, Major Lennox,' Lady Ruth greeted me coolly. 'I believe you take yourself for a sleuth?'

'Erm …' There didn't seem to be much of an answer to that.

'No sleuthing, young man, I will not permit it,' she proceeded to lecture me. '*I* am organising this wedding, and I will brook no distractions. You will behave yourself. Do you understand?'

Well, really, what did she know about it? I was just about to open my mouth to inform her that there was actually a murderer in the vicinity, when Caroline broke in:

'Lennox, will you walk Dame Gabriel into dinner, please? You're seated between her and Daddy.'

'What?'

I was approached by a very round lady sporting some fairly startling make-up. She was brightly dressed in yellow silk and had a ridiculous feather-and-diamante concoction in her curled hair.

'You must be Heathcliff, how delightful!' she gushed. 'Such a heroic name, Heathcliff. You must simply adore it.'

It was the soprano. I turned to scowl at Caroline, who laughed. 'Serves you right for bringing that policeman here,' she hissed.

Benson materialised to bang the dinner gong with a wobbly hand, and the beaming soprano grabbed my arm and dragged me into the dining room. I helped her into her chair and with a suppressed sigh sank into my seat. The sight of the magnificent room cheered me though — it was an ancient place with rich mahogany panelling reflecting flickering candlelight from the glittering chandelier. The high ceiling above was deeply carved in rococo plasterwork and the carpet was thick as fleece underfoot. Despite its size, it felt cosy and companionable — a warm refuge for a feast with friends.

The Brigadier couldn't hear a thing amongst the clatter of plates, cutlery and chit-chat, so he either ate in silence or roared orders at me.

'Lennox, tell those idiots in the mess my soup is cold.'

'Yes, sir,' I replied loudly, although the whole house could have heard him. I turned toward Dame Gabriel.

'I hope you are recovered? After the accident?' I asked her.

'Oh, it was a dreadful shock but I am quite restored, dear boy. I brim with good health! – though I grieve for poor, poor Crispin. A wonderful talent lost to the world and in his prime, too,' she expounded, make-up creasing around her eyes. 'I have had to break-in the new man. It has been quite exhausting, but he is coming along under my guidance. I have exacting standards, Heathcliff.'

'Erm, my name is Lennox, actually.'

'Really? But Caroline expressly informed me that you are *Heathcliff*.' She raised painted eyebrows.

'That is Caroline's idea of a joke.' I turned back to the subject of the extinguished tenor. 'Who is the new chap – the one who's taken over from Crispin?'

'The Understudy. Young and quite inexperienced but with a good voice. If it were not for the dreadful circumstances, I'm afraid he would never have had the chance to take the lead.'

'Really, and who did you say he was?' I enquired, wondering if said tenor had kiboshed Crispin to gain top billing.

'Andrew Dundale. He wasn't able to attend dinner this evening. Both myself and the leading man are always invited to dinner. The rest of the troupe take their supper in the Dower House,' Dame Gabriel informed me while swiping the remaining bread roll.

'You don't mean Lord Dundale's son, do you?'

'Oh, yes, we are all top-drawer, you know. No hoi-polloi in *our* group,' she laughed. 'Are you acquainted with him?'

I nodded. Andrew Dundale had been better known as Andrew Dumbdale because of his wooden-headed intellect. Andrew's nature was harmless, but he had *very* little brain. We'd been at school together, where he'd excelled at attendance, and that was pretty much the sum of his achievements. Although I do recall his enthusiasm for drama and singing – qualities no doubt requisite to play lead tenor for the Noble House of Opera.

'Major Lennox, muster the men at dawn for Inspection. This is a shambles,' the Brigadier suddenly snapped, making me jump.

'Yes, sir. Will do,' I shouted, and returned to Dame Gabriel. 'Is Andrew leading the opera company now?'

She tittered gaily. 'Oh, no. *I* have stepped into Crispin's shoes. It is such an honour. And I may add, we did need freshening up. I mean, Crispin was a marvel but he was rather set in his ideas and he could be quite forceful.

There were times when we were not a happy crew …' She looked at me over her wine as she took a sip; lipstick smeared on the glass.

'And were these "times" frequent or just now and then?' I asked.

'Well, I don't wish to speak ill of the dead,' she began, knowing damn well she was doing exactly that, 'but Crispin could be a bit of a Tartar and quite disruptive when he was in one of his moods, and that was really quite often. But he was an *artiste*, you know, and the greater the talent, the greater the desire for perfection. Sometimes it is necessary to crack the whip.'

'So he terrorised the company?' I said as a plate of spring lamb, new potatoes and various greens was placed in front of me. 'Will you be doing the same?'

'I … No … No. But the performance is paramount. We must give our all, we must …' She spluttered to a halt, having flummoxed herself. 'Do excuse me, there is something I really must discuss with dear Ford.' She turned to Hiram's father on the other side of her.

At least that shut her up. I enjoyed the excellent repast and quietly observed the guests, my gaze lingering on Florence, who was wearing a pale tartan jacket over a cream silk blouse. She was amongst the animated crowd at the other end of the table, seated next to Hiram; they were laughing and chatting. Caroline was talking to a smooth-looking chap I hadn't met, although judging by the jocular manner in which he spoke to both Caroline and Hiram I had him down as the best man. He was around thirty, much the same age as me and the rest of the younger set.

The Brigadier held a dislike for modernity and the room was entirely candlelit. Beneath the chandelier, gleaming silver candelabra holding creamy candles were ranged along the centre of the table radiating a warm glow and lighting people's faces as they leaned in to exchange small talk, anecdotes and jokey gossip. I watched Florence as she took a sip of wine and looked at me over the rim. I smiled, she smiled, and then turned her lovely face back toward Hiram.

The table was so wide it was almost impossible to converse across it, saving me from small talk with Lady Ruth Chisholm, who was sitting opposite me. I took a longer look at her. Must say, she didn't look much like Hiram: a long, lean face, sharp nose with a slight hook at the bridge, and steel-grey hair cut to the nape of the neck. She noticed my attention and stared back, so I offered my best grin but she looked away, evidently unimpressed. The Prussian, von Graf, sat next to her, and she ignored him, too – although I noticed he made eyes at Dame Gabriel next to me. I'd wager she was the recipient of the stolen roses.

Benson doddered about, a napkin hanging from his arm, hands trembling as he served the Brigadier. Fortunately Dicks was also on duty and chivvied the other servants. Our plates were cleared as they were finished, napkins retrieved when dropped, wine glasses refilled when empty – it was all smoothly and elegantly done.

An unknown lady, discreet and inquisitive, was taking more of an interest in the conversation than her food. I think she was a neighbour: grey hair tied in a neat bun, thin, bird-like in manner and looks, she was watching with bright eyes, and then turned to say something to Ford. There was another strange name – Ford – where *did* parents get their ideas? And Hiram? Maybe it meant Henry, or was a version of Heinrich, or some such. What was wrong with normal names? My mother had landed me with Heathcliff. *Heathcliff*, for God's sake – what was she thinking!

'The girl, Lennox.' The Brigadier broke loudly into my meanderings.

'Yes, sir.'

'Marrying a foreigner, you know. He can speak the language. Big fellow. He'll need a mount. Find something in the stables for him, would you?' he bellowed huskily in what he must have thought was *sotto voce*.

'I will see to it, sir.'

'I think he'll do,' he continued, staring straight at Hiram, who was pretending not to notice, though the chatter around the table suddenly became muted.

'Yes, excellent choice, sir.' I leaned in to reply.

'Good people, Americans – your mother was one, Lennox.'

'She was, sir. But she spent most of her life in England.'

'I remember her, marvellous woman. Good heart, very kind. They beat us once, you know. Seventeen eighty-three. On our side now. Whole divisions of them on the Western

Front. It will make a difference.' The Brigadier slammed a hand down on the table, making the silver jump. 'Damned Russians have turned, the bounders! Not the Americans – they won't turn. Steadfast people.' He stared down the table, his eyes slipping out of focus as he lapsed back into the past and the murmur of conversation rose again. Benson removed the Brigadier's plate as a number of footmen cleared the way for pudding. The Gurkha, Kalo, remained silently behind his master's chair; there was little for him to do, but he was never far from the old man's side.

'Didn't happen to know that Crispin had a habit of bleeding, did you?' I thought I'd drop a minor bombshell into Dame Gabriel's ear as she bit into her Eton mess.

She coughed and spluttered bits of meringue. 'Well, well ... I knew, but he was so careful. He said he had "the disease of kings". Haemophilia, you know. He didn't bandy it about but it wasn't a secret either.'

'And you fell on top of him, didn't you?' I continued.

'Major Lennox, it was an accident!' She said loudly.

People turned to scowl at me – well, Lady Ruth and Caroline did. I finished my pudding in silence.

Dinner broke up amidst chatter and we gentleman made our way towards the smoking room for brandy and cigars. The ladies headed for the drawing room to do whatever they did there. Hiram fell in beside me and I enquired if he had a fancy for a spot of pigeon shooting.

'I sure do, old man. I seen any number around and I've been wanting to take a shot at them. They eat the corn faster than we can plant it back home.'

'Excellent, I suggest we…' I was cut off suddenly and rudely hailed.

'I say, you're Major Heathcliff Lennox, aren't you?' It was the chap I assumed was the best man. He held his hand out, which I shook sparingly.

'Yes, greetings, old chap,' I replied.

'Geoffrey Jarvis – old friend of your cousin Adam Kingsley.'

'Kingsley is not my cousin, he is a lawyer and a snake,' I told him quite clearly to lay any doubt on the case.

The Brigadier and the other chaps had continued on to the smoking room but Hiram had turned and was quietly waiting and watching.

Jarvis laughed. 'Excellent, Heathcliff, old boy. He told me you were a wit.'

'Nonsense, I'm nothing of the sort.' I took a step back. 'And don't call me Heathcliff.'

'Said you were a clever cove, too. Even got away with murder.' Jarvis grinned.

I really took offence at this. 'Absolute rot! What the devil do you mean by that?'

'You know – last Christmas, at Melrose Court. You should have been fingered for murder but you managed to pin it on someone else. Great wheeze!' He held the grin on his face, which was smooth-shaven, pale brown eyes and hair, lightly pock-marked, but open, friendly, and entirely at odds with the accusations he was now throwing at me. And, I realised, had probably batted into other ears, too.

I was aware of Hiram standing like a monument in the passageway, quietly taking in the exchange.

'Now, you may be best man and a guest in this house, but I am damn well not going to allow you to spread filthy slander about me. I'll have your bloody hide if you repeat that accusation.'

He simply laughed – thought it was funny. I was in half a mind to hit the fool. 'Oh, I'm not the best man,' he replied gaily. 'I'm the Chaplain.'

CHAPTER 6

The Reverend Jarvis went off chortling as though everything were a huge joke.

I raised my eyes at Hiram, who was regarding me with a slight furrow to the brow.

'Damn strange sort of chaplain infesting this parish,' I remarked, still seething, 'and he's not even wearing a collar!'

'I thought the same ma-self,' the Texan replied in that slow drawl. 'But I reckoned it must be jus' the way folks are out here.'

'Well, they aren't. And for the record, I haven't murdered anyone – ever.'

Hiram smiled, his teeth very white in the lamplight, and I returned the grin. 'Come on, old chap, let's get a snifter before we have to join the ladies.'

The Brigadier was seated and silent in an upright wing chair by the fire, now alight and crackling, the Gurkha standing sentry behind him. The German had disappeared somewhere, which suited me as I'd no desire to bandy words with that blighter.

We settled in deep cushioned chairs and were soon discussing the merits of various shotgun mechanisms, particularly in relation to pigeon shooting. Hiram and his father were very knowledgable about guns. Ford slipped a hand into the extraordinary boots he wore and pulled out a neat little Derringer pocket pistol with walnut grips, and passed it to me. I turned it over, eyeing it closely as it gleamed in the firelight, and realised it was loaded. Brows raised, I handed it back, carefully.

'Where I come from we'd be naked without a gun,' Ford drawled. 'Even my dear wife packs a pistol. Pearl handled grips it has. I bought it for her myself when we was wed.'

'Pa was a wild-catter,' Hiram explained. 'Drilling for oil in the boondocks, way outside of the proven oil fields. Took a few years of grit and guts before he struck a load. It was crazier than the gold rush.'

'An' just as dangerous,' Ford laughed. 'I sure did like the adventure, though. But ranching is my real desire. I sold all my oil fields an' bought myself a farm. It's a fine homestead and my wife has made it finer, God bless her.'

I was trying to imagine Lady Ruth as a rancher's wife on a Texas range when the Brigadier announced we were to join the ladies. Caroline grabbed me as I arrived in the drawing room, my snifter still clutched in my hand.

'Lennox.'

'What?'

'This is Miss Isabelle Busby,' Caroline informed me. 'She's terribly interested in crime and detecting. You have first-hand knowledge, so I thought you'd like to chat to her.' She smirked as she said this, knowing full well I had no desire whatsoever to make small talk with Miss Busybody or anyone else. It seems I was still being punished for introducing Swift into the place.

I stood to allow the lady to take her seat, then fetched a chair to sit beside her while Caroline went to sit between Florence and Hiram.

'Are you really a murderer?' Miss Busby immediately asked as Dicks offered her a pale sherry in a dainty glass. She took it with thanks and a bright smile.

'No, of course not. Ask anyone. Ask Chief Inspector Swift of Scotland Yard, he'll be here tomorrow morning.'

'I didn't think you were. But chaplains can be quite credible, you know. Although I'm not quite sure this particular chaplain is what he seems,' she mused.

We both looked toward Jarvis, who was alone on a sofa behind the family group. His face had turned florid as he knocked back the brandy and held his glass up to a footman for a refill.

'How long has he been ministering in the parish?' I asked.

'Not long. But he's not our Bloxford parish vicar, he's the house chaplain, he ministers for the family at the private chapel here at the Hall. He's supposed to care for the old chantry too, but he hasn't taken much of an interest. And he has no excuse, as his rectory is almost next door to it. I'm surprised the Brigadier accepted him – he's not the usual sort at all.'

'Hum. Well, he seems pretty rum to me.'

'Yes, quite!' she said, sipping sherry.

Maybe Miss Busybody wasn't such a birdbrain after all, actually I was beginning to realise that she was really rather astute. I eyed her more closely – she'd been pretty once, many years ago. The lines around her bright eyes spoke of a sense of humour, the slight upturn to her furrowed lips was a smile engraved by time. My mother would have liked her.

'Were you at the opera the night of the accident, Miss Busby?' I asked.

'I was, yes, indeed. It was an adequate performance. I'm rather fond of opera, although I prefer something more traditional. *Aida* is particularly moving.'

'Wouldn't know, I'm afraid,' I replied.

'You don't support the arts?' she asked, a note of teasing in her voice.

I eyed her. She was prevaricating, and I wondered why. Probably weighing me in the balance before deciding to open up – or not.

'Where were you sitting during the performance?' I asked.

She returned my gaze, then smiled. 'You don't think it was an accident, do you?'

'No,' I replied.

'My nephew is the local police inspector – Inspector Watson – my sister's eldest. He attended that evening and became terribly excited that it may have been murder. There was quite a debate at the time, then I think pressure was brought to bear and he decided it was nothing of the sort and lost interest. He's a chump,' she added.

'There's still a body at the mortuary; that can't be so easily dismissed. What about Crispin's family?'

'Two elderly aunts in Sussex, a bit gaga, from what I understand,' she told me. 'The accident was explained to them, they made the usual expressions of regret and released the body for burial.'

'But there must be an inquest?'

'Ah, but there is an earl and a wedding, isn't there. Nobody wants a fuss and it is generally believed that there is no reason to create a fuss. A quiet funeral will take place shortly. It will all be forgotten.'

'Hum,' I replied, weighing her words. I wasn't about to confide in her that Swift would already have acted to prevent any internment.

'Unless *you* take an interest, of course.' She looked at me with arched brows.

Dicks came over to refill our glasses. I must say, the Brigadier kept an exceptionally good cellar.

'Miss Busby,' I said after a sip of my snifter. 'Investigating requires the gathering of information and evidence. There is very little evidence, but someone with an enquiring mind may be able to offer information – such as where everyone was seated at the time of the accident.' I looked pointedly at her.

She laughed, a trilling laugh. 'Very persuasive, Major Lennox. Very well ...' Her voice dropped a notch as she became more serious. 'I was near the back, almost in the last row. It was a very long performance and the audience were not aficionados, so there was quite a lot of fidgeting. At the time of the accident, the family, including the Texans, were seated in the boxes. The young couple in the left-hand box, the older members in the right. I couldn't see them when the performers fell, but the lights were turned on almost immediately afterwards and they leapt to their feet and leaned over to stare at the stage. Except the Brigadier: he remained seated, but I saw him clearly,' Miss Busby added.

'Very good.' I nodded. 'Who was missing? There must have been some empty chairs in the auditorium.'

'There were,' she replied. 'Quite a few, actually. The Chaplain wasn't there, nor was the German gentleman. There were a small number of others absent, but they were local farmers. The understudy wasn't in his spot either.'

'You mean Andrew Dundale?' I prompted.

'Yes – he caught my attention, he has a very good voice. I do hope he keeps it, because he does sound rather strained,' she digressed. 'He was supposed to be among the chorus at the rear of the stage. They were silent as the soprano began her aria, but I was watching carefully – he wasn't there.'

'Interesting,' I noted. 'What happened after the trapdoor collapsed?'

'The young American took over, the groom, I mean – Hiram. He ordered people out and called for a doctor, who came immediately. I went below, they were rolling the soprano off the tenor,' she paused for a sip of sherry.

'She was making a dreadful fuss - he was distinctly dead. Quite ghastly, with his tongue hanging out and bloodshot eyes bulging. It seemed obvious what had happened: the plank holding up the trap-door gave way – and yet, one must ask, why had it not happened sooner?' She looked at me with a question in her eyes. 'I take it you are seeking answers to that puzzle?'

I nodded silently, not wanting to spill any beans.

'And of course there is the little door at the back of the theatre, the one that allows direct access to the traps below the stage,' Miss Busby mused.

'You know about that?' I asked, watching her more closely.

'I am an old friend of the family, I often walk in the grounds here.'

'You know where the spare key is?' I asked.

'Of course.'

'And anyone can gain access, if they know about it?'

'Yes, and I suspect a good many people who live or work in the house do know,' she stated with an arch of the brows.

'Hum. Any suspicions?'

She laughed. 'Indeed, yes, but no one I could point the finger at. It was too dark to see anything, apart from the orchestra.'

'Who *are* the orchestra, by the way?' This was a question I'd been wanting to ask for a while.

'I had the same thought,' she said. 'According to my chump of a nephew, they are from one of the Oxford colleges and play in their spare time. They were all present at the time of the accident, and before. It was easy to see them as they each had a lighted candle over their music stand, and I know none of them was absent.'

'Hum.' I nodded and switched the subject. 'What brought about the change of chaplain? Jarvis?'

She laughed lightly. 'For an investigator, Major Lennox, you don't seem to have discovered very much.'

That brought a frown to the brow. 'Well, I've only just started,' I protested.

'And nobody wants to tell you, either, do they?' She smiled again.

I laughed at the teasing, she was a spirited lady. 'Perhaps you might throw some light, Miss Busby?'

A slight frown gathered on her face as she recounted the tale. 'Well, the previous chaplain stole some silver and ran away. Or that was the story, anyway. He was an odd chap, quite reclusive. Jeremy Bartholomew, he was called. I tried to befriend him as he seemed rather a lost soul, but he remained elusive. I think he had suffered some sort of shock in the War. He stuttered rather badly and had a tremor, you know.'

I nodded. I knew there were a lot like him. Some recovered, many didn't.

Miss Busby continued: 'When he disappeared, my nephew investigated.'

'Inspector Watson?'

'I have only one nephew,' she retorted archly. 'He found letters in the Reverend Bartholomew's cottage signed by a woman from Brighton. It appeared that Bartholomew had been involved with this lady and that they planned to start a new life together on the Isle of Wight. All his belongings had gone, and so had some of the valuable church silver. It caused quite a stir at the time.'

'When was this?'

'Late last year.'

'Did the police find him in the Isle of Wight, or Brighton?'

'Not a trace,' she answered. 'But they said he would have changed his name, and she probably did too.'

A shadow loomed next to us.

'Miss Busby.' Von Graf arrived and bowed with a smart click of his heels. He then lifted the lady's hand and kissed it reverentially. 'Fraulein, it is always a pleasure to meet with you,' he smarmed.

'Major Lennox, have you met Count von Graf?' Miss Busby asked.

Yes,' I retorted sharply.

'Ja, Major.' Von Graf raised thin eyebrows at me. 'My friend Jarvis tells me you are a murderer, nein?'

'No, I damn well am not,' I retorted with feeling.

'Ha-ha, this is a joke, is it not? Your marvellous British humour. I like it very much. I am very British, don't you know, old man,' he laughed, then noticed my hostile regard and took a step backwards. 'Well, I must push off. I will be seeing you.' He raised a hand in mock salute, clicked his heels again, flashed a smile at Miss Busby and went over to join Jarvis, still sitting alone on a sofa.

'There's no need to scowl, Major Lennox.' Miss Busby was smiling. 'He can be quite amusing, you know, and he is very knowledgeable about art.'

I was about to tell her about the filched flowers when Caroline broke into our conversation by standing up and clapping her hands. 'You will all be delighted to hear that Dame Gabriel has agreed to sing for us. And Hiram's mother, Lady Ruth Chisholm, has offered to accompany her on the piano.' She looked around, commanding silence.

'Just need to see to my dog, old thing,' I told Caroline. I nodded to Miss Busby and the assembled, and made for the door.

'Lennox, come back!' Caroline snapped at me, but I'd had enough for one night, and besides, I had quite a lot of information to digest.

On returning to my room, I picked Fogg up and stuffed him under my arm. The kitten was asleep and I had determined not to have my dog-walking routine dictated by Fogg's infatuation with a small cat.

Foggy ferreted around the front gardens startling birds in the bushes while I stood gazing at the dark heavens strewn with stars. The night air was cool and fresh and suffused with silence. It cleared my head of the buzz of conversations, particularly the irritating ones. I stood quietly on the lawn, hands in pockets, and looked up at the house – a handsome place, its mellow stones settled into the gentle Cotswold landscape. Elaborate chimneys rose from steeply pitched roofs, black against the sky. Light shone yellow from various windows – tall, delicately latticed and framed in stone, the place looked inviting and warm and I called Foggy to come back with me indoors.

The bedroom fire had been lit and was blazing against the night chill. I took up my chair at the desk as kitten and dog settled on the hearthrug to watch the flames together.

Evidence that Dicks had been present was everywhere. My pens, pencils, ruler, knife-opener and ink were lined up precisely to the right. Empty jam jars stood in a serried row and my blotter was placed to the left along with my magnifying glass and, dead centre, my brand new notebook.

I lit the oil lamp and opened my notebook, which I'd brought for this very purpose. It was rather smart, I thought, with a dark leather binding and thick cream pages run across with faint red lines. I filled my pen with fresh ink and wrote all the details given to me by both Clegg and Miss Isabelle Busby. I ended with a large question mark next to the name of the absconded chaplain, Jeremy Bartholomew, and dabbed each page with the blotter. Tomorrow I would share some of my findings with Swift – provided he didn't spend too much time eliciting the company of the lovely Florence Braeburn.

CHAPTER 7

Breakfast is better taken in solitary peace, apart from the company of my dog, of course. Generally, when not at my own home, I take it alone in my rooms, but I thought I might bump into Florence today so I trotted down to the morning room with Fogg under my arm. I was the first to arrive as it was still only a touch before seven o'clock. I tucked in to my bacon and eggs, enjoying the quietude as footmen trod softly behind me.

I liked this room, it was filled with sunshine from large windows overlooking the gardens. Light reflected along the walls, washing the pale pastels with bright hue. As an interlude between dawn and the coming day, the morning room provided a gentle launching pad. I was musing quietly on the genius of designers of old when my serenity was abruptly broken. Andrew Dundale plonked himself opposite me.

'Heathcliff! You here?' Andrew said as he stuffed the corner of his napkin under his double chin.

'Patently, Andrew, and don't call me Heathcliff.' I reached for the newspaper and opened it in the hope that it would put him off. It didn't.

'Rumour has it that you're doing a spot of *detecting*. Probing into Crispin's extinction and all that?' Andrew retained the angelic phiz I recalled from our school days: eyes, cow-like in bovine blockheadedness, with a round face, pink cheeks and blond hair.

'Nothing for you to worry about, Andrew,' I muttered, staring intently at some tedious article in the Times.

A footman delivered Andrew's plate, almost overflowing with fried bacon, sausages, eggs, black pudding, kidneys, a sliver of steak, mushrooms, fried bread and onions. I didn't need to worry about him bothering me for long because he'd shortly be dead of a heart attack.

Before that, however, he leaned in close across the white tablecloth. 'You don't think it was an accident, do you? There wouldn't be anything to detect, if it were.'

I didn't answer, it would only encourage him.

'The thing is, old man,' he told me, shaking salt copiously over his meal. 'It should have been me.'

'What?'

He stopped spraying salt and looked around the room, then stared at me. 'It was me, not Crispin. They were after *me*.'

'Wait a minute. Are you saying you think someone wants to kill you?'

'Yes, that's what I said, Heathcliff. I thought you were detecting. You're not going to get very far if you can't follow the string of a sentence.'

'Andrew, if you call me Heathcliff again you'll be wearing that meal.'

'Well, really, old man. I came to tell you that my life is in danger and all you can do is object to my calling you by your own name.'

I tossed the newspaper aside. 'Start again, Andrew, and keep it simple, will you.'

He finished another mouthful. '*I* was supposed to sing the lead that night. Crispin told me he had something terribly important to do. "More important than squandering my talent on that bunch of Philistines", he said. But when Dame Gabriel heard about it, she threw a huge tantrum. Berated him in front of the whole troupe, called him a rank amateur and worse. Anyway, he crumbled in the end, performed the whole caboodle, and ended up getting squashed by said Dame.' Andrew gazed, round-eyed at me while chewing.

'Andrew,' I remarked. 'Anyone would realise it was Crispin on stage. He was older than you, for a start.'

'Yes, but once we were in make-up it was hard to tell between us. We're the same build and height and all that. Even hair colour.'

I eyed him narrowly: those round blue eyes in a chubby face topped by golden curls – perhaps he was cherubim to Crispin's seraphim.

'Why would anyone want to kill you, or him, for that matter?' I asked as I finished my food and dropped half a rasher Foggy's way.

'I don't know, but they do.' He nodded solemnly.

'Wouldn't be connected to the Black Cat Club, would it?' I asked.

He spluttered pieces of bacon. 'How the devil do you know about that?'

'Crispin's frocks. Oxford. And I recall how you used to like dressing up in school plays. Not too difficult to make the connection, really.'

'Is that detecting?' His brows rose in genuine surprise. 'Jolly good if it is. Did you really murder someone, Lennox?' he asked as he dunked toast in his egg.

'No, I did not! But if I ever do, that damn chaplain will be at the top of my list.'

'There's no need to shout, old chap,' he said.

I ran my fingers through my hair. 'Just tell me what happens at the Black Cat Club.'

'Ah, well … This isn't going to go any further, is it?'

'No,' I lied. 'Spit it out, Andrew, or we'll be here all morning.'

'Um, it's just a bit of fun really. Bunch of chaps laying on some light-hearted entertainment. Like we used to do in the Army. Concerts, that sort of thing,' he said.

'Yes, and …'

'Well, we used to have an act together, Crispin and I, in the Division Theatre Group. We were on loan from the Oxfordshire Hussars. When the War ended, we came back and just sort of carried on.'

'The Oxfordshire Hussars were under the Brigadier, weren't they?' I asked.

'Yes, but I don't think he cared for any dramatics; sent us off to HQ and told us we could stay there for the duration.'

'He knew you and Crispin, then?'

'Wouldn't say he knew us, old chap.' Andrew paused for a slurp of tea. 'Said we were unfit for service and sent us packing. Crispin's bleeding affliction, you know – and I'm a flatfoot; so we weren't much use in the soldierly sense. They let us in as Non-Combatants.'

'Hum.' I digested this snippet and ordered some toast and marmalade. 'This act you had, were you dressed in drag?'

'Yes – yes, that was the point: we were the "ladies". We were stars back in the War, you know. Putting on shows. The men used to adore us. Everywhere we went, they'd call out to us, "Give us a song", or "Show us a leg". When we sang "Take Me Back To Dear Old Blighty", everyone joined in, top brass too. It was very moving, actually.' He suddenly broke into song. '"There's a long, long trail a-winding / Into the land of my dreams. Where the nightingales are singing / And the white moon beams …"'

I remembered it, too, from when I was at the front; and he was right, it was very moving. I shook myself out of it.

'All right, Andrew. Quieten down, man,' I told him as the footmen turned to stare. 'So you continued your act at the Black Cat Club in Oxford?'

He sighed. 'We did, but it wasn't the same. Much smaller house, of course; and I have to tell you, Lennox, there are some strange fellows down there. I mean, we're supposed to be the ones in drag, but so are quite a few in the audience. Most of them, actually. Crispin thought it was all marvellous, but I have doubts, you know …' He trailed off.

'Is there anyone else at the Club that you know or recognise from here or the opera company?' I questioned.

'Good Lord, no!' He almost jumped at the thought. 'You won't tell them, will you? Especially Dame Gabriel. She is an utter martinet – terrifying woman. If she knew, it would be the end for me.' He looked at me with round-eyed consternation.

It was my turn to sigh. 'Andrew, I'm not here to judge or tattle. I am here for Caroline's wedding and casting a cool eye over Crispin's death while I'm about it.' That's what I told him, anyway.

'I'm not going anymore. Not now,' he said, and forked the remaining sausage.

'Where?'

'The Black Cat Club. I told them last night, I can't do it on my own – not without Crispin. My heart's not in it, so I'm going to stick to opera.' He sighed suddenly. 'But it lacks fizz, you know. The crowd doesn't sing along – well, they can't really, can they? Awfully difficult to hit those sorts of notes … but yes, I miss the shouting and the clapping. The troops were always so happy to see us. I'm not sure I'm suited to opera.' He sighed again and finished his meal. 'But you will get him won't you, Lennox? The blighter that did for Crispin – because he'll still be after me. If it *was* me, and I think it was, because it would have been me if –'

I stood up, cutting short his wittering, my patience and wits exhausted. 'I'm going now, Andrew. Goodbye.'

Underneath the brainless meandering, Andrew did have a point – why did anyone want to kill Crispin? Or Andrew for that matter – not that I thought they did. He was always a dramatist, needing to be the centre of attention even at school. No, I didn't believe for a moment anyone had it in for Andrew, but Crispin? What had he done? And who had he done it to?

Florence was coming in through the French windows from the garden as I was crossing the hall, lost in thought. The sight of her snapped me out of my cogitating. She was wearing a peach-coloured frock and looked a peach herself. Fogg raced up, tail wagging, for a fuss and a ruffle; I grinned like an idiot.

'Greetings, old thing,' I said, without managing to make a fool of myself.

'Hello, Lennox, it's a beautiful morning, I couldn't resist a walk in the gardens and I picked some wild flowers. Adorable, aren't they?' She smiled and showed me a bunch of weeds.

'Um, yes, very nice. There are proper flowers in the garden, you know.'

Her smile faltered. 'These are proper flowers. They are a gift, Lennox, from nature.' She held them up.

'Really? Well, thank you.'

I took them from her, not sure what to do with them, but tried to look appreciative. She stared at me rather oddly.

'I didn't, um... Well, never mind. We're having a dress fitting this morning. Caroline and I, that is. The other two bridesmaids are coming to join us. Bunty and Agatha from the hunt. Do you remember them?'

'Erm, no. Don't think so. Should I?' In the bright sunlight I noticed Florence had freckles across her nose. I'd never thought of freckles being remotely appealing until that moment.

'Yes, we all rode out with the local pack when we were youngsters, it was such fun.' She looked up at me. 'Don't you remember?'

'Erm ...' I cudgelled my brains. 'I had a big-boned roan. Fifteen hands, wouldn't shy from anything, just threw his heart into it and jumped. Had him for years, even after I outgrew him, he was called Red.'

'I meant people, actually.' A small frown formed between her brows. 'Anyway, Caroline has organised a hack; we're taking a picnic lunch with us. The stable boys are getting the horses ready and we wondered if you'd like to join in. Hiram and his father are coming too, it's not only girls,' she laughed lightly.

'Yes, I'd be delighted. If they've still got the bay gelding called Toby, I'll take him.'

'I'll ask them. And you'll bring doggie?' She bent to ruffle Fogg's long ears.

'Fogg, he's called Mister Fogg.' I wanted to talk to her further – tell her how delightful she was and pretty and something about lighting up this fine spring morning, but I seemed to have frozen to the spot again.

'Well, see you later then, Lennox and Mister Fogg,' and off she went, waving. I waved back with the weeds and watched her go.

Dicks had been left in charge of the kitten so I didn't feel the need to return to my rooms just yet. I headed off with Fogg for a walk through the sprawling formal gardens at the rear of the house, heading for the chantry. I knew Swift would want to visit the Dower House when he arrived and interview the opera troupe, and before that tedious event, I thought I'd take a quiet look around.

I strode through fragrant flower gardens, then took a path between avenues of tall yew hedges and followed on through squared plots of medicinal herbs edged with lavender, still dormant in the cool of early spring. The chantry was set on a hill; it was very old, pre-dating the house by a number of centuries. Some sort of monastery had stood here once, but the greed of monarchs and men had stolen the lands and buildings away until all that remained was the simple structure where the monks had once chanted to God. It was tall and narrow, as these places were, being only as wide as the length of the joists that had been used to span the roof. Slim windows fitted with leaded glass were cut into the rough stone walls. The only decoration on the building was around the arched doorway, where ancient hands had carved a frieze – now eroded away to indecipherable knots and loops. The door was on the latch; it squealed as I pushed it open. I entered quietly and walked to the front to sit in a pew. Fogg was always well behaved in church, and he sat at my feet as

I bowed my head and sent a silent prayer for my parents and the many friends and comrades who lay in the rich soil of Flanders' fields and beyond.

Squat candles flickering with flame were fixed to a stand near the altar, which was covered with a white cloth embroidered with the Bloxford family crest. I laid the posy Florence had given me at the foot of a gleaming brass cross set on a high stone window sill. There were more candles in a box and I picked one up, lit it from another and placed it in the wrought-iron candlestick with a half dozen others, then turned to look around. It was a spartan building: high wooden roof blackened with age, plain white walls, various marble and brass plaques in memory of the family dead, an ornate bust of a plump lady, another of a Cavalier wearing a plumed hat at a jaunty angle, and a recumbent medieval knight carved from yellow Cotswold stone. It was dust-free and smelt of candles and beeswax and the scent of fresh flowers, which were prettily arranged in vases around the nave. Exquisitely embroidered kneelers hung from the ancient pews. I imagined it was Miss Busby caring for it all, as she'd mentioned that Jarvis wasn't doing his duty by the place.

The rectory was down a meandering path, set beyond a hill bearing a mausoleum, standing in lost grandeur amidst an overgrown graveyard awash with bluebells. Fogg chased pigeons in the copse behind the house as I raised the knocker to rap on the door. No one answered, I rapped again, very loudly, and then tried the handle. It was locked. The rectory was little more than a two-storey cottage with an elevated title. Thatched roof turned green with moss, whitewashed walls peeling and faded to grey, it looked unkempt and unloved. I peered through a small lattice window: dirty dishes were piled up and empty bottles strewn about the kitchen. I walked around the side through a tangled garden of weeds and looked through grimy windows into the sparsely furnished living room. A cloth-draped canvas was propped on an easel; there was a low table next to it laden with brushes, a palette and contorted tubes of oil paints. The paraphernalia was set up in the far corner, where the brightest light was to be had. Jarvis was obviously an artist as well as a man of the cloth. I tried the door again, then gave up and retraced my steps.

'The Lord is my Shepherd, I shall not want. He maketh me to lie down …'

The sound of prayer reached my ears. It was muttered in a low tone – a man's voice, coming from the direction of the graveyard. The hairs rose on the back of my neck. Fogg suddenly froze. One paw held off the ground, nose sniffing the light breeze drifting down from the hill, he stared towards the soft murmuring amongst the headstones. Then he turned and ran, ears and tail down, racing full tilt back towards the house and no doubt the safe sanctuary of his basket and the kitten.

An old man, dressed in a long dark cloak and leaning on a shepherd's crook, was softly reciting the prayer, almost as hymnal music. It was plaintive and lilting, haunting in the quiet of the ancient graveyard. His back was towards me but his black and white collie dog turned its head to stare for a moment, then went back to watching whatever held the attention of its master.

The shepherd reached the end of the prayer and finished with, 'Amen.'

'Amen,' I echoed.

He didn't move, just stood with lowered head. I went to join him and we both looked down upon the body of the Reverend Geoffrey Jarvis. He lay sprawled, crucifix-like upon the grave of someone long dead. A sentinel sword pierced the ground at his head. His black cassock was stained with a bloom of dark blood across the chest and his glazed eyes gazed unseeing at the clear blue sky of the fresh spring morning.

CHAPTER 8

'Dead,' the shepherd informed me.

'Indeed,' I replied. 'Have you been here long?'

'No, I were looking for me ram. 'E's not got nought to do and the lambs is being born, so I weren't watching him as close as like. 'E's gone searching for new pastures, 'e has. They be like that – rams,' he told me in voice heavy with the burr of the Cotswold Hills. 'And it's going to rain, tha' ken.'

'Really?'

'Ay. Yon cows be lyen', don't tha' see.'

'Yes,' I nodded, not entirely comprehending what he was talking about. 'Didn't happen to see anyone else around, did you?' I asked. 'The blighter who murdered the Chaplain, for instance?'

'Nary a soul.' He shook his head. 'The Reverend were like this when I found 'im, not but a short while ago. Thought I should say a word, 'im being of the cloth an' all.' He looked up at me – a bent old man; beneath the cloak he was clothed in ancient tweeds, tied at the waist and gaiters with thick twine. He had a long nose, thin and crooked, straggling eyebrows like brambles over the brow, and eyes blue as the sky, that watched me closely as we spoke. 'Weren't you as did it, were it?'

'No, it was not,' I replied briskly, although I only had my dog as witness, but then, so too did he. 'I think he's been dead for some time, actually.' I moved forward to take a closer look. Jarvis was frocked in the usual chaplain's garb: long black cassock, somewhat grubby dog-collar, and two-tone Oxford brogues – rather raffish for a chaplain, in my view.

The blood had seeped around a wound to the man's chest and spread in a wide stain. By the slightly charred hole in the fabric, I'd have wagered it was caused by a bullet at fairly close range. Quite a large bullet, actually, and it had probably gone right through him. I glanced at the old gravestone behind him, but there was nothing to be seen other than mottled moss and lichen.

The sword had been struck into the ground just a couple of inches above his head. It was a rapier, rather a handsome one, and judging by the blazon on the pommel it came from Bloxford Hall – I recognised the family crest of swans and lions rampant.

I ran my hand through my hair, somewhat nonplussed.

'Didn't hear a whisper,' the shepherd said.

'What?' I asked.

'No gun shot. This mornin', I didn't hear owt, but then the wind be blowin' down to the woods, an' I was up of it.' He indicated the direction with his crook.

'Ah, yes,' I snapped out of my momentary reverie. 'I doubt anyone would have heard it, unless they were near the Rectory.'

'Aye,' he nodded. 'I'll be away, then. Ram'll be catched in a hedge or ditch if I don't garner 'im up.'

'Very well.' I nodded to him. 'Didn't catch your name?'

'Seth,' he replied, and left with a steady tread along a slim track between the bluebells and leaning gravestones, his dog silent at his heels.

I straightened up, hand on chin, and took a walk around the body. Other than the blood on his chest, there wasn't much to see. There was no apparent injury to the hands or face and I wasn't going to lift his frock. From his expression you'd think he'd found it a joke because his face wore a distinct smirk – the same expression he'd worn last evening; not so amusing now, I thought.

I felt under his chin: no pulse of course – his skin was stone cold and slightly damp, there was a layer of dew on him, and his jaw had already started to stiffen. I lifted one arm and let it drop. It was flaccid, so he'd been dead at least two hours, but not much longer as rigor mortis was just creeping in. He wasn't wearing a watch, but I withdrew my fob from my waistcoat pocket and noted the time at eight twenty hours. Swift could check the dead man's clothing – the police were better suited to that distasteful task, in my view. I turned towards the house in search of the Inspector.

There was another argument in the hall, I heard it as I approached, could hardly miss it actually.

'I can go wherever I consider necessary. I do not need your permission,' Swift was shouting at Dawkins.

'No one as given me no orders, so's ye can't do nuffink,' Dawkins retorted. 'More 'an my job's worth, doing somethin' without orders.'

I sighed. 'Dawkins, what the devil do you think you're doing?'

'Major Lennox, sir.' Dawkins's shoulders drooped as he saw me. 'I was just sayin' –'

'Don't.' I held up my hand and then pointed in the direction of the boot room.

He shuffled away, muttering, 'Dogsbody, I am. Nothin' but a dogsbody, no one tells me nothin' 'cept do this, do that ...'

I nodded at Swift, who yanked the belt of his trench coat tighter and fell into step with me.

'We need to interview the opera group,' Swift stated.

'Not now, Swift. Something more important.'

A silent footman swung the French windows open for us.

'I'm not answerable to you or anybody in this house, Lennox. Nor am I going to be chaperoned about the place.' He swung round to face me. 'I am an officer of the police and I am investigating this incident as I see fit.' He raised his voice. 'ON MY OWN. Is that clear?'

'Fine,' I replied, turning away as he headed in the direction of the theatre and the Dower House. 'I'll telephone the local constabulary about the body.'

He stalked a few more steps along the gravel path, then stopped and swung round. 'What?'

I carried on towards the distant hill beyond the walled gardens; he had to break into a trot to catch me. I walked in silence for a while, then told him about the expired Reverend.

Irritating as Swift was, he knew how to listen without breaking in with pointless questions, so as we strode uphill I briefed him on the conversation I'd had last evening with Miss Busby about who was missing on the occasion of Crispin's death. I chose to omit Andrew Dundale's wittering nonsense until I'd given it a little more thought myself.

We were a touch breathless as we reached the corpse stiffening in the sunshine behind the chapel.

Seth, the old shepherd, was gone and I hadn't mentioned his role to Swift as it would only complicate matters; Miss Busby on the other hand was fully present and staring with consternation at the bloodied body.

'Ah, good morning, Major Lennox.' She turned to me with a tight smile. 'It seems we have a tragedy.'

'I'm sorry you've had to witness this, madam,' Swift said, and introduced himself.

'Perhaps we should let the Inspector do his job, Miss Busby?' I suggested, and moved away a few steps. She followed whilst keeping a close eye on Swift's examination of the extirpated Jarvis. He was very carefully surveying the body with a magnifying glass in one hand while poised with a pair of tweezers in the other. I would rather have liked to be doing the same, but hadn't brought my whatnots with me and also felt I should be on hand to support Miss Busby in case she were suddenly overcome.

'I visited the chantry earlier this morning,' I began, 'there were lit candles. I thought it may have been your work?'

'Yes, indeed,' she said, 'I come here most days.'

'Would you like to wait in there?' I asked. 'I can escort you.'

'No, really, Major Lennox.' She smiled. 'It isn't necessary. I nursed injured soldiers here at the house during the War – it was given over to convalescence. I have seen worse.' She looked back at the body. 'He wasn't a nice man, you know.'

'Can't say I took to him either.' I would have used stronger language in other circumstances.

Swift looked towards me. 'Nothing to be found.' He pocketed the glass and tweezers. 'We'll turn him.'

I went to help and we heaved the Chaplain over. It wasn't easy, as he was stiffening up quite rapidly. There was little to be seen other than more dried blood, although something flickered into my brain and flew out again before I could register it. I straightened up as Swift continued to search the body.

'Bullet went all the way through,' he remarked. 'We'll have to search the area for it.'

'It looks like he was killed here,' I remarked.

Swift glanced at the Chaplain's shoes. 'Yes, there are no scuff marks, so he wasn't dragged. He could have been carried, I suppose.'

'Unlikely,' I remarked. 'The killer would have been covered in blood and the blood would have run down the man's cassock.'

'Yes,' Swift agreed, cooly, 'he was either standing on this spot, which seems unlikely, or he was ordered here at the barrel of a gun.'

'Or sword point.' I added.

Swift looked back down at the corpse's fingers. 'There's paint under his fingernails and on his clothes.'

'Oil paint, probably,' I said. 'He was an artist of some sort.'

'He was a very good artist, actually.' Miss Busby came to stand beside us; she was evidently made of pretty stern stuff. 'It was the only good thing about him.' She watched as we rolled the body back. 'Why do you think the sword was struck there, just behind his head?' she asked.

Swift and I looked at it for a moment, then each other.

'I don't know,' he said and closed his lips firmly.

Neither did I, but I knew that it must have considerable significance.

'He was killed sometime after dawn, I'd say,' I remarked, changing tack.

'Agreed,' Swift replied. 'About half-past six this morning.'

'Whose grave is this?' I asked Miss Busby, trying to decipher the worn lettering on the headstone.

'Frederick Benson. Old Benson's grandfather,' she replied. 'The Bloxfords are in the vault.' She turned to indicate the stone mausoleum surrounded by bluebells at the centre of the graveyard.

'We'll have to call the local constabulary,' Swift said wiping his hands together. 'And an ambulance.'

'Oh, I already have,' Miss Busby put in. 'My nephew is on his way.'

'He's the local Inspector,' I told Swift, and turned back to Miss Busby. 'He's not coming in by the main gate, is he? Because I haven't warned them at the Hall yet …'

'No.' She shook her head. 'There's a lych-gate just beyond the hill, it opens onto the village. He will be here very soon, he was just finishing his breakfast.'

The piercing blast of police whistles broke into our conversation, quickly followed by the sound of heavy boots running up the hill.

'Well, Swift,' I said, moving in the other direction. 'I think we'll leave you to it.'

'Stop right there!' A voice bellowed at us from the direction of the trampling boots. 'Don't you be touching a thing.'

There followed another loud blast of whistles.

A platoon of police arrived red-faced and panting, led by a doughy individual whom I took to be Inspector Watson.

We had arranged the body back into its original position and the uniformed constables gathered around it, agog with excitement. One of them collapsed in a heap.

'Take no notice,' Watson ordered, 'Walter always faints at the sight of blood.' He was near bald with small eyes and pink cheeks; beads of sweat were gathering over his sparse brows. His creased suit was slightly too small for his girth and his paunch threatened to burst his waistcoat buttons.

'Why did you bring him, then?' I asked.

'He's the Sergeant,' Watson replied. 'Got to have a sergeant present. Takes the notes, he does.'

'Not from down there he doesn't,' Swift retorted.

'Oh, it's you, Inspector Swift?' Watson recognised him and sketched a salute. 'I've come to inspect the scene of the crime, sir.'

'I haven't seen no one killed afore,' one of the bobbies said.

'You ain't been in the War, you ain't,' an older constable responded.

'Is 'e gone stiff yet?' another asked.

'Why's that sword stickin' in the ground?' someone piped up from the rear.

Watson knelt down next to the body and began prodding the corpse, then looked up at Swift and me. 'He's been shot. I hope you haven't touched him?'

We glanced at each other and remained silent.

'I'll be needing statements and fingerprints, we'll do it proper, like,' Watson continued.

'Don't be ridiculous, George,' Miss Busby told him. 'I am not going to have my fingerprints taken.'

'Aunty Bella,' he hissed, 'don't be showing me up now.'

'Do you think the bullet went right through?' another copper said, leaning in closer.

'Yes,' I informed him, 'it did.'

'How do you know that?' Watson snapped, pausing in his search of the body for papers or anything interesting.

'Um …'

'Was it you' as found him?' Watson looked at me accusingly.

'Yes, but he'd been dead a couple of hours by then,' I replied.

'Where was you two hours before, then?'

'At the house – and I have a number of reliable witnesses,' I informed him, although Andrew Dundale could hardly be described as reliable.

'I can vouch for him,' Swift backed me up, which made a change.

'Can I touch 'im, sir?' another constable said, reaching a finger towards Jarvis, who was taking on a mottled hue under the warming sun.

A shrill jangle of bells reached us from the direction the police had come.

'That'll be the ambulance,' Watson said, getting up off his knees and brushing grass from his trousers. 'Doctor'll be here. Enough gawping now, lads. Search the area. Apprehend anyone you find. Look for clues, and find that bullet,' he shouted, waving his arms about. 'And you folks, you can make your statements to Walter when 'e wakes up.' He eyed us firmly.

'You'll find me at the house,' I said, turning on my heel. I'd had enough policemen for one day.

'Lennox, you can't just leave,' Swift started to argue.

I ignored him and walked off; Miss Busby followed.

'You're going to the rectory, aren't you?' she said as we trod the path toward the cottage and the copse of trees.

'I assume you telephoned your nephew from there?' I said.

'I did, yes.' She was little out of breath trying to keep up with me, so I slowed my pace.

'And you know where the key is,' I stated.

She nodded. 'Yes, under the flowerpot next to the front door. What are you looking for, Major Lennox?'

'Paintings, Miss Busby. There are a few empty spaces up at the house, I noticed them when I arrived.'

'Ah.' She stopped suddenly and smiled. I turned to face her.

'What?'

'The Chaplain wasn't working on the sort of paintings one would exhibit in open view.'

'Really,' I raised my brows. 'Why?'

She giggled. 'They were all ladies. Naked ladies.'

'Good Lord. Perhaps you'd better stay here.'

'Certainly not,' she said, marching off ahead of me. 'One of them is me!'

CHAPTER 9

I stood irresolute with hands in pockets as Miss Busby took a firm grip of the rectory door and tugged it open. I'd charged into perilous situations during the War, but this one brought me into hitherto uncharted territory. The question playing uppermost in my mind was: how recent was the portrait? And why on earth was she *naked*?

The place was more disordered inside than it had appeared from my glance through the windows. I had to duck – the beamed ceiling was low – but I made my way safely to the easel where Miss Busby had tugged the white linen cloth off the canvas resting on the paint-spattered bar.

'What do you think?' she asked meditatively.

'Um … doesn't look awfully like you, frankly.'

'It isn't,' she replied.

I regarded it more closely. 'Isn't that …?' I began, then suddenly recoiled. 'Good God, that's Lady Grace!'

Miss Busby laughed. 'Rather good, don't you think?'

To my relief the picture was not actually naked, although it wasn't difficult for the imagination to fill in the areas draped in silk and gauze. Caroline Bloxford's eyes gazed steadily back at me, except that it wasn't Caroline, it was her mother. A lady whom I recalled as being warm, sparkling, and old to my child's eye – and always fully clothed. This was an entirely new vision of her and it came as a bit of a shock.

'Jarvis can't have painted this,' I said. 'Lady Grace has been dead for almost two decades.'

'He didn't,' Miss Busby answered. 'He was restoring them. There are over a dozen that I'm aware of, but they're supposed to be under lock and key at Bloxford Hall. They're known as the Bloxford Beauties.'

'Including you?' I frowned, unable to make sense of it.

She smiled, then grabbed the linen cloth, wrapped it back around the portrait and shoved Lady Grace into my arms.

'Come on. We're not having the police leering at this. Quickly now, my nephew will be here shortly.'

'Are there any more here? I asked.

'Not that I could find,' she replied, 'and this one shouldn't be here either.'

I followed her into the copse behind the house and we followed a muddy byway that led back toward the village and stopped at the lych-gate.

'Miss Busby –' I began.

She held her hands up to silence me. 'I will explain, truly, Major Lennox.'

The swift march through the trees had brought colour to her cheeks; she looked younger, and rather exhilarated by the clandestine thievery. 'Would you care to come to tea, later this afternoon?' she asked.

Intrigued though I was, the thought of the picnic lunch and ride in the company of Florence held far more appeal. But I realised I wasn't going to join them now. I must talk to the Brigadier and break the news to him that not only had he lost his chaplain, he was also about to be invaded by the police whether he liked it or not. And Caroline would have to know. Damn it, this was exactly the sort of hue and cry everyone had been trying to avoid.

'If I can,' I replied as I arranged the wrapped painting more firmly under my arm.

'Lavender Cottage,' Miss Busby smiled. 'Goodbye.'

I avoided the graveyard and the police and strode quickly back to the house. I was just in time to see the riding party trot off down the drive. Hiram and his father were riding in the most extraordinary fashion, with high-pommel saddles, and seated as though they were almost falling asleep on their horses' backs.

My mother was American, but I don't recall her ever riding in such a singular fashion.

Benson was in the hall tottering about with a small tray of the day's mail, his sleeves falling over his wrists. 'Ah, Major Lennox,' he wheezed. 'They've gone, I'm afraid we couldn't find you. I asked young Dicks, but he didn't know where you were. You could hurry, sir, catch them.'

'No, no, old chap. I'm off upstairs to see the Brigadier, must have a word. And Benson?'

'Yes, sir,' he rasped.

'Find Dicks. Tell him to stand by the door, would you. The police are on their way.'

He looked at me as though the lights were going out, then perked up suddenly and nodded. 'Yes, sir,' he said again, and tottered off.

I placed my hand on the carved wooden bannister rail to go upstairs, then halted. The missing paintings from the hall had been returned. At least, I assumed they were the same artworks, as they fitted very well into their spaces. There was a fine thoroughbred horse with long legs, an excellent pair of hunting hounds and a landscape of the area with some sheep in it. I went over to take a closer look, noticing they seemed very spruce – in much better condition than the rest, actually, which were dusty with soot from the many log fires that had burnt in the huge fireplace. I gazed for a moment, then turned and bounded up the stairs to my rooms, where I pushed the wrapped portrait of Lady Grace under the bed and dashed onwards to the upper floor.

Kalo the Gurkha let me in and silently led me through to the Brigadier, who was again seated before a roaring fire, staring into space. I took a chair opposite and broke the news to him loudly.

'The Chaplain?' he bellowed.

'The Reverend Jarvis, sir,' I repeated. 'He's been killed. Shot. And a rapier from this house was left next to him, sir.'

'Who killed him? The damn Boche? Must have crawled under the wire. Shoot 'em. All of them.' He slapped his hand down on his knee.

'Jarvis was your chaplain here at the house, sir,' I tried again.

The Gurkha brought him something muddy in a cup that may have been tea.

'Herbal. Want some?' the Brigadier asked, sipping it.

I shook my head.

He looked directly at me, eyes slightly blurred by the blue haze around the irises, then suddenly he focused quite clearly. 'Lennox. Are you telling me that imbecile Jarvis is dead?'

'I am, sir.'

Whatever was in the tea seemed to have done the trick.

'Good, never liked him. Who did it?'

'No idea, sir,' I persevered. 'What was he doing here, apart from ministering?'

He stared at me, a tic flickered on his cheek, but he made no other movement. 'You are digging, Major, into things that do not concern you.'

'Like the Bloxford Beauties?' I replied.

He continued to stare directly at me, then spoke coldly. 'How did you learn of the Beauties?'

I could hardly spill the beans on Miss Busby. 'I discovered the nature of his work. And I need to know if it was sanctioned by you.'

I was fishing in the dark; it was very clear that the Beauties were a closely guarded secret. I decided not to tell him that I had squirrelled away Lady Grace under my bed.

He stared at me with hostility, then spoke.

'There was a storm. Some windows blew in, caused damage. The paintings needed restoring. I agreed to the cleaning and whatever these Johnnies do. Started in Charles the Second's day. Sixteen sixty or thereabouts. Family carried it on. No smut, first class artists and all that. One by Gainsborough. Not for public view, they're in the Long Gallery, locked up. Going to hand them over to my new son-in-law. Hiram. He can look after it. Soon have it all anyway.'

So the Brigadier knew he didn't have long – or I took that to be his meaning.

'Why would anyone kill Jarvis?' I asked again.

'Man knew how to paint, but he wasn't a man of the cloth.'

'How did he come to be here?'

'Bishop sent him. No, no, it wasn't. Ask the Americans, the mother. And Lennox …' His voice trailed off.

'Yes, sir?'

'I wanted it to be you. Thought if you came here, perhaps she would think again. But I watched her. And him. They're happy, aren't they?'

'They are, sir.' I sighed, saddened to see the old man failing. He was lost to us most of the time and soon he would be gone altogether. 'Caroline and I were as close as siblings, but it was never more than that. She made the right choice.'

'We all hoped, when you were young. Grace and your mother. Your family came to stay before the War. You should have seen them, the girls. Grace was named well, and your lovely mother, too, Mary-Rose. They were good friends. Led me and your father a merry dance …' He drifted off, into days long ago. At least he wasn't fighting the War. I rose, gave him a smart salute, left him to his memories and trotted downstairs.

I could hear raised voices in the hallway as I descended. The constabulary had arrived. Dawkins was remonstrating, and the police were all arguing with him. It seemed like an excellent time to make a few notes in my book so I turned tail and took the stairs two at a time to arrive at the sanctuary of my rooms. Dicks was there, tidying up – what could possibly be left to tidy up, for heaven's sake!

'Benson didn't happen to speak to you, Dicks?

'No, sir. Would you care for coffee, sir? I can bring some.'

'Um, yes please, Dicks, and sandwiches. Been a busy morning.'

'Certainly, sir. Mister Fogg returned without you, I gave him a snack.'

'Excellent, thank you. We found a body – he dislikes anything dead. Hopeless as a gun dog,' I remarked while filling my pen with more ink, some of which dripped onto the desk. Dicks didn't even notice; he was standing motionless with a small brush in his hand.

'You, mean a – dead person? Somebody dead, sir. Actually dead?'

Really, people do get excited about bodies, you'd think no one had ever been murdered before.

'Yes. It was the Chaplain – Jarvis.' I blotted the ink-spots myself as Dicks seemed to have lost interest in cleaning.

'Another one?' Dicks stared at me wide-eyed.

'Yes, why? Do you know something about the previous chaplain?' I asked, eyeing him more closely.

'No, no. I meant another dead body. You know, after the opera singer. This is like the moving pictures. Was it with an axe?' Dicks asked, eyes open even wider.

'No, shot at close range. What moving pictures?'

'At the new picture house at Oxford, sir. I went to see *The Face at the Window*. Scared stiff, I was. It was wonderful, sir.'

'Ah, moving-picture houses – never been. You mentioned coffee, Dicks?'

'Yes, sir. Right away, sir. Erm, sir, won't the police want to talk to someone, sir?'

'Probably. You will find them downstairs, Dicks. And don't let them run amok, will you.' I turned back to my notebook and wrote down the time and details of this morning's intriguing incidents. I halted for some moments while I considered the Bloxford Beauties. Was there a direct link between Crispin Gibbons and Jarvis, and if so, was it art or was it theatre, or both? Or neither? The ink dried on my nib as I pondered, then a sharp rap on the door snapped me from my woolgathering.

'I brought coffee and dainties for two, sir.' Dicks came in with a huge tray.

I didn't have to ask why he'd supplied sustenance for two because Swift stalked in right behind him, a deep frown between his brows and the rapier closely wrapped in a striped cloth.

'No fingerprints, I take it?' I said.

He shook his head and sat on the edge of one of the club chairs beside the unlit fire. 'All wiped clean or the killer wore gloves. But I found this.' He held up a flattened bullet between finger and thumb. 'It hit a gravestone at the rear of the cemetery.'

I moved in his direction and took it from him to roll around in my palm.

'Above forty, possibly forty-five, I'd say. Difficult to say, it's been terribly deformed.'

'Do you have any firearms of that calibre here?' he asked.

I laughed. 'Yes, and so has everybody in the house. And if not, they'd certainly have access to one.' I eyed him closely. 'Come along, Swift, you know what it's like. This country is awash with guns brought back from the war.'

His shoulders sagged a fraction. 'Yes, I am quite aware of that.' He stared me in the eye. '*You* didn't do it?' he asked.

'No.' I turned to Dicks, busy setting the table whilst listening to our conversation. 'Dicks, what time did you come in this morning?'

'Six thirty-five, sir,' he confirmed.

'Just as I was leaving for breakfast,' I said.

Swift nodded. 'Very well. Any idea who did it?'

'No.'

'Would you tell me if you did?'

That gave me pause. 'Probably.'

'Is that a sword, sir?' Dicks came and stared at the wrapped rapier. 'Was the Chaplain shot *and* stabbed?'

'No, he wasn't,' Swift said.

'Can I see it?'

'No,' Swift snapped. 'It's evidence in a murder case.'

'Dicks,' I reminded him, and nodded at the table where the kitten had clambered up and was sniffing the contents of the milk jug. Dicks moved smartly to grab the little cat.

Swift was still in a black mood, and confronted me. 'You and the old lady, Miss Busby, removed something from the rectory. The piece of art Jarvis was working on at the easel.'

I regarded him quietly, wondering how he'd discovered that piece of news.

'You've got paint on your sleeve,' he said. 'It's the same colour as the wet oil paint I saw on the palette.'

'Ah,' I replied, with a smidgeon of guilt.

Fogg went to sit next to the reading table where Dicks had finished spreading a tablecloth and had set two places with plates, coffee cups and saucers and the usual whatnots. He was now standing with a white napkin over his arm, like some ginger-haired French waiter from a bistro.

I checked my sleeve as Swift went to sit in the chair. The damn paint wouldn't come off – well, at least it was green. I sat down and thanked Dicks, telling him we didn't need him any further.

As there was just the two of us, I opened up over coffee, and spilled the beans about Lady Grace and my conversations with Miss Busby and the Brigadier. Swift responded reasonably but he wanted to see the painting, so I lied and told him I'd left it in Miss Busby's hands.

'Later,' I told him. 'And we'll need to track down the other Bloxford Beauties. The Brigadier said they were in the Long Gallery. But, Swift, I have to warn you, it's a sworn secret held by an ancient and honourable family — there will be hell to pay if it gets out.'

He regarded me silently for a long moment, taking in my words. Then asked, 'what's the Long Gallery?'

'It's usually a large room built under the eaves, at the very top of the house. All the fashion in Elizabethan days; designed as an indoor skittles alley originally, and somewhere for the children to play and run off steam when the weather forced the family indoors.'

'Pretty much thought of everything, didn't they. The nobs, anyway,' Swift replied, unable to resist a dig.

'Oh, cut the chip off your shoulder, Swift. It's churlish and unwarranted,' I told him. 'That was then and this is now. Owning a place the size of Bloxford Hall is one long headache and don't pretend you don't realise that.'

'Humph,' he muttered, helping himself to a generous slice of shortbread.

'If one of these Beauties is by Gainsborough, it'll be extremely valuable,' Swift commented.

'All the paintings are by leading artists,' I replied. 'Each one of them will be valuable. But it's a private family collection — they're the mothers, grandmothers and great grandmothers of this house. None will ever be sold, whatever the circumstances.'

He regarded me unblinking for a moment, then nodded.

'What's the story on the rapier?' I asked.

'I'm sure you recognise the crest. You know it's from here,' Swift said. 'I'll search the house shortly, see if I can discover where it's missing from.'

I laughed, he scowled at me. 'Swift, there are almost a hundred rooms in this place and every one of them is packed. How many gewgaws, souvenirs, and war booty do you think the family has accumulated over three hundred years. Take a look, by all means, and if you don't return in the next couple of months, I'll send out a search party.'

He didn't seem to think that was amusing.

The door swung open and Benson tottered in. 'Policemen,' he said through short breaths, 'In the house, Major Lennox, sir. His Lordship is upset. Taken his shotgun to them, sir – he's on the upstairs landing.'

CHAPTER 10

I jumped up and made for the door, Swift followed, tossing his napkin aside as the sound of a gunshot echoed through the house.

'Brigadier,' I yelled as we ran. 'They're ours, sir. Tommies. Don't shoot.'

He didn't hear me and blasted another volley down into the hall, then caught sight of me.

'Damn their eyes. Bloody Boche have got into the camp. Where are the guards? They'll be court-martialled for this. Bring your gun, Major,' he shouted back while reloading. Kalo was passing him ammunition from a leather cartridge case.

There was the sound of running boots and shrieking coming from downstairs. I heard someone calling out that they'd been shot - it sounded like Dawkins, so it wasn't all that bad.

I shouted again. 'They're our boys, sir. We've driven the Germans back. Better call a ceasefire.'

He fired off another blast. 'What?' he bellowed, 'Speak up, man.' I could hear him reloading as we reached the landing.

'Call a ceasefire, sir. They've retreated,' I shouted as best I could through sharp breaths.

'Scarpered, have they? You're sure? Very well.' He stood up and bellowed over the balustrade: 'Cease fire!'

He handed his gun over to Kalo, who swivelled it expertly in his hands to bring it to rest at his side, then stood stiffly to attention while the Brigadier marched back to his rooms, before turning smartly about to follow his master.

Swift and I leaned over the bannisters to see if there were any signs of bodies or blood; fortunately, everyone must have gone into hiding, as the hall was entirely vacant. We raced down to find Inspector Watson and his men sheltering behind the stairs and Dawkins leaning against the wall with a bloodstained handkerchief held to his ear. A bobby was fingering a hole through his helmet, and the Sergeant had fainted to the floor.

'Watson,' Swift yelled. 'What the hell is going on here?'

'That idiot there –' Watson pointed at Dawkins '– started arguing about us going upstairs to see the Earl and then suddenly a gun goes off. I'll have you in gaol.' He made a sudden grab for Dawkins, who took to his heels, heading toward the kitchens.

'Outside! All of you!' Swift marched them out of the door as Dicks held it open.

I watched them parade out of the house, then returned to my room and my notebook, somewhat irked by all these interruptions. The kitten had woken up and was playing with the pens on my desk, scooting them over the edge. I gave its ears a rub and put it in my pocket where it purred itself to sleep as I continued my jottings.

Swift returned, red in the face and scowling.

'I've sent them back to the station,' he snapped. 'They were only supposed to interview the servants.'

'Did they discover anything useful?' I enquired.

'Apparently the family don't use the old chantry anymore, apart from burials, but Jarvis comes every day to hold a service in the house chapel. Nobody ever attends of course, but the Chaplain is required to be there. He didn't arrive this morning.'

'What time was the service?' I asked, my pen poised to note these vital pieces of information.

'Seven o'clock every morning except Sunday when the main service is held at nine,' he said, grabbing another piece of shortbread from the abandoned table. 'I imagine he was on his way here when he was waylaid.'

'Where were the servants? Between six and seven?' I asked.

'Mostly having breakfast or preparing it. A couple were in the morning room.'

'So the staff are all accounted for?

'They are,' Swift confirmed. 'Apart from that idiot Dawkins. The cook said he was probably 'shirking as usual'. Her words, not mine.'

I turned back to my book and wrote these snippets down.

'Lennox,' Swift began, and halted. I turned in my chair to face him. 'Lennox, listen a moment, will you. I work alone, always have. Won't have a sergeant, or a partner. But I admit –' he paused again '– I don't understand these nobs. This world of lords and ladies. And I will not allow my work to suffer because of my own shortcomings.' He folded his arms and looked at the ceiling. 'I would accept your help if you were to offer it.'

I laughed, then looked at him speculatively. It probably took quite some fortitude for a professional like Swift to admit he needed help, particularly from a rank amateur such as myself. And we'd been at daggers drawn last time our paths had crossed, too.

'My hand, old chap, and I'll do what I can to be of assistance.'

We shook on it. I can't say it was a gesture of friendship but it was an acknowledgement of a camaraderie of sorts. And *pax*.

'I'll take a look at this house chapel,' he said,' wherever it is.'

'Fine, I'll come with you.' I took the sleeping kitten from my pocket, put it in the basket and led the way into the corridor. Swift gave me a curious look and muttered something under his breath about eccentricities.

We took a couple of wrong turns because I hadn't been there since the memorial service for Lady Grace, and had very little memory of it.

The house chapel proved to be an ornate affair. The high ceilings were decorated with angels on clouds holding trumpets and golden harps. Tall stained-glass windows filtered sunlight in harlequin hues and richly carved saints stood poised in niches built into wood panelled walls.

It should have been a peaceful sanctuary but today we found the place full of women. They were yanking rolls of white gauze and silky stuff out of boxes that had evidently not long arrived. Hiram's mother, Lady Ruth, was barking out orders and pointing up at something or other while aproned maids ran about.

She advanced on us with a tight smile. 'Good day, Major Lennox. Who is this?'

'Chief Inspector Swift,' I told her. 'Scotland Yard.'

Her eyebrows shot up. 'Major, I distinctly told you –'

'Brigadier gave his permission,' I cut in.

'Really, well, I am most surprised.'

'Delighted to meet you, your Ladyship.' Swift offered a brisk nod of the head. 'I assume you are dressing the place for the nuptials?'

'Yes, evidently, and you are detaining me, gentlemen. I have vital decorating to arrange and I will not tolerate interference.' She pulled back the sleeve of her lilac tartan jacket and glared at her watch as she upbraided us. 'We are expecting the Reverend Jarvis to arrive. He is late.' She turned to stare at the door as though commanding Jarvis to appear.

'He's dead,' I said.

'Lennox!' Swift cut in. 'Leave this to me. I've had training to break news like that.'

'Dead?' Lady Ruth replied, brows raised. You'd think he'd done it deliberately from the air of annoyance she exuded.

'I'm afraid so,' Swift replied. He opened his mouth to carry on with whatever platitudes were deemed suitable to the occasion, but she interrupted.

'Well, really. What are we to do now? The ceremony is in three days,' she snapped. 'And I believe this is the second chaplain already lost in the vicinity. As you insist upon being here, Inspector Swift, you can tell me what Scotland Yard is doing about it.'

'They, um ... Well, I'm investigating,' he muttered.

'With the help of Major Lennox, I assume. Really, if this is the best the constabulary of this country can achieve I'd be surprised if the next chaplain lasts a week. I bid you good day, gentlemen.' With that she turned and marched off, rapping out orders to maids as she went.

I raised my brows at Swift who frowned and then we turned towards a closed side door. It was warped with age and Swift had to give it a good shove to open it. We walked into the vestry, a dusty room, high ceilinged, black beamed, with plain whitewashed walls and cobwebs in the corners. There was a small window allowing a shaft of light into the room, alleviating its cheerless aspect.

Some of Jarvis's clothes were hanging from pegs – a collarless shirt, trousers hooked with braces, and two pairs of shiny shoes. Swift rifled through the pockets and pulled out cigarettes, Vesta matches and a crumpled handkerchief. I took a look in the small desk drawers, pulling them out and laying papers on the desktop blotter. There were pens and pencils jumbled next to an ornate silver box, an empty ink-pot to match, a heavily chased goblet, an exquisite silver jug, a number of sculpted candlesticks and whatnots of similar ilk. Swift stopped to pick up an exquisite salt cellar. He turned it carefully in his hands, then raised his eyebrows at me.

'Jarvis had expensive taste in silverware,' he remarked dryly. 'Should this be here?'

'No,' I replied, casting an eye over the items on the desk. 'There will be altar-ware for the church services, but they would be kept locked in the ambry. I'd say those items are from the house.'

'The ambry being a cupboard in the chapel,' he stated.

'Yes,' I agreed.

'Jarvis was a thief,' Swift asserted.

I didn't reply. Swift had a habit of making hasty accusations, although in this instance I suspected he was right.

There were a couple of chairs and Swift and I each drew one up to read through the papers. They proved to be sermons and liturgies, copied out neatly from somewhere; they were well fingered and creased. There were seven sets, one for each day of the week. I imagine he rotated them.

Swift put the papers back in the drawer and closed it firmly, shoving the small desk backwards as he did. It left it rocking on the uneven stone flags, so I bent down to reposition a torn piece of card that had been pushed under one of the feet. Rather than replace it, I turned it in my hand to read the lettering, then straightened up to hand it to Swift.

'The Black Ca …' He read the words from the torn section and looked at me. 'Must be the Black Cat Club?'

'Yes, and proof of a connection,' I said, rather pleased with myself.

Swift placed the card between pages of his notebook, silent and thoughtful. It was another clue to point us along the way, though we continued to search for another twenty minutes, just to be sure we hadn't missed anything.

We escaped through the chapel under the haughty eye of Ruth Chisholm and returned to my rooms, where Foggy jumped up to greet us and the kitten yawned.

Swift unwrapped the sword and took a long look at it. 'My father was a cavalryman,' he remarked.

'Then you'll know the rapier was for fencing. Duels and all that.'

'I do, and this is probably one of a pair,' Swift said, feeling the sharpness of the slim blade. 'I checked with Benson to ask if he recognised it, but he just said that the Bloxfords were a military family and there were enough swords in the house to arm a battalion.'

I was about to say that I'd told him so, but then decided to move to neutral ground. 'Which regiment did your father belong to?' I asked.

'Imperial Light Horse. South African. I was brought up there, Johannesburg. He was killed at the Battle of Ladysmith. Then my mother brought me to London.'

'Considerable contrast,' I remarked.

'Johannesburg and London? I couldn't say – we actually lived out in the country; there were lions, giraffe and zebras in the bush. It was extraordinary and very beautiful.'

'You liked the animals?' I asked.

He nodded. 'Noble creatures, a damn sight less complicated than people,' he remarked with a sigh.

I smiled, realising he was another loner, more comfortable with a dog or even a cat for company than the strange paradoxes of the human race.

He picked up the striped cloth, raised the rapier in salute and left, presumably to secure his evidence and report back to Scotland Yard.

I returned to my jottings. I drew a simple line image of the sword and spent more time over the details of the hilt and insignia, then made an inky rendition of the torn card from the Black Cat Club while it was still in my mind. There wasn't much point in trying to illustrate the squashed bullet so I merely noted the approximate calibre. I paused to stare at the empty jam jars in which I'd hoped to gather evidence. Swift had all the whatnots, and as he was the official in charge I suppose he would always commandeer the booty. I would have to make do with my inexpert drawings.

The lunch gong sounded and despite the recent snack our activities had left me peckish. I turned into the morning room, where lunch was customarily served, to find the damn Prussian seated alone and already wearing a napkin under his chin. He was leaning over a plate of mash, liver and bacon. I started to back out, but he spotted me.

'Ah, the famous aeronautical Major Lennox. Come – come. I would talk with you,' he called out, waving a fork at me.

Benson was tottering about, and fortunately Dicks had come down and was organising the servants serving the food. He lifted the domed lid with a flourish. 'Would you like a napkin clip, sir?'

'No, Dicks, I am not in my dotage yet.'

'Very good, sir,' he grinned. He seemed to possess quite the chirpiest nature I'd come across. 'I believe the Brigadier is resting now, sir, and will not be joining us.'

'There were noises, I think, in the stairs. What was the cause?' von Graf asked between mouthfuls.

'Policemen, sir. In the hall,' Dicks replied as he fussed around.

'Is there a revolution? Ha-ha!' von Graf laughed. He dyed his hair: I could see grey bits that he'd missed behind the ears; and he wore eau de cologne, I could smell the damn stuff from across the table.

'No, bit of a misunderstanding, that's all,' I said. 'You recommended Jarvis to the household, I understand.' I knew that wasn't the case but tossing a bit of bait his way might bring some titbits to the fore.

'The Reverend? It was the Lady Ruth who did so. She knows both him and I. Jarvis is a good man. He was much help to me during the troubles, you know.'

'You mean the War?' I slipped some liver into my handkerchief to save for Foggy as he'd declined to come with me.

'I was with the Allied forces. Helping.' He ate very quickly; you'd think he was anxious to be elsewhere.

'Were you a traitor or a spy?'

'Nein, nein. Major Lennox, I protest. I was an adviser on art. Before the troubles I was in Paris, I owned my own gallery, and before that I was in London. I am quite an expert, you know.' He leaned forward and fixed me with blue eyes.

'So how did you and Jarvis meet?' I asked him.

'He is excellent artist, very good. I departed Paris when the bombs began falling. I fled to find the British and some old friends from London. I speak German, I offer to be a translator. Jarvis, he is Chaplain at this place and when the men, the Tommies, you know, when they find artworks, they show me. Jarvis, he can make the mending if the art is damaged. We worked together at this, for the Army. We always reported everything. Nothing missed.'

'Which regiment?'

'The Royal Highlanders. Scottishers. We were with the Headquarters.'

'And after the War?' I had finished my lunch, which I must admit was very tasty, despite the company.

'I returned to Paris, of course. It is my home. But the French, these people are not happy, and there is not enough food and money. Jarvis writes to me, he is at Braeburn Castle. The Laird of Braeburn was also in Headquarters and he has trust in us, knows we are experts in the world of art. Jarvis says the Laird is in need of selling some pieces. The Schloss, it is not good, the roof has water falling in, the stones are tumbling down. I know very well how to sell art and Jarvis, he can mend it and clean it. Make it in first-class order so we can sell it for the old chap for the first-class price.'

Von Graf had become animated during the exchange, smiling and gesticulating. Perhaps he wasn't as bad as I thought. After all, some jolly decent people had invited him into their homes. He began telling me about some incident with a chap in a kilt during the war – rather funny, actually. I watched him as he talked, he could be jolly and amusing – perhaps I'd been hasty in my first impressions.

'And you met Lady Ruth there?' I asked.

'Ja,' he nodded. 'All the Chisholms, I meet them. They are family of the Laird. We become good friends, Lady Ruth and I. She is a cultured lady. She lives in a desert you know, a cultural desert, I think, ha-ha-ha!' He laughed loudly at his rather feeble jest.

He unhooked his napkin from its chain and placed it on the table. 'But I must leave you now, Major. I go to see Dame Gabriel. The next opera, it is to be *Carmen*. Quite vunderbar. And Jarvis, too, he is at work, you know.' Von Graf tapped the side of his nose. 'Special work for the Brigadier. Quite delightful,' he laughed. 'But he must finish painting the set now for the opera. It is time.'

'Might be a bit of a problem there, old chap,' I told him as he tossed his napkin on the table.

'Ja?'

'Jarvis is dead. Murdered. Where were you at six thirty this morning?'

CHAPTER 11

He blanched, his mouth fell open and then quivered, his eyes widened in shock. It all looked pretty genuine to me.

'Dead?' He sounded quite astounded.

I nodded, didn't even eat my pudding, just watched him.

'B-but …Jarvis, dead,' he stuttered, then straightened his back and stared at me. 'Was this the cause of the police? They were here. Is this why?'

'Yes,' I said and dug into my jam roly-poly and custard.

He stood up to leave. 'This is a tragedy. What will we do? The paintings, the opera, Oh, Gott im Himmel, this is terrible, terrible.'

If he was acting it was pretty good, but then he was an aficionado of art and opera, so maybe he could act, too.

'One moment, old man.' I stopped him. 'You didn't mention where you were early this morning.'

'In bed. Asleep, of course, what else would I be doing!' He stalked out, his stacked heels rat-tatting on the wooden floor as he went.

I finished my meal and went in search of my rooms and my notebook to jot down the findings of the interview.

Foggy greeted me enthusiastically and I shared the purloined liver between him and the kitten. I sat down, opened my book and started my list of possible culprits. Count von Graf was about to be noted as suspect number one. The ink dried on my nib as I pondered who else I could add. Watson and his bobbies had determined that all the servants were accounted for; only the idiot Dawkins was absent. Much as I found Dawkins an irritation, I couldn't see him as a murderer – he didn't have the gumption, for a start. I had no idea of the Chisholms' whereabouts, nor Caroline or Florence either, but the mention of Braeburn Castle had given me pause. That was Florence's home and I had met her coming in from the gardens this morning.

No, I refused to go along that route. The mystery must lie within the opera group or the Black Cat Club and, like it or not, I would have to go with Swift and interview them. I drew out my fob watch and wondered how long it would be before the Inspector returned. I probably should have warned von Graf not to talk to anyone. And he'd said he was going off to hobnob with the soprano. Damn, he was probably letting the cat out of the bag even now. I stood up – I would go, even if it did mean tackling that bunch of warblers entirely alone.

Voices rose from the hall; I heard Caroline giving orders and Hiram's deep tones as I descended.

'Oh, Lennox, you didn't come,' Caroline said when she caught sight of me. 'We had such a marvellous time down by the river – you know where it widens out between the trees? The old boat was there and we rowed up-river, it was simply heaven!' She gave me a peck on the cheek; she was looking vibrant, with rosy cheeks and a wide smile.

'Well, there was a bit of an emergency, old stick. Got rather held up.' I opened my mouth to explain further but was cut off.

'We had one, too: poor Florence turned her ankle,' Caroline interrupted. 'She battled on, of course, but it's really quite swollen now. Luckily your chap Swift was on hand when we arrived back here and he carried her up to her room in his arms. Quite the romantic, isn't he?' she laughed.

'Yes,' Hiram drawled, 'He's a real good guy. Well-mannered, too.'

'You can sure tell a man by his friends, Lennox,' Ford added. 'An' you've got good uns.' He patted me on the back as he said this.

I was virtually speechless. Damn it! Swift was a total sourpuss most of the time; now they thought he was charming and he'd carried Florence off in his arms, leaving me to break the news about Jarvis.

They took it reasonably well: Caroline immediately said she would rope in the local vicar, whom everyone preferred to Jarvis anyway. I didn't ask where they were when Jarvis had been dispatched this morning; it seemed rather infra dig and I had already put a damper on the day.

'Listen, old thing,' I told Caroline, who was holding onto Hiram, her hand lost in his huge one, 'your father's had a bit of a run-in with the local law. Swift is handling it, I'm supporting him, but you should go and calm him down. We don't need any more excitement.'

Hiram replied, 'We'll go up there now, Lennox, old man. I thank you for your help right kindly.' He nodded and led Caroline upstairs.

'I have informed your wife, sir,' I said to Ford, who was still in the hall, watching and listening to events.

'And how did she take that?' he grinned. 'I'll bet she pursed her mouth up.'

'Um, well she wasn't *terribly* pleased about it,' I replied.

He laughed. 'She's got all uppity about this wedding and she likes things runnin' smooth. And Hiram's our only child. Truth to tell he's mine – his Ma died when he was still in diapers. But Ruth, when I wed her she took to him like he was her own little chick. A remarkable woman is my Ruth.'

'She's Scottish – is that where you met her? Scotland?' I asked, wondering what diapers were and why Hiram wore them.

'No, I ain't never set foot outside the United States in my life until last year. Her folks left Scotland when she was a small child, I met her in Dallas at some oil tycoon's party that she and her old folks was attending. They've got blue blood all the way through and Ruth don't ever forgit it. She keeps the old ways, even in the Texas plains.'

'And she's related to the Braeburns?'

'She sure is: her father was the junior son of the old Laird. She's young Florence's great-aunty. You can see the resemblance – when I see Florence, I see my dear wife when we were first introduced.'

'Good Lord, really?' That was a bit of a shock – I tried to vanquish images of Florence as Ruth Chisholm.

'Well, I'll go and find the good lady. You have a good day now.' He raised his wide-brimmed hat and ambled off.

The sound of singing reached my ears a hundred yards from the Dower House. It wasn't far from the theatre, making me wonder why on earth they didn't just go over there and practice. As I reached for the door-knocker on the rather handsome little house an ear-shattering note sang out from an open mullioned window. I took an involuntary step back, then took a grip of myself and knocked loudly. The singing stopped. A head appeared from an upstairs window. 'Yoo-hoo,' the lady sang rather than said. 'Gosh, you are handsome.'

'Um, greetings,' I called up. 'I'm Major Lennox, from the house. Friend of the family. Lady Caroline, the Brigadier, and all that.' I had a habit of babbling when nervous and the buxom lady leaning from the window was making me very nervous indeed.

The door was yanked open.

'We're busy,' a large gentleman with a handlebar moustache told me. He was wearing a bullfighting costume complete with red cape, and began pushing the door closed as he spoke.

'Fine, fine.' I beat a retreat but didn't get very far as Swift arrived behind me.

'Open up. Police,' he said, and held up a badge.

I was quietly impressed because it did the trick: the door was immediately flung back open. It wasn't the moustache this time, it was the buxom lady with curly dark hair piled up on her head.

'Oh, are you the police? My goodness, I simply adore a man in uniform,' she almost purred, while flashing very long eyelashes at Swift. 'And as for you …' She reached out and slid a finger down my tie.

'Erm …' we both mumbled at once.

Swift recovered his wits first. 'Madam, I am not wearing a uniform.'

'I know,' she drawled, 'that's even better: a man *without* his uniform.' She was leaning against the door, almost wearing a scarlet silk dress with sleeves drooping across her bare shoulders. It was some sort of gypsy costume, I think, although any gypsy wandering the countryside dressed like that would be immediately arrested – assuming the policeman could keep an adequate grip on himself, that is.

'Lizzie, clear off.' The moustache reappeared and tried to shoo her away. It didn't work.

'They are the police, Ferdinand, and they simply must be allowed in.' Lizzie tossed her head, lifting a hand to a stray curl.

Swift tightened the belt of his trench coat. 'Madam,' he barked, 'we're here about Sir Crispin's death.' He stepped across the threshold driving back the theatre folk. I stood back in admiration: it takes a brave man to tackle a lady in that state of undress.

'Oo, you are forceful,' she giggled, and backed into the interior. 'But I like you.'

They were all dressed in gaudy get-ups. There were five in view, the two from the doorway and another three leaning over the bannisters from upstairs. Then another lady in scanties came to join them, and a rotund chap with thick dark hair and a goatee. I didn't spot Andrew Dundale or Dame Gabriel among them.

'We're doing *Carmen*,' Ferdinand the moustache boomed by way of explanation. 'I'm the baritone, Escamillo,' he announced.

'Thought you were called Ferdinand,' I said.

'Oh, really! Utter bourgeoise.' He rolled his eyes. 'You are not opera lovers, are you?'

Swift broke in. 'Go and sit down – NOW! We'll interview you all in there.' He indicated the large room beyond the hall.

That brought about a babble of voices and more ladies and men descended the stairs chattering as they came.

'How exciting,' Lizzie trilled, and led the way from the crowded hallway through the open double doors into the drawing room.

It was very elegant, with an ornate plaster ceiling, prettily decorated walls with patterns of peacocks and whatnots and large portraits of rather pretty ladies. I wondered if these were the same Bloxford Beauties, albeit fully clothed.

There wasn't much time to admire anything; the babble grew more clamorous as they squabbled over seating on the three large sofas set around an unlit fireplace.

'Silence,' Swift shouted. He pulled up an ornate chair and placed himself between two couches where he could see them all. There was only one place left and Lizzie patted it for me to come and sit next to her.

'Lennox, will you sit down,' Swift snapped as he tugged out his notebook and pen.

I sat on the edge of the sofa while Swift told them who we were and that we were here about Sir Crispin's 'accident'. He hadn't mentioned Jarvis yet; I assumed he was holding it in reserve. Lizzie walked her fingers across my leg, making me jump. 'I'm Carmen, you know. Mezzo-soprano,' she whispered.

I backed into the corner.

'Where was everybody at the time Sir Crispin and Dame Gabriel fell through the trap-door?' Swift called out.

That created another cacophony of noise.

'Quiet,' he yelled again. 'You.' He pointed to the moustache. 'Where were you?'

'On stage,' he snapped back. 'We all were.'

'Except Andrew Dundale,' Lizzie broke in. 'He had sneaked off and didn't come back until after darling Crispin had been squished by Madam Whiplash.'

They all giggled. I was calculating how far it was to the door and how long it would take me to reach it if I vaulted over the back of the sofa.

'I assume you're referring to Dame Gabriel.' Swift raised a brow and then noted this down as more laughter broke out. 'Where is she? And Andrew Dundale?'

'At the big house, stuffing themselves while we sing our hearts out here. I mean, really, who do they think they are?' Ferdinand the moustache groused.

A tall man, haughty and thin, came in from a side door. He was wearing a tailor's smock with pins and threaded needles stuck into it, and a tape measure around his neck; he didn't have to explain that he was the wardrobe master. He minced across the drawing-room rugs, smoothed his bouffant hair with a limp hand, and stopped to look at us, hand on hip.

'Ooo, are you the boys in blue? How simply darling, you can handcuff me anytime.'

Right, that was it.

'Swift, I'm going to see about the naked ladies. I'll see you later.'

All eyes instantly swivelled in my direction. As exit lines go, that was probably one of my better ones.

CHAPTER 12

Lavender Cottage was full of budding roses, trailing wisteria, late tulips, bluebells and various other spring flowers, but not much in the way of lavender. It was an archetypal Cotswold cottage, with a thatched roof, mellow stone walls and a low beamed ceiling, which I ducked beneath.

'Oh, hello, Major Lennox. You are earlier than I expected.' Miss Busby stood aside to let me and Fogg in.

'Um, yes.' I sat down as directed on a chintzy chair beside a merry fire. Miss Busby had, no doubt, set it burning against the drenching rain that had suddenly blown in under scudding clouds. The kitchen was through an open door, and I watched as she put a copper kettle on an old iron range.

She tilted her head to one side, a habit I'd noticed before. 'You're wet and rather flustered.' She was perceptive as well. 'And your poor doggy is dripping.' She found an old blanket to wrap around Fogg and he sat by the fire looking embarrassed.

'Caught in the rain,' I mumbled. I dug in my pocket, pulled out the kitten and gave it to her. 'Got a bit damp too.'

'Ah,' she said, and took it into the kitchen for a rub-down, then placed it next to Fogg. 'Little boy.'

'What?'

'Your kitten is a boy.' She gazed at me with mischievous eyes. 'I checked.'

'Oh.' I'd already made a brief inspection, but had been none the wiser.

'What do you call him?' she asked.

'Kitten.'

'Is that his name or title?' she smiled.

'Erm,' I thought about it, 'better give him a name.'

'Yes,' she said, 'any thoughts?'

'He's grown rather tubby. How about Mr Tubbs?'

'Shows a modicum of imagination at least,' she laughed, and went to pour the boiling water into a flower painted teapot, then came back with it on a tray, along with cups, milk jug, flapjacks, hot buttered scones and whatnots.

'I have one,' she said.

'One what?'

'One of the kittens – he's asleep upstairs.' She laughed.

'Oh.'

'He's ginger. I called him Pudding. He's become a little fat, too, just like his brother.'

'Whose brother?'

'Your Mr Tubbs. My kitten is one of the abandoned litter from the theatre.'

'Oh,' I said again, then realised I had been rather distracted. 'Miss Busby. Are you acquainted with Florence Braeburn?'

'I am.' She nodded. 'She's pretty, isn't she.'

'Um …' I mumbled through a mouthful of scone.

'Are you sweet on her?'

'Well …' I wasn't sure what to say. 'Do you think she's like Hiram's mother, Ruth Chisholm?'

'Lennox.' Miss Busby sipped her tea. 'People are what they are. Not what you want them to be.'

'Um,' I mumbled again, my mind elsewhere, and then turned to look directly at her. 'You mean "yes", don't you.'

'I mean, Lennox, that you need to view her without the romanticised imagery you've conjured in your mind's eye. Talk to her, don't worship from afar. Get to know her as a real person.'

'Yes. Well, yes, I will.' I munched a bit more. 'Not very good with the fairer sex, you know. Bit of a mystery.'

'I rather thought so,' she smiled. She waited for me to reply, but I couldn't think of anything to say.

'Did you want to ask me about the Bloxford Beauties?'

I nodded. 'Why are you one of them?'

A shadow flitted across her face, causing the smile to falter.

'The Brigadier, Neville, was not the elder son. Did you know that?'

'No,' I confessed. 'Before my time.'

'Randolf –' Her voice broke across his name, she took a breath and continued. 'We were engaged, a long, long time ago. And as a young bride-to-be I was asked if I'd like to become one of the Bloxford Beauties. The portrait was meant as a wedding gift to the groom – this was the tradition and has been for a few hundred years. Not everybody said yes, but I jumped at it. I was a madcap young thing in those days, you know. Riding to hounds, out with the shooting parties, dancing the night away at local balls. We had a marvellous time. The Hall was always bustling: the older Bloxfords liked to entertain and we even put on our own shows at the theatre. It was such fun, so full of laughter and music. Poor Caroline has missed all of that. I do hope she and Hiram can bring the house back to life again.' Miss Busby paused to sip tea, her eyes gazing into the distance.

I waited in silence. The kitten, 'Mr Tubbs' as he was now designated, clambered up to sit on her knee; she stroked him quietly.

'The Bloxfords are military men. Born to be soldiers, they used to say. Randolf was no exception, his regiment was sent to fight the Boers. He died there shortly before he was due home for our wedding ...' She forced a smile. 'Typhoid killed him. Not a heroic death. Agonising and utterly wasteful, but not heroic. And so he was dead and buried in Africa and I never saw him again.'

'I'm sorry,' I said; all I could say really.

'Grace and Brigadier Neville were wed a year later. Caroline didn't come along for a long time, too long probably, and Grace's health never really recovered, poor soul. I remember your mother, you know. Mary-Rose, a lovely woman. They were close friends.'

I regarded her, thinking about how her life would have been – the wife of the Earl, probably a mother and even grandmother by now.

'I taught.' She sipped tea and took up the conversation again. 'After Randolf died I became the local schoolteacher. I enjoyed it. The people who live here in the village are all friends, and my family of sorts. I feel very blessed, you know.'

'Why do you visit the chantry?' I asked. 'And care for it?'

'I was born in this village, I have a relatively humble background and I find the house chapel very pretentious,' she smiled. 'I wanted to be wed at the old chantry, where my parents were married. And that is where I hold my memories of Randolf. Even if his body isn't buried there, I feel his presence. And I go to say thank you to God, for the life I have led. A long life now and not too many aches and pains –' she smiled '– for an old lady.'

I echoed her smile. 'No regrets? You would have been lady of the manor, patron of the arts, a grand dame, if your fancy had taken it.'

'None at all – and I would have never been a "grand dame".' She laughed. 'Enough of days gone by, Major Lennox. What have you discovered? You and Inspector Swift?'

I told her about Crispin and Andrew and the Black Cat Club, and Clegg and the switched planks, and then the ridiculous members of the opera group, finishing with my luncheon discussion with the German, von Graf. Miss Busby listened quietly without interruption.

'It may not be related to this Black Cat Club at all, you know,' she mused. 'It may be something that happened at Braeburn Castle.'

'Possibly. I think von Graf made the arrangements for Jarvis to come here, through Lady Ruth. And von Graf was instrumental in bringing the Noble House of Opera to the Hall,' I replied. 'And Ruth agreed to that too.'

'Oh dear. It's all quite complicated, or seems to be,' she remarked. 'Major Lennox, do you fear there is some sort of mad killer on the loose? Because I would hate to think that any of the wedding party are in danger.'

I pondered this, a thought that had already troubled me.

'I believe not,' I said. 'I'd say the motives lie in the past.'

'I do hope you are right,' she said.

So too did I.

Fogg, Tubbs and I retraced our footsteps. The rain had blown away as quickly as it had appeared and the walk through the walled gardens was damp underfoot, giving off the scent of new-grown grass and wet earth. I placed Tubbs in Fogg's basket and left them in my bedroom.

I had Andrew Dundale in my sights now; there were a number of questions I wanted to ask. Just as I was heading downstairs to find him, I was diverted by Dicks, rather red in the face.

'Lady Caroline has been looking for you, sir. Seems to be in a bit of a tizzy about that dead chaplain.'

'Ah, yes. I thought she'd taken the news rather too well. By the way, Dicks, the kitten's a boy. Called him Mr

Tubbs. Better get him some milk and take up a treat for Mr Fogg. We were caught in the rain – got a bit damp.'

'Certainly, sir,' he grinned.

I tracked Caroline down to her rooms in the west wing. She was indeed in a tizzy and had been crying, too, by the looks of it.

'Greetings, old stick,' I hailed her upon walking in.

'Oh, Lennox.' She climbed off the bed and came to peck me on the cheek. 'It's beastly. No-one liked that awful man, but there are now two chaps dead in a week. The ceremony is only three days away and we will simply be awash with people. Should I call it off? Are they in danger, do you think?' She looked up at me, hair tangled, eyes red-rimmed; she was still dressed in riding gear and her white chambray blouse was now badly creased. I assume she'd been lying on the bed working herself into a flap.

I made her come and sit in the window seat, a place where we'd spent many hours in our childhood, reading books and plotting mischief.

'What does Hiram think?' I asked, putting my arm around her shoulders as she sniffled into a handkerchief.

'That we should carry on. The deaths weren't actually in the house and he thinks it's to do with some sort of dispute between the players in the opera group. I said we should send them packing but he thinks Swift will uncover the culprit and that will be that. And Ruth is absolutely determined that the next opera must go ahead, so I'm really rather cornered, aren't I?'

Indeed she was, and that was very likely the crux of the problem. Lady Grace had died young and Caroline had spent most of her life being the only child of a loving but absent father. She'd had the run of the house and ordered everyone in it pretty much as she liked. Now she was about to wed and had Hiram to contend with, not to mention a single-minded stepmother-in-law. Kind though they both undoubtedly were, Caroline was no longer calling the shots in her own home and the realisation had probably hit her hard.

'I agree with Hiram. There is no need to cancel because of Jarvis, no one will miss him.' I squeezed her shoulders, trying to gee her up. 'You've found a good chap there, in Hiram, I mean. He'll be a rock for you. A mountain, actually.'

She gave another sniff. 'He is rather vast isn't he. We had to give him one of the draft horses to ride, he looked ridiculous on the others.'

'I saw the saddles,' I remarked.

She laughed. 'They brought them with them, he and Ford. Can you imagine what the hunt master will say when we turn up for a meet?'

I laughed with her. 'He'll be a breath of fresh air, Caroline. Bring some life to the old place.'

'But he may chafe against the bit here — you know how stuck in our ways we are. I do wonder if I'm expecting too much of him. And if he really knows what he's letting himself into.'

'As you said, old thing, he's a big chap – he can think it

out for himself. More to the point, are *you* ready for this marriage?' I asked without quibbling.

'Lennox,' she began, then halted as people do when about to utter something ticklish. 'Um. Do you know why Daddy was so keen for you to come before the ceremony?'

'Yes.'

'You do?' Her brows shot up.

'Yes, I just said so.' I unwound my arm from her shoulders.

'Why on earth didn't you tell me?'

'Why should I?'

'Well, what do you think?' she asked.

'About marrying you?' I said.

'Yes.'

'Not a chance, old stick. Run a mile first. Actually – I'd run a lot further.'

'Oh, thank heavens,' she said and relaxed back against the cushions. 'Hiram and I were concerned and we weren't sure how to broach it.'

'You didn't seriously think I was harbouring feelings for you, did you, Caroline?'

'Well, it's hard to tell with you, Lennox. You're so utterly hopeless at romance.' She stuffed her damp handkerchief in her pocket and sat up.

Why was it that absolutely nobody ever credited me with the ability to do a damn thing? Not even to declare a few soft words when the time was ripe? Or solve a murder?

'Why does Hiram think Swift will apprehend the killer and not me?' I demanded.

'Swift is from Scotland Yard, he's a professional. Why wouldn't he find the murderer? And he's awfully sweet. We all think he's quite charming,' she told me, with a straight face.

I was becoming rather annoyed by this. 'No, he's not. I'll have you know he wanted to hang me, and would have done, given the chance. Really, Caroline, I do wonder about your judgement sometimes.'

'There's nothing wrong with my judgement.' Her eyes flashed. 'Are you trying to tell me you don't like Hiram?' she accused.

'Of course I like him. That wasn't what I meant at all.' It was time to leave, Caroline was turning decidedly waspish for no reason. She'd been like this ever since she was a child.

'You always said I should look before I leap. You're not going to play 'Sir Galahad' are you Lennox, and start meddling?' She accused me.

'No, I was just trying to help,' I retorted loudly. 'You're always throwing yourself into things without a damn thought in your head.'

'That's so typical of you, Lennox, you think I can't be trusted to make my own mind up. I would never have married you!' she shouted, and flung a cushion at me. 'Not ever, you total stinker, Lennox!'

I opened the door and stalked out. Benson was in the corridor with a tray of tea and biscuits.

'I'm terribly sorry to hear that, sir,' he said as another cushion flew out through the door. 'We had all hoped –'

'Benson, don't even think about it …'

Damn it, words failed me.

CHAPTER 13

I'd had absolutely enough of talking to insensitive people who never listened to a damn word I said. And I had spent almost my entire time trying to track down a murderer, interviewing people, including that gaggle of farcical theatricals in the Dower House, and all the thanks I get is to have cushions thrown at me. I was in half a mind to return to the peace and quiet of my house, the Manor at Ashton Steeple.

'Hello, Lennox.'

'Um … Greetings.'

'I was about to go through the gardens, would you like to come with me?' Florence asked.

Well, this was unexpected. I nodded dumbly and shoved my hands in my pockets. A footman opened the French windows and I followed her onto the terrace.

She looked awfully pretty wearing a pale pink jersey, silk scarf and cream wool skirt just below the knee, with stout country shoes. Her plaited blonde hair gleamed in the fitful sunshine. I noticed the soft line of her cheek, the curve of her lips as she smiled and the blue-grey of her eyes as she glanced at me.

Miss Busby's advice came to mind and I thought I'd better say something – it would have helped if she'd mentioned what to say.

'Do you remember pushing me out of the hayloft?' she asked.

'Um, no. I'm awfully sorry if I did. Accident, probably.'

'No, it wasn't! You pushed us all out and then declared yourself King of the Castle,' she laughed.

I tried not to smile.

'And the hunt. It was our first proper ride to hounds and you were supposed to watch out for Caroline and me. She was thrown from her pony when she over-faced it at a fence, and you came over on your horse and ordered her straight back into the saddle and told her to get a move on because the pack was already over the hill.'

'I remember that. Nearly missed the whole show thanks to her bawling. I gave her my handkerchief and she still wouldn't get back on.'

'Yes, and you said she'd never get blooded at that rate, and she was simply covered in the stuff from a nosebleed. Then we all started laughing, because it was such an absurd thing to say.'

'I must have been a dreadful tick!'

'Oh, you were quite gallant in your own way. You just had a strange manner of showing it, that's all.'

'Yes, Caroline just mentioned the same thing,' I wasn't about to say she'd actually yelled it at me.

'I think she's rather het up with everything,' Florence replied.

I hesitated, half a mind to open up, but decided I'd had enough of sensitive subjects for one day and sought to change tack.

'When was the last time I saw you?' I asked. 'I remember so little of those days.'

'Caroline and I were about nine; you would have been around twelve or thirteen, I suppose. I think your mother was quite ill and it's probably clouded your memories. That sort of thing often will.'

She was right about my mother; and after she died, my father packed me off to school, holed up in the house and never went anywhere. I think it left a chasm in our lives that neither of us ever managed to cross.

'So what have you been doing? Well, since you grew up, anyway.' I asked her.

'Singing mostly. During the War I joined a local concert party – I sing soprano. Recently I have been training in Edinburgh with a marvellous teacher.' Her eyes lit up with enthusiasm. 'It requires terrific dedication, you know, but I'm rather good at discipline. I do so admire people who are utterly single-minded, don't you?'

'Um,' not much I could say to that as it was a complete anathema to me, although I had to admit, this sleuthing had rather gripped my mind of late.

'I'd simply love to become professional,' Florence continued unabated. 'But I'm just not quite up to the level. The singers here are divine, I'm terribly in awe of them. When I heard about the Noble Opera from Caroline, I decided to come to Bloxford early so I could watch them at work.'

'Really?' Good God, what was she thinking? The poor girl was completely deluded. 'One of them's probably a murderer,' I told her.

'Yes, Andrew Dundale. I do think it's such a shame, he's an excellent tenor. Jonathan is going to arrest him when he finds him. He's on his trail at this moment. He's terribly brave.'

'By *Jonathan* I take it you mean Inspector Swift?' I asked.

'Yes,' she replied gaily. 'I was such a twit, hurting my ankle, but he carried me up to my room. It was terribly gallant of him.' She laughed. 'And he sent one of the footmen to fetch ice from the icehouse to put on my leg. It's much better now. Isn't he wonderful!'

'No.'

'Oh, Lennox. You are funny,' she laughed. 'Jonathan sings Gilbert and Sullivan with a group of friends. He's offered to take me to a show in Oxford this evening. Caroline and Hiram are coming. You're very welcome to join us if you wish.' She stopped to face me, eyes alight with excitement. She looked beautiful in the sunshine; we were under a couple of cherry trees, the blossoms just bursting into bloom, birds were twittering above us full of the joys of spring. It was the most romantic of settings, and yet I felt my heart sink.

'Um, busy actually, old girl. Can't be done. Sorry. My dog, Mr Fogg, needs walking, you know.' I closed my mouth to stop myself babbling.

'Well, if you do change your mind, we're leaving early

to take dinner in town,' she said, not appearing to be in the least dismayed by my rebuff. 'I am heading to the theatre now. The opera company are having a dress rehearsal and I'm desperate to watch. Do come, please, Lennox.'

We were indeed near the theatre. 'Afraid I must dash, Florence. But I'm sure you'll have a marvellous time,' I took her hand and pecked it lightly.

'Yoo-hoo,' a voice sang out. It was that damn woman, Lizzie or whatever she was called. The whole pack of them were following her, trotting down the path toward us dressed in the same outlandish costumes they were prancing about in earlier. Andrew Dundale wasn't amongst them.

I beat a rapid retreat and trod the path back toward the sanctuary of my rooms, hands shoved in pockets and my heart heavy with sadness and regret. I dropped into the chair by the unlit hearth as Foggy came to push his wet nose into my hands. I ruffled the silky tan-gold fur on his head as he gave me a lick of support. Tubbs clambered up my trousers to sit on my lap and we three sat for a few quiet moments while I silently remonstrated with myself about my utter stupidity in upsetting Caroline. And, it seems, my failure to make any dent upon Florence's tender emotions.

A knock on the door broke into my morose meanderings. Caroline came in with a cushion clutched to her chest. She'd change and looked fresher, though her eyes were still rather red.

'Here,' she shoved the cushion into my hands. 'You can throw it at me, if you like.'

I grinned, put Tubbs down and gave her a hug. 'I'm sorry, old girl.'

'I am, too. It's just…' she waved a hand in the air.

'I know, and dead bodies don't help.'

'Can you keep it out of the house, Lennox? Away from the wedding?'

'As far as I'm able, yes I will,' I promised.

She looked up at me, the cushion clutched in her hands. 'Still my 'almost big brother'?'

'Always,' I told her.

She laughed, kissed my cheek, and made for the door, then turned. 'Oh, I forgot. Hiram gave me this.' She came back, handed me an envelope and skipped off with a wave and a bright smile.

I went to my desk. The envelope was scrawled with heavy handwriting. I slit it open with my letter opener.

'Howdy, old man. I'll kindly take you up on the offer to go shoot pigeon. Tomorrow at around 6.30 a.m. Suggest we meet out front. I have my own guns. Hiram Chisholm.'

Feeling a trifle better, I went to retrieve my pair of Purdeys from the dressing room and began the task of stripping them and putting them in good order. Whilst my hands were occupied with the cleaning and oiling of my guns, my mind turned to the puzzle of the murders.

I could understand Swift's desire to apprehend Andrew Dundale, given that he'd taken Crispin's role as lead tenor and was missing at the time the trap-door collapsed. And I suspect Swift had learned about Crispin and Andrew's partnership during the war and latterly at the Black Cat

Club, which would make him even more determined to drag him off to the cells.

Andrew amounted to the perfect suspect – but Andrew had neither the brains nor the backbone for such an enterprise, and it wouldn't take Swift long to realise this. No, I was convinced it wasn't Andrew. Von Graf was missing at the time, too, as was Jarvis, and either or both of them could very easily have exchanged the plank. But unlike the machinations leading to Crispin's demise, the murder of Jarvis was neither devious nor disguised. Whoever killed Jarvis chose a very vivid act of murder. And they left the sword at the scene. Why?

I replaced my guns in the safe cupboard in my dressing room and locked it. The kitten had woken up and scrambled onto my desk. It sat on my notebook and stared at me with round eyes and long whiskers.

'Down,' I ordered him. Nothing. Completely ignored me. He had very large ears. If they carried on growing he'd look more like a bat than a cat. Maybe I should rename him? I could call him 'Batty', perhaps? He meowed. I think he was hungry. Dicks had left a jug of milk on the windowsill; I went over to pour some into the saucer by his and Fogg's basket. When I turned around to fetch him, he'd scattered all the pens, pencils and whatnots off the desk. Dicks came in just as I was carrying the kitten to the saucer and quietly remonstrating with him about his juvenile behaviour.

'Sir.' Dicks regarded the mess on the desk.

'It wasn't me!'

He placed a fresh jug of milk for Tubbs on the window-sill, returned to the desk and quickly tidied everything back again, then walked off with an air of hurt martyrdom. Damn it, he was turning into his Uncle Greggs.

Swift came in as Dicks went out.

'You went to school with Andrew Dundale, didn't you? Is that why you didn't tell me about his partnership with Sir Crispin at the Black Cat Club?'

'Who told you about that?' I asked.

'One of the troupe; apparently it had been kept secret. But I think you found out?'

'Listen, Swift, Andrew Dundale is too dumb to commit anything, never mind murder. Chasing him merely detracts from the search for the real culprit.'

'That's for me to judge,' he snapped. 'I knew nothing about it, but you did. You're obstructing my work, Lennox. I'll cut you out if you hide evidence from me – you're just protecting one of your own, aren't you?'

'Utter nonsense, man. You really are going to have to drop this Socialist resentment if you're going to achieve anything.'

'I don't need to kowtow to nobs to succeed in my work,' he argued.

'I wasn't referring to your work,' I retorted.

'What are you talking about?'

'If you want your romance with Florence to blossom, you need to know that she's actually Lady Florence of Braeburn Castle. Her father is the Laird of one of the oldest aristocratic families in the country and Florence is the sole heiress.'

CHAPTER 14

He fell silent, then raised a hand to his chin. I thought he was going to turn on his heel and storm out, but he didn't, he stared at me, or rather through me. Then he let out a sigh and slumped down in one of the club chairs next to the unlit hearth.

'Lennox,' he began.

I waited because it seemed he had more to say.

'Lennox ...'

'Yes? Do spit it out, old chap.'

'Are you going to pursue Florence? Because I'd rather know.'

'No,' I said.

'No?'

'No.'

'Well, why not? She's a marvellous girl. The best. Anyone would want to be with her. How could they not?' He was becoming quite worked up. 'She is probably the most beautiful thing I've ever set eyes on. And an intellect to match, do you know –'

'Yes, yes,' I cut in on him before he got carried away

with the rhapsodising. 'But she has a very different nature to mine. And she sings, and she likes all that highbrow sort of stuff. Opera and whatnot. And I don't, and I never will. Not even for a girl as lovely as Florence. And I don't think she's particularly interested in me, either.' I finished with a silent sigh.

'Really? Are you just telling me this – trying to throw the wool over my eyes?' he accused.

'Swift, you are the most suspicious fellow I've ever come across,' I retorted. 'If you think you and Florence can make a go of it, I wish you the very best of luck.'

'But she's one of *you*, the aristocracy,' he said, and ran a hand through his hair. 'She'll never look at *me*.'

'She has already taken a look at you, old chap, and I'd say it was a very favourable look.'

He continued to stare in a perturbed state at the far wall.

I rang the bell for Dicks – this was the sort of occasion where only brandy will serve. Dicks came and fussed around, setting up small tables, brushing them down, polishing the goblets, and then dusting the bottle of best Napoleon. I took it from him in the end and shooed him out of the door.

'Here.' I held out the snifter for Swift. 'And do not say one word about drinking on duty.'

Whatever year the brandy was made, it was an extremely good one. A couple of sips of the amber liquor had us both in better spirits.

'I have nothing to offer her, you know,' Swift said.

'Times have changed, old man. She'll follow her heart. If that's what you're offering, let her decide whether to take it or not.'

'Is she wealthy, then?' He looked at me, the hawkish expression he habitually wore replaced with a furrow of doubt.

'Poorer than a church mouse,' I told him. 'Castle is falling about their ears, debts up to their eyes, and all she can do is sing, which isn't going to do a damn thing to restore the family fortune.'

'So she needs to marry a rich chap like Hiram,' Swift maundered.

I topped up his snifter. 'Nonsense, the days of selling off the prettiest daughters has gone. We live in an enlightened age, Swift. Poorer, but happier – or something akin to that.'

He didn't seem entirely convinced, but the brandy had blazed a course through his blood and I think he was prepared to square up and hazard his heart. I hoped he would, anyway.

'I'll deliver Andrew to you in the morning,' I told him. 'But take my word for it, it isn't him. We need to get back on the trail of the real culprit, old chap.'

'Yes, you're right. Been rather distracted. We're erm … Lennox, we're going to a show this evening. Would you like to come?'

'Already made my apologies.' I told him.

'Ah, very well. It seems you're ahead of me.' He focused his eyes on me. 'You're sure it's a good idea? You know, it's all rather –'

'Swift,' I told him firmly. 'Faint hearts, and all that. Go and win the fair maiden.' I opened the door and pointed the way.

He finished his brandy, placed the glass carefully on the table at his elbow, stood up, swayed for a moment, and wove his way to the door. He turned to face me, yanked the belt of his trench coat tighter and raised a hand in farewell.

'Back in the morning,' he told me, and departed.

I closed the door behind him. I had a free evening and would spend it tracking down that oaf Andrew Dundale and finding out what the devil he'd been up to the night Crispin was killed. And a bit of dedicated detecting would also keep me from contemplating the loss of the lovely Florence Braeburn.

I headed for the Bloxford Arms, which was where I thought Andrew would be. Even at school he'd take a sniff of the hard stuff before bounding out onto the stage or cricket pitch or whatever the event.

I'd brought Foggy with me as it was a pleasant stroll down to the local hostelry. We were met by a mix of scents at the door: dry hops, spilt ale, pipe tobacco, wood smoke and wet dogs. The ancient walls were lined with old pews and assorted locals were sitting chatting quietly upon them. A chap in the corner was singing a folk song in the local dialect, and soon a few more joined in, the words lifting to the smoke-blackened rafters.

'You here, Heathcliff,' Andrew greeted me from his perch at the bar.

'Clearly, Andrew.' I could see he was in his cups. I ordered a tankard of beer from the landlord.

'The old Bill are persecuting me, Heathcliff.' He addressed his large tumbler of whisky.

'Why?' I asked, although I knew most of it already.

'Crispin. Black Cat Club. One of the troupe spilled the beans, probably the wardrobe master, he loves indulging in tittle-tattle.'

'You didn't tell me where you were when Crispin dropped through the trap-door, did you, Andrew. And don't call me Heathcliff.'

He sniffed, looking morose and guilty at the same time.

'Don't tell me it *was* you,' I warned him. 'I've just spent the last hour persuading the police of your innocence.'

'Why did you do that?' he responded.

'Because you're too stupid to have killed him,' I said, taking a sip of the excellent local ale.

'Absolute rot! I could have done, if I'd wanted to, not that I did, but – you know, you really are quite rude, Heath –' he looked me in the face '– Lennox.'

'Where were you, Andrew?'

He reddened. 'You won't tell, will you?'

'Yes, I damn well will because you need an alibi for murder, so spit it out, man.'

'Oh, all right. I was meeting Dawkins behind the theatre.'

That almost made me choke. 'Dawkins? You mean that idiot footman from the house? What the devil were you meeting Dawkins for?'

'Brandy and wine. Excellent examples. I'm actually a bit of a connoisseur, old chap.'

'You've been buying the Brigadier's best brandy and wine from that toad Dawkins? Is that what you mean?' I may have raised my voice.

The singing in the corner stopped suddenly and heads turned in our direction.

'Yes, just said so, didn't I?'

'Knowing that Dawkins was stealing it?'

'Well, I wasn't going to sneak in and steal it myself, was I,' he expostulated, then deflated in defeat. 'Do you think they'll arrest me?'

'I bloody well hope so.' I put my beer down on the bar. I'd lost my taste for it and the company. 'Eight o'clock in the morning you will report to my room with all the Brigadier's bottles intact. Do you understand me?'

'Well, really, Lennox,' he spluttered. 'I protest. I paid good money, you know.'

'*Eight o'clock*,' I reminded him forcibly. All eyes followed my departure, then no doubt, turned toward the red-faced thief.

Fogg and I returned through the still settlement where thatched cottages fringed the village green. Woodsmoke hung in the air – kitchen stoves would be alight, warming pies or puddings or kettles for tea. The scent of damp grass mingled with the fragrance of flowers from close-tended gardens. A black iron hand pump stood sentinel, a horse trough beside it, the stone stuccoed with dark moss. Ducks huddled together at the edge of a still pond, their heads tucked tightly under downy wings. Fogg ran ahead, nose to the ground, I whistled him quietly to come by my side and we trod softly together across the grass, lest we disturb the peace.

Benson tugged the door open. He seemed rather more sprightly this evening – perhaps the spring weather was adding a bit of zest to his old bones.

Greetings old chap,' I hailed him warmly, pleased to see him in better fettle. 'Looking for Dawkins.'

His eyes slid in the direction of below stairs so I trotted down, ignoring sideways glances from various maids and minions, and caught my quarry coming out of the kitchens with a slice of fresh baked bread in hand. He dropped it when he saw my face and backed away.

'I ain't done nuffink,' he shouted.

'You've been stealing from the Brigadier's cellars, you snivelling worm.'

'Only a few bottles, that's all it were.' He had backed into the whitewashed wall and started wheedling. 'I was asked by that opery singer. He's a nob; I was just doing as I were told, I was. He told me to get him some an' I did.'

'You'll answer to the police in the morning, Dawkins. Tonight you're going to be locked in the coal cellar. That will give you time to think about your thievery.'

'No, don't, sir. Don't. Can't stand being closed in, sir. Please. It were just once. I'll tell you what I saw, sir, that night. If you leave me be, I'll tell ye what I saw.'

I stared down at the blighter, lank hair around his thin face, eyes wide, slack mouth open.

'What did you see?' I demanded.

'It was in the dark, sir, behind the theatre. That night the singer fell dead. I said to Mister Andrew I'd bring the bottles round the back next to that little green door as goes under the stage. There wouldn't be no one about, cos they was all inside, listening to the singing. Mister Andrew, he comes out the door and comes over to me. He gives me the dosh – that's money, that is – an' I gives him the bottles. Two of brandy, three of burgundy, being all I could carry. He's all dressed up in his finery, and rushes off to hide the bottles back at the Dower House. I stayed counting the money. He gave it me in all little bits of coins, pennies, threepenny bits, tanners, couple of shilling and two half-crowns. Well, I dropped a half-crown and was feeling about in the grass when another bloke comes by and he's panting cause he's carrying this big bit of wood. I didn't know what he was doing in the dark of a night, but I stayed hid away till he'd gone, then I stood up again.'

'Did you see who it was? With the plank?'

'Ay, sir. It were that chaplain. One as is dead now. Wasn't wearing his cassock, but I knew it were him.'

That made me stop and take notice. It was the evidence we needed and it put a very firm finger on the culprit. If I weren't so damn furious about the thefts, I'd have been rather pleased.

Dawkins gabbled on. 'Then Mister Andrew comes back, but he can't get in the green door. "Locked," he says. "Where's the key?" Well, I'm already spooked, and

I don't want to tell on no chaplain cos we shouldn't a been there, so I didn't say nuffink. I took to my heels and scarpered.'

We were interrupted by a noise behind us that sounded like the sort of snort a bull at a gate would make, and turned to look. There was a crowd of astonished servants, including Dicks – they must have heard the commotion and come to find the cause. The snorting came from the cook, a lady of short stature but a girth as broad as her height. She was pushing up the sleeves of her aproned dress; her large fist was wrapped around a rolling pin and her small eyes shone with the wrath of a good woman's fury.

'Dawkins,' she yelled out, the noise filled the stone-flagged corridor and reverberated along to the rooms beyond. 'You snivelling snake, you've gone an' done it now.' She advanced on the wretch.

Dawkins's eyes widened in horror, he cowered, he shook, and then he turned tail and ran hell for leather. The enraged cook bellowed and followed, thundering along in hobnail boots with rolling pin raised above her head. 'Dawkins,' she bellowed again.

They disappeared around a bend. I turned to see the other servants staring after them, their eyes bright in the lamps hanging above from the ceiling. A few shook their heads and turned away to go back whence they came, muttering amongst themselves.

Dicks came to join me.

'Rather think retribution has presented itself, Dicks,' I said.

'Indeed, sir, and Cook has a mean hand. There'll be no escape for Dawkins now.'

'You think she'll catch up with him?' I asked. 'I'd have wagered he was fleeter of foot.'

'Maybe, maybe not, sir. But that lady with the rolling pin isn't just Cook – she's Mrs Dawkins. There's no escaping an incensed wife, sir.'

'Ah, yes. A wife is a treasure and a trial, Dicks.'

'Indeed, sir.'

I gathered up my dog, who had chosen to accompany me, the kitchens being one of his favourite spots, and returned to my rooms.

Not only was the house now short of a cook but most of the guests were elsewhere. The senior Chisholms, Ruth and Ford, had gone to Oxford in the company of the younger set. The Brigadier was being served by the Gurkha in his rooms, and I had no desire to eat a cold collation with anyone else who chose to turn up in the dining room.

Dicks proved himself the good soul that he was and put together a tray of game pie, ham, various sticks of greenery, chunks of stilton and cheddar, Cook's best homemade pickle and thick slices of buttered bread attended by a glass of rich red wine. I lit the fire against the damp night air, and with my dog at my feet and my kitten on my lap, I feasted in solitary splendour. I think it was the most restful meal I'd had since arriving at the Hall.

The remainder of the evening was spent at my desk, pen in hand, thoughts turning over Dawkins's revelations.

Jarvis had exchanged the planks, and no doubt been killed for his murderous deed. To my mind, that made von Graf even more suspect and I underlined his name in my notebook with a heavier stroke of the pen. But what about Lady Ruth? And where did Florence fit in? Or the opera group for that matter? But the Gainsborough was a glittering prize, almost beyond value.

The motivation must somehow be related to art, I thought. Jarvis and von Graf were involved in art – restoring it, selling it, maybe even stealing it. What could Crispin have done to warrant his murder? Was he sold a dud, or did he stumble upon their duplicity? Should I go and confront von Graf now? But Swift should lead the interview: I'd more or less promised not to act without him. And we didn't have any evidence; although perhaps if I confronted him …? I reined in my musings – we needed facts, not meanderings. A trip to Oxford and the Black Cat Club may well reveal some evidence, I thought, or, at the very least, an example of what a den of iniquity really looked like.

CHAPTER 15

Early light saw me on the front doorstep, Purdey under one arm, dog under the other. Hiram arrived as the sun rose over the green-hilled horizon in front of the house. He was wearing a blue outfit such as his father had worn, with a white shirt and black cord for a necktie. Once accustomed to it, I thought it had style of sorts and was probably a great deal more comfortable than the stiff tweed he'd sported the other evening. Our habitual green and browns reflected the colours of the countryside around us; I imagine his blue and white suited the open skies of Texas. Perhaps he was homesick and wearing a reminder of his native land.

'Greetings,' I said.

'Howdy,' he replied.

Formalities complete we ambled off in the direction of the old woodshed and the pigeons I'd spotted in the vicinity.

'How was the Gilbert and Sullivan performance last evening?' I asked in a friendly manner.

'I never seen anything like it,' he replied in his slow drawl. 'Got more life 'n that opera Ma's so keen on, but my preference is for a hoe-down.' He took a pot shot at a pigeon and brought it down, then another and reloaded his Holland & Holland to bring down two more. He was an expert shot – a great deal better than I.

I fired off a couple of blasts and landed one. Fogg refused to even look at the dead birds, so we gathered them up and put them in our game bags. There were plenty more pigeon near the hay meadows and we strolled up there.

'I understand Ruth is related to Lady Florence,' I tossed in as an opener.

'She sure is,' Hiram confirmed.

'You were visiting Braeburn Castle? Home of Ruth's family, the Braeburn clan?' I persevered as we cleared the brow of the hill.

'Met my fiancée there. She's a great gal is Caroline. Great gal.' He lifted his barrel and fired a couple more shots, bringing down two fat wood pigeon. I emptied a barrel which merely succeeded in scattering the rest of the flock.

'Indeed, yes, she is. Known her since we were knee-high,' I said.

'She told me you don't hold no hard feelings about our being wed,' he said.

'None at all.' I stopped to face him. 'Hiram, much as I admire Caroline, we are friends and only friends. Believe me, I wish you both the greatest joy.'

'Why, thank you kindly.' He took my hand and crushed it enthusiastically. 'She was fretting over telling you, and I think her pappy had it in his mind that you were the man for her.'

I extracted my hand and shook some feeling back into it. 'Maybe at one time,' I said. 'But I happen to know that he's delighted with Caroline's decision.'

'Lennox,' he said. 'Would you do me the honour of being my best man? I know Caroline would like that.'

That caught me unawares. I stammered, 'Well, erm, yes, yes, of course. I mean – yes, delighted. Honoured, actually.'

'You know this is just a small wedding,' Hiram explained. 'Around a hundred folk coming over for the chapel ceremony and the ball. We'll be having a proper Texas celebration at the family ranch next month. You don't have to come, though, if you don't want to. I have a friend out there will be standing by my side.'

'Ah, good. Well, if you don't mind, old chap, I'll give that one a miss,' I told him. 'Sounds like you've been planning this for quite some time.'

'We sure have. I fell for Caroline as soon as I clapped eyes on her. A happier man than me you're not going to see, my friend.'

'Excellent,' I said as I called Fogg to heel. 'Why were you visiting Braeburn?'

'Ma – Ruth, that is – has been fretting to visit her ancestral home for many years. So Pa wrote to the old Laird and got us an invite. Came over last summer on the White Star ocean liner, we did. I didn't want to go, but I'll be forever grateful that I did. Made my eyes open wide to see what is out there in the world.' He paused to search the skies for pigeon, but there were none, so we carried on our slow walk, guns ready in hands. 'That old castle was sure a sorry sight,' he continued. 'Florence and her pappy, the Laird, did what they could to make us comfortable but the place is falling into the loch. It troubled Ruth and she made this plan for Pa to buy it.'

'Your mother wanted to buy Braeburn Castle?' I was somewhat incredulous at this piece of news.

'She offered the Laird a blank cheque. Didn't come out right, though; the old man wouldn't sell so much as a stone. I think he was offended, myself.'

'Um, yes, unfortunate.' I imagine he was extremely offended, but there was no point in saying so. I sought to change the subject. 'I assume Caroline came to keep Florence company?' I asked.

'She did. I think Florence had her matchmaking hat on, and I'm mighty thankful for what she did.'

I suspected Ruth had her matchmaking hat on when they persuaded Hiram to go to the Castle with her and Ford. She must have been terribly disappointed when Hiram and Florence didn't fall for each other.

'What did you make of Jarvis and von Graf?' I asked.

'Thieves is what I make of them,' he said without preamble.

'Really? Are they actually thieves, then?' I asked, relieved we'd finally broached the subject.

'I can't prove it, but I believe they are. Ma won't hear a word of it. She has a good heart but a head full of fancy ideas.' Hiram suddenly stopped to fire off two more shots and brought down two birds that I hadn't even spotted.

'What made you think Jarvis and von Graf were stealing?' I said once he'd collected his birds. Fogg sat by and watched him.

'They were selling paintings for Florence's pappy.'

'And you thought they were pocketing some of the proceeds?' I asked.

'I did. Florence told me they had sold poorly. I questioned Jarvis, he said the market was swamped and the cost of sales were high, but I didn't think that was so. Florence showed me the ones they kept back: there was cattle and meadows, mountains and forests. She said the others had been even better. I said they were mighty fine, but Jarvis and von Graf laughed – told me I didn't understand art. Well, that may be so, but I can tell a good painting from a bad un. Those paintings were sold cheap and I reckon they were skimming the profits.'

'And who did you tell about your suspicions?' I asked.

Fogg ran ahead, saw a squirrel and started to bark, sending a bunch of wood pigeon into the sky. I raised my Purdey and downed one, Hiram hit two, reloaded, and hit two more at extreme range.

'Everybody, at some time or another: the old Laird, Florence, Ma and Pa, Caroline, even the Brigadier. None of them agreed with me. That chaplain sweet-talked them all. He said every darn house in this country had old paintings like that on the wall and half the folk were selling on account of their homes being in a state of disrepair after the war.'

Actually, I did have to agree with the defunct Jarvis on that point: such works may seem rare to a Texan, but here in the old country they were as common as wood pigeons.

We picked up the birds and headed for breakfast, dropping the birds off with an unsuspecting footman as we entered the house.

The morning room was full of women, Caroline, Florence, Ruth and two others whom I assumed were bridesmaids – Bunty and somebody-or-other. The place was alive with chatter of weddings and I beat a retreat. Hiram was made of sterner stuff, and besides, Caroline spotted him and came over to drag him in by the arm.

I escaped to my room and rang for Dicks. Tubbs had rearranged my desk again. He flicked the remaining pen off the edge and sat down in the middle of my bare desktop and stared innocently at me. I placed him back with Fogg in their basket just as Dicks arrived with a tray of fried eggs and bacon. He looked at the items scattered on the floor, frowned, plonked the tray down on the reading table, didn't even lay the knives and forks – just stalked across to the desk, replaced Tubbs's best efforts and walked out without a word. He didn't give me a chance to explain.

He came back after I'd enjoyed my excellent meal.

'The cat did it!' I told him quite clearly.

'Huh.' He went off again with an air of indignation and the emptied tray; not even a 'sir' was spoken.

I turned the pages of my book and jotted down a few notes from this morning's conversation. My quiet solitude was broken a short time later as Swift came in, ready for action.

'Where's Andrew Dundale?' he said, without so much as a good morning.

'Greetings, old chap,' I replied. 'He's right behind you.' Which indeed he was, for Dundale now shambled in with an obvious hangover and a sheepish demeanour.

'Sit,' Swift ordered Andrew, who sat in one of the club chairs. Swift leaned over the back of another, facing Andrew and scaring him out of what little wits he possessed. It didn't take long for the whole story of the stolen wine and brandy to tumble out.

'Where are the bottles?' Swift demanded.

'With Benson,' Andrew answered, his voice shaking. 'I gave them to him when I came in. You can ask him if you like.'

'I will,' Swift said. He withdrew his notebook and began writing in his careful, precise hand.

'Are you going to arrest me?' Andrew asked. 'Because I don't think it's fair. I paid for them, you know. And now I have given them back and I'm out of pocket a great deal of money, so I don't see how you can –'

'Quiet.' Swift cut him off. 'We are not arresting you – yet. But don't leave the estate. Now get out.' And Andrew did, as fast as his feet would take him.

We watched him leave and I closed the door behind him. Swift dropped into a chair, crossed his legs and yawned.

'Last night went well?' I asked.

'Hum,' he nodded with half a smile.

'I had a word with Dawkins,' I told him, and recounted the incident and the news about the plank and Jarvis's proven guilt. I concluded with the retribution brought upon him by Mrs Dawkins.

Swift laughed – the first time I think I'd heard him laugh. He wrote it all down and then snapped his book closed.

'So it was Jarvis.' He looked up at me. 'We have two killers, or rather, we had.'

'Yes, and now it's a question of who murdered the murderer,' I agreed. 'We should talk to von Graf.'

'He's next on my list to interview,' Swift said, pocketing his notebook.

'Has anyone taken statements? The whereabouts of people when Jarvis was shot, that sort of thing?' I asked.

Swift smiled. 'Quite the professional, Major.' He teased me. 'Yes, Watson's gang questioned the locals in the village. Nobody saw or heard anything.' He paused to look wryly at me. 'And I asked everyone at dinner last evening where they were — very politely!' He added, then continued with a slight frown. 'None of them actually has a sound alibi apart from Caroline who was chatting to a maid. Lady Ruth said she was bathing, Ford was reading the newspaper, Hiram was still asleep.'

'And Florence?'

He turned a little pink. 'She, erm, she went for a walk in the gardens, but she didn't hear anything. And there was no-one about,' he added hastily. 'And they've all got guns, before you ask, and know how to use them. As you've already observed, this is a military household.'

I nodded silently, then said. 'You didn't find anything at the rectory?'

He shook his head. 'No. You and Miss Busybody took the only item of interest. Where is the painting, by the way?'

'Miss Busby, actually,' a voice from the doorway corrected him. We both spun around as the lady herself walked in, preceded by Dicks acting as her escort. He left as silently as he'd come, still not talking to me, apparently.

We hastened to our feet and Swift had the grace to apologise.

'No matter, Chief Inspector,' she said as we offered her a seat. She sat on the edge, perched upright, hands crossed on her lap, wearing a pale green woollen suit, jersey and a scarf. Her shoes were damp: she must have come through the gardens. 'I have been thinking,' she announced, with a slight frown and raised a finger, 'about *bluebells*.'

'Y…es …' I replied, with some hesitation.

'They spread very slowly, you know. They have bulbs that split off and produce new flowers. They seed too, but it takes many years. Once the bulbs are disturbed they will die if not handled carefully.'

Swift was gazing at her with a deep frown and, no doubt, a shortening temper.

I caught on first, being a country chap.

'Oh, well done!' I exclaimed. 'The grave was covered with grass.'

Now I realised what it was I'd missed.

Swift glared at me. 'Will somebody tell me what possible significance bluebells could have?' he snapped. 'Because I've got better things to do than discuss horticulture.'

'In spring,' Miss Busby told him, 'the graveyard behind the chantry is covered with bluebells. But there was merely grass growing on the grave where the body of the Reverend Jarvis was found. There can only be one reason why there weren't any bluebells.'

'Because someone dug it up last year and destroyed the bulbs,' I answered.

'Exactly,' she said. 'They probably stripped away the turf and relaid it afterwards. Of course the grass would continue growing, but not the bluebells.'

I looked at her appraisingly. 'And you think that's where the body of Jeremy Bartholomew was buried.'

'Indeed, I do,' Miss Busby replied.

CHAPTER 16

'Right.' Swift bounded to his feet, yanked the belt of his trench coat tighter and made for the door. We went through the gardens; Swift kept up a brisk pace and Miss Busby was a little breathless by the time we approached the old cemetery. Sounds of digging greeted us as we arrived. An old man was excavating the grave where we'd found the body of Jarvis yesterday. He worked with a steady rhythm and was already some two feet down, the turf carefully cut and stacked to one side, a pile of reddish brown soil heaped upon the other. The surrounding bluebells were bent and bruised having been trampled during the activities of the police the day before.

'Good morning, Graves,' Miss Busby called to him.

He stopped and looked up at us, his narrow face wrought with deep lines, grey stubble upon his chin. He leaned on his spade and called out.

'Mornin' to ye all. 'Ye from t'ouse then?'

'Yes; this is Major Lennox, Graves,' Miss Busby told him.

Graves touched his grimy cap.

'Greetings,' I said. 'Jolly good name for a grave digger – Graves.'

'I'm called that because it's me job, ye clod,' he replied.

Miss Busby persevered. 'And this is Inspector Swift from Scotland Yard.'

Graves eyed him closely. 'Not from yon station, then? They be a right daft bunch, they be. Wouldn't a dug this hole if it weren't Miss Busby 'as asked me. Not for yon police. They can do it the'selves.' He spat on his hands, took up his spade and dug the shovel deeper into the soil. ''Tis the first time I've dug one up, ye know.'

Swift stepped forward for a closer look. 'Has it been disturbed recently?' he asked.

'Aye, that it has,' Graves replied, digging as he spoke. 'Loose, ye see, not barted doon like ye'd expect.'

We all leaned in to look.

'So there may be a body buried down there?' I asked.

Graves grinned. 'Ay, lad, old Benson is down here. That's one of the eighteen hundreds Bensons, not the old, old Bensons, cos them's over yon.' He nodded towards a group of worn stones. 'And the even older Bensons lie beneath *them*. But the plot got a bit crowded and they give up and came down 'ere.'

'Um … right,' I said, and decided not to ask any more idiotic questions.

Graves dug on, working along a six-foot trench about three feet wide.

I glanced at Miss Busby – she was looking rather

anxious. To my mind, attending the excavation of mouldering bodies wasn't a suitable experience for a lady.

'Miss Busby, would you prefer to –' I started to ask her, but my words were interrupted as Graves's next shovelful brought a sickening stench up with it.

'Wait.' Swift called out. 'That's enough, man. You've found it.'

I reached for my handkerchief.

'Ay, and summat more,' Graves called, apparently impervious to the abominable stink. He clanged his spade against something metallic in the grave, then reached down and yanked a sword from the dirt, letting loose the most retchingly putrid odour that I'd ever had the misfortune to encounter.

He held the sword up above his head, filthy with soil, slime and God knows what on the blade. Part of the hilt glinted in the sunshine.

'Eee, 'tis like that sword in the stone, so it is,' he said, glee in his voice.

I had to retreat along with Miss Busby and Swift, both of whom were holding handkerchiefs to their noses.

'Graves,' I said, 'it is absolutely nothing like the sword in the stone. Not remotely.'

'Hand it over, man.' Swift demanded.

''Tis I what found it,' Graves argued. 'And a rare thing it is,' he said, tugging up some grass to wipe the blade.

'Police evidence,' Swift snapped, and took it from him after a short tussle. He carried it upwind of the opened grave and we gathered around to peer at it.

'It's rather fine, isn't it,' Miss Busby remarked as Swift turned it in his hands. Graves came to join us - I tried to stay upwind of him as he was beginning to whiff a bit.

Swift cleaned the blade as best he could with handfuls of grass. I sacrificed my handkerchief to the hilt, wiping the pommel clean of soil until we could make out the blazon on the hilt.

'*Not* the Bloxford family crest,' Miss Busby remarked.

'No, but the crown and thistle doesn't make it too difficult to guess which side of the border it came from,' I said.

'Scotland,' Swift said. 'Is it the Braeburn insignia?'

We all looked at each other.

'I'm afraid I don't know,' Miss Busby answered.

'Better go and find out, then, hadn't we,' Swift said quietly, and turned to march towards the Hall.

'Stay and guard the place, would you, old chap,' I told Graves.

''Twas I as found it, ye know. Like that mystical sword, that is.'

'No, it *isn't*, Graves,' I told him quite firmly.

Swift stopped at the mirror pond in front of the Orangerie and dunked the sword into it, scattering the golden carp that had come to see if we had bread for them. He kept plunging it under the water and then rubbing off the foul ordure until it shone clean and bright. Then he carried it to the house, his sleeves wet, his hands dripping.

We entered through the French windows and went into the hall. Florence was up on the first floor and looked over the balustrade to wave a small envelope at us.

'Hello,' she laughed gaily and ran down the stairs, pretty as ever in the same peach dress of a couple of days ago. 'Jonathan, I have just written a note to you, to say thank you for the roses this morning. They're quite beautiful.' She smiled at him, but the smile faltered as she saw the look on his face.

'Do you recognise this?' he asked, holding up the sword.

She came closer to examine the detail on the hilt. 'How strange.' She took it from his hands to hold it to the light, and then swung it expertly around. 'Finishing school,' she laughed. 'Fencing was the only thing I was good at, apart from singing.' She offered it back, the hilt held toward him. 'The insignia is ours, but I've never seen the rapier before. It looks quite old. Where did you find it?'

'Buried in a body,' Swift replied.

Well, that dropped a bombshell into the conversation, but then, the mention of corpses tends to do that. Florence stepped backwards.

'You mean it was actually *in* a body? Someone was murdered? Who?' she raised one hand to her cheek.

'Probably the old chaplain, Bartholomew,' Swift replied. 'Strange that the sword should come from your home.'

'Ah,' Florence uttered. 'I see – that makes me a suspect, does it? Well, thank you for having some faith in me. Obviously I would come here with one of our own swords to murder someone I've never even heard of.' She was getting rather worked up. 'What a simply ridiculous suggestion. I do hope you find your killer, Inspector Swift, because it most certainly was not me!' With that warm retort she crumpled up the envelope she held in her hand and threw it at his feet. Then she turned and walked upstairs, head held high, back straight, every inch the fine lady that she was born to be.

The Inspector looked after her for a moment, then picked the paper up, shoved it in his pocket and turned away, rather red-faced.

'I'm going to the station,' he declared. 'Need to call out our medical investigators from London.' Sword in hand, he stalked off, though he had to wait for Benson to pull open the front door, which rather spoiled the drama of the exit.

'Oh dear,' Miss Busby said.

'Yes,' I replied, and pushed my hands in my pockets. 'Too suspicious and too quick to accuse,' I remarked.

'Indeed,' Miss Busby replied.

We returned to my rooms and sat at the reading table.

'I am sure the body was that of poor Bartholomew,' she said.

'Yes,' I nodded. 'Unlikely to be anybody else,' I observed, and rang the bell for Dicks.

'Who do you think may have done it?' She was sitting upright, hands held together. The kitten spied her and came to clamber up onto her lap. She stroked it absently.

'Jarvis probably, or von Graf. I expect one of them stole the sword from Braeburn Castle.'

'They were all here, you know, when Bartholomew disappeared,' she said. 'Except Jarvis.'

'Oh,' That rather clouded the issue. 'Um, could you tell me again what happened, please, Miss Busby, around the time Bartholomew was supposed to have run off with the silver and the lady from Brighton.'

'Yes, of course.'

'No, wait,' I told her. I went to my desk for my notebook, pen and ink-bottle and returned better equipped to carry out a proper interview.

Miss Busby smiled as she watched me fill my pen with ink, blot the stray drops and then look up at her with brows raised.

Dicks came in with a tray laden with a teapot, cups, saucers and dainty whatnots.

'Mister Benson told me to bring some refreshments, sir,' he said, spreading the table with a white cloth and placing the items from the tray with his usual precision. He fussed about, though he wasn't his usual self.

'Thank you, Dicks,' I told him.

'Hummph.' He went off, still rather miffed with me.

Miss Busby poured the tea and began. 'It was late last summer, at the end of September – I remember because the apples were falling from the trees. Caroline had just returned and she had Hiram with her, and his parents, Ford and Ruth, and Florence, too. Von Graf arrived a day or so later, but not Jarvis.'

I wrote this down; she waited for me to finish as I was rather slow.

'Was this the first visit from Hiram and his parents?' I asked, taking a bite of Madeira cake, still warm from the oven.

'Indeed it was, and it caused quite a stir. Caroline

had met Hiram at Braeburn Castle and subsequently sent a telegram to the Brigadier to say that she was bringing her new fiancé home to introduce him,' she told me, her eyes thoughtful as she recounted events. 'That ruffled the Brigadier's feathers because it wasn't the right way to do things at all. But a letter from Hiram arrived in the next post. He requested a visit to Bloxford Hall to formally ask the Brigadier's permission for Caroline's hand. Well, the Brigadier couldn't really say no, but he put them off until the following week. In the meantime questions were asked, discreetly, of course, about Hiram's family background. By the time they all arrived at the Hall, the Brigadier was prepared to receive them.'

'Do I take it that you were the one who made discreet enquiries about the Chisholm family, Miss Busby?' I asked her.

'Indeed I was,' she smiled. 'I have many acquaintances, and they do like to gossip, I'm afraid.'

'And your friends thought the Chisholms passed muster?'

'Very much so. A family of substance and good standing. Which was a great relief to the Brigadier's mind.'

'Where did they go?' I asked her. 'The Chisholms, I mean, when they left here before coming back again recently.'

'London, to visit historical sites and museums, theatres and art galleries. A cultural tour, in effect.'

'Did Caroline go with them?'

'No, good heavens, that would have been most unseemly.'

'And this from one of the Bloxford Beauties,' I teased.

She laughed and poured more tea into our cups. 'It's a question of perception, Major Lennox.'

I smiled and jotted down her remarks then turned to the subject of today's corpse. 'Bartholomew,' I reminded her.

'Ah, yes.' Her face fell. 'What a sad ending, poor man – and I really could not believe he had run off with the silver, or a lady. It seemed so unlikely a tale. He wasn't the sort at all.'

'Do you know where the letters are, the ones that were found at the rectory after he disappeared?' I asked.

'I do,' she said, and suddenly looked quite mischievous. 'I stole them from my nephew this morning. Wasn't that naughty of me!' She laughed and placed the sleeping kitten on the table to retrieve her handbag, from which she drew out a few sheets of paper.

Must say, that made my eyes open. 'What on earth made you think to do that?'

'Once I had it in my mind that poor Bartholomew may be lying in that grave, I thought we would need to examine the letters. So I went to the station and while my nephew was distracted I persuaded the clerk, Miller, to lend them to me. I taught him, you know, Bobby Miller; he was very slow to learn his three 'r's and I spent a great deal of time instructing him after school.'

She spread the letters on the table between us. They were signed from a Miss Margaret Pearson. The paper was ordinary, everyday sort of stuff. The hand was well formed and regular, and all were written in the same colour ink, a shade of brownish black. There were no dates and the address had been merely noted as 'Brighton'.

I read them carefully and found that they rather lacked heart. No soft words of tenderness or mention of missing the other's presence, or even reminiscences of times spent together. They were mostly instructions about when they were to elope, which railway station to meet at, and to be sure to bring sufficient funds.

'Where are the envelopes?' I asked, spreading the papers in front of me.

''There weren't any,' Miss Busby replied, watching my actions closely.

'Doesn't that strike you as strange?'

'Yes, and I said so to my nephew at the time. But I doubt he's ever written a love letter in his life and he does rather lack imagination, so he thought nothing of it. I still have all the letters my fiancée wrote to me – they are in their envelopes, tied with ribbon.'

'Precisely – nobody throws away envelopes containing love letters. And the envelopes would require an official post office date stamp, and that would be very difficult to forge.' I fetched my magnifying glass. There was a splatter of tiny ink drops across the writing on all the pages, I realised. It looked as though someone had shaken a pen that held a drop of ink on the nib. I manoeuvred them until the small blots joined up across the edges of each page. 'The ink is exactly the same colour as the ink that was used to write the notes,' I said, staring intently through the magnifying lens. 'And the spots sprayed across the pages were made when all the letters were together in one place.'

She caught on quickly. 'Which should not be possible, because each letter was supposed to have been sent on a different date.'

'Exactly,' I said. 'These are fabrications. This is nothing but a smokescreen.'

I gave her the glass so she could see for herself and she bent over them, nudging the pages with her fingers and studying each one to examine the colour and texture of the ink.

'It was very carefully devised,' she added.

'As was the death of Sir Crispin,' I replied. 'But the killing of Jarvis was entirely different.'

'I have been thinking about that. Retribution, do you think?' Miss Busby asked.

'Yes,' I mused. 'But for what?'

'The death of Bartholomew?' she suggested. 'Someone determined who killed him, and left Jarvis's body as a sort of "x marks the spot", don't you think?'

'Possibly, but if it were von Graf, he may have killed Jarvis and Bartholomew and made it look as though Jarvis did the first murder. Or …' I paused and looked at her. 'I think we need to unravel a little more of the knot, Miss Busby, because there is much here to think about.'

CHAPTER 17

'Indeed! And I really must be going, Major Lennox.' Miss Busby smiled at me, her eyes once again bright and shining. 'Inspector Swift will be asking for these at the station and he will blame poor Bobby Miller if he discovers they are not there.' She gathered up the letters and returned them to her handbag.

I rang for Dicks, who must have been lurking nearby, for he arrived swiftly at my rooms. He escorted Miss Busby out, opening doors for her along the way and chatting as they went, because no doubt news of the discovery of Bartholomew would already have begun to spread.

Despite his sleepy state, Tubbs had returned to my desk and was even now shoving the remaining pen from the tooled leather top to drop onto the rug. I scolded him to his face; he stared back with wide blue eyes and an innocent air. I returned him to the basket, opened the desk drawer, tossed everything into it, including my notebook, pens, pencils and whatnots, and closed it again. Enough kitten nonsense, I decided.

I knew I should visit the Brigadier and tell him about the latest dead chaplain, but first I wanted to take another look at Lady Grace. I felt under the bed to pull out the wrapped canvas and carried it to my desk in the window embrasure. I scrutinised her carefully in the bright sunshine coming through the mullioned glass. It was still a bit of a shock to see her so young – and déshabillé.

The pale green paint that I'd managed to smear on my sleeve when Miss Busby and I were at the rectory was quite distinctive. I checked my jacket again and compared it with the artwork in an attempt to find the same colour on the canvas. It wasn't there. Jarvis may have been restoring Lady Grace, but he must have been painting something else. What was it, and where was it?

I wrapped the canvas and returned it under the bed and was grovelling about on the floor as Dicks returned.

'Sir,' he said. 'Lady Ruth requests your presence in the library.'

'Just a minute, old chap.' I bent to pick off fluff and bits of Foggy fur from my trousers.

'I have a brush, sir.' Dicks whipped it out and advanced.

'No, Dicks, how many times do I have to tell you. No brushes.'

His face fell but then he spotted my vacant desk.

'I say, sir, you tidied up!' He flashed a wide grin.

'Indeed I did, Dicks,' I replied, and moved to sit in my chair.

'Um, I think she means now, sir.'

'But I was. . . .' I looked at his earnest young face, 'oh, very well.'

Lady Ruth was sitting at the desk in the cluttered, somewhat dark and masculine room, books lining the shelves almost to the ceiling. Her angular face was bent over a pile of papers. Pen in hand, she was underlining sections of a very neat list with a firm hand. She wore prim spectacles, and the same tartan jacket she'd sported before with a simple cream blouse and high collar – she looked very much the stern aristocrat.

'Ah, Major Lennox, sit down, will you,' she ordered, her grey eyes made larger by the lenses of her glasses. 'My grand-niece, Lady Florence Braeburn, is upset. You and your friend Inspector Swift are the cause.'

'Um . . .' There wasn't much I could say, really. Swift was the guilty party, but I'd feel like a snitch if I tried to pin it on him.

'This delving about for bodies has got to stop,' Lady Ruth commanded. 'I cannot have Lady Caroline's and my son's wedding disturbed just because you have a fancy for sleuthing. You must not cause any further distress to the family. It will not be countenanced. The ceremony is the day after tomorrow and you are wandering about the countryside in search of corpses. It is utterly thoughtless of you, Lennox, and – I must use the word – selfish.'

Well, that was a bit rich! Here we were, doing our best to hunt down a murderer and all she could do was rabbit on about some damn bean-feast.

'I –'

She cut through the protest I was about to utter. 'You have already found a dead chaplain, the Reverend Jarvis, who, I may remind you, I had arranged to officiate at the wedding. Now I am to believe you have dug up another one! What next, the parish priest? This will not do, Lennox.' She raised her voice. 'I will not have it. I have talked to the Brigadier and he agrees with me. No more police and no more detecting. Really, young man, it is quite preposterous.'

'Mrs Chisholm –' I began, and received a frozen stare '– I mean, Lady Ruth, Inspector Swift and I are trying to prevent any further deaths –'

She interrupted again – she wasn't prepared to listen to a word I said.

'You are about to be the best man, Major Lennox, and I expect you to take your duties seriously. I have made a list of your tasks and responsibilities for before, during and after the ceremony. Here it is.' She pushed two closely written sheets of paper over the desk at me. 'I want no more of this nonsense and absolutely no more bodies. I hope I have made myself clear. Now, off you go.' She wafted her hand at me as though I were some minion. 'And take these with you,' she added, holding out the papers, which I'd failed to pick up.

I found myself on the other side of the door rather nonplussed. What the devil did she know about detecting? And why *shouldn't* we find bodies? There was a murderer on the loose and someone had to put a stop to it before someone decent was killed. If there were to be another victim, it would jolly well serve her right if it were her.

I heard the lunch gong ring. I wavered: I had no desire for more of the same company, but I was hungry and having a tray sent to my room would take at least half an hour. Hiram came into the hall as I was dithering.

'Howdy,' he grinned with a flash of white teeth. He noticed the papers crumpled in my hand. 'Ma cornered you, did she?' he laughed. 'Here, you know the best thing to do with these?' He took them, crushed them into a ball and tossed them into the empty fireplace. 'Come have some lunch with me, Lennox,' he drawled. 'We'll go to that old inn down in the village. I don't fancy another preaching while I eat my grub, and if we stay here that's just what we'll get.'

'Ha, my thoughts exactly!' I grinned; now here was a far better solution. We set off at a cracking pace. 'You're sure the girls don't want to come?' I asked as we reached the village green.

'They've got their heads full of flowers and flounces. I can hardly get a word of sense from any one of them,' he said.

He was wearing the blue trousers and jacket again today, and as it had started to rain he'd topped the outfit with a wide-brimmed hat. We drew some strange looks from the locals as we strolled through the village. Hiram raised his hat to all the ladies we met, making them giggle.

He turned to talk to me. 'Florence told me about the

sword in the dead guy you dug up this morning. I think your friend Jonathan could have handled that situation a whole lot better.'

'Swift has a tendency to suspect everybody,' I told him. 'Strange, though, the rapier being from Braeburn.'

He glanced sideways at me, brows drawn together. 'Why do you believe it came from Braeburn?'

'The insignia on the handle, it's the blazon of the Braeburns.'

'Yeah …' he held the word as if he were in thought. 'But there was a Braeburn married to a Bloxford in seventeen hundred and something. Maybe it came here with that fair lady?'

'Really?' That made my eyes open, although I shouldn't have been surprised: these old families were always intermarrying. 'How do you know that?'

'Ma's an encyclopaedia on the subject. She knows every twig and branch of the Braeburn tree and she'll lecture on it without end if you don't stop her.'

We reached the pub, my mind turning over this new piece of information. The landlord hailed us as we walked in and it wasn't long before we each had a pint of beer in hand and a steaming steak and kidney pie with mash on the table in front of us. Heaven on earth for the paltry price of a shilling and sixpence apiece.

We cleared our plates in no time and Hiram produced a heavy silver cigarette case and drew out a cheroot. He offered one to me, but having recently foresworn tobacco, I shook my head.

'Don't happen to have heard of the Bloxford Beauties, by chance?' I asked.

He leaned on the table, cheroot between his lips and looked me in the eye, then said slowly, 'Yeah, I have.'

'How did you hear?'

'Lennox, the Beauties are a family secret and I'm sworn to keep it.'

'By whom?'

'The Brigadier, my future pa-in-law,' he drawled, smoke drifting from his lips.

'Well, I know about them too. Did he show them to you?'

'No. Like I told you, we're not wed yet, so I ain't family. I'm surprised to hear you're in on the secret.'

I returned his regard. 'I was told in confidence. Listen, old chap, I think these murders could be related to the paintings. So I'd appreciate you opening up.'

He thought about it, chewing on his cheroot. 'I knew something about it before the Brigadier told me, but I didn't let on. Like I said, Ma is an expert on anything pertaining to the Braeburns.' He paused to take a draught of beer. 'Florence's father gave Ma the keys to the Castle's muniment room and she spent many a day in there, taking notes and copying things out from all them old family papers. She said they'd been badly neglected and were going to ruin. Had new chests made for them – big wooden ones with fancy locks, although I don't know why she thought they needed locking up. Anyway, in some of them papers she found a note about a young

Braeburn bride, Lady Eleanor Braeburn, wedding a Bloxford man and having her portrait done. It was mentioned as being part of the Bloxford tradition. There was a note in French, which she gave to von Graf and he translated it. He laughed and told her these brides wasn't wearing any clothes.'

'Hum.' That gave me pause. 'Why did she involve von Graf?' I asked.

'She involved them both,' Hiram said. 'Jarvis was real good at deciphering the lettering on old wills and deeds, and von Graf can translate Latin and French, so they spent a lot of time with her over them old manuscripts.'

I eyed him over my tankard. 'Any mention of Gainsborough?' I asked.

'Sure was. That was the name of the artist who painted Lady Eleanor Braeburn. Ma was very excited by that,' he flashed a grin.

'I can imagine,' I replied. 'And so she learned about the nature of the Bloxford Beauties?'

'She did, and she asked Caroline if the tradition had been kept up. She told her it had, and that it was a secret, and not to spread the word about. Trouble is, it was too late: Jarvis and von Graf knew. She swore them to silence, but I wouldn't trust either one of them an inch.'

'But your mother did?'

'She did,' he nodded.

'Did she speak to anyone else, such as the Brigadier, about it?'

'You'd have to ask Ma for more on that, but I wouldn't recommend doing it right now.'

'Ha, no, I was planning on giving the lady a wide berth actually.' I grinned, then turned my mind back to the matter – it did explain who'd let the cat out of that particular bag.

He tossed the remains of his cheroot into the flames of the fire blazing in the hearth beside us, and looked momentarily glum.

I eyed him, realising he was a fellow who had things on his mind. I may have been concentrating on tracking down a murderer, but Hiram was about to make a life-changing commitment.

'Haven't been a best man before, old chap,' I began. 'But I think one of the duties is to check that the groom is entirely filled with confidence that he's made the right choice.'

'You going to try to talk me out of it, Lennox?' he laughed dryly. 'Wouldn't want to be in your shoes if any of the gals get to hear of it.'

'No,' I laughed, 'but I'd like to hear your side of it.' I called the landlord over for another pint each.

'I'll reassure your mind, my friend. I couldn't be happier in my choice of bride. She's all a man could want, and more. A prettier, kindlier-tempered woman I never did meet. And clever with it, knows how to fix and mend just about anything – and she can ride a horse better than the cowpokes back home. That's saying something, that is, cause them boys have been all but raised in the saddle. Amazing lady, my Caroline.'

Well, the man really must be besotted, I thought; because apart from the horse riding I wouldn't have recognised Caroline at all from his rosy-eyed description.

'Pleased to hear it,' I replied, although I could still detect a certain disquiet in his demeanour.

He let escape a sigh. 'But I don't like all this wedding fuss and bother. The women are all a-fluster, and we gotta sit through another darned opera. You know, Lennox, she's got a mind to do it all over agin back at the ranch an I'm going to have to lay down the law. We ain't doing it and that's that.'

'You mean Ruth wants to run your Texas ceremony on similar lines to this one?'

'She sure does, but we're having an old fashion hoedown whether she likes it or not. No opera and none of this fancy-dangle dressing up. I just haven't had the heart to tell her, but I'm going to have to do it.'

'If I were you, old man, I'd wait until after this wedding is over and you're on the boat home. That way she'll have a few days to get used to the idea. If you do it now, she'll be upset through the whole damn bean feast, and it's bad enough as it is.'

'Yeah,' he drained his tankard. 'I'll take your advice. She can have her way over this wedding – but in Texas we'll do it the way me and my lovely bride wants it.'

'What are your plans for the future?' I enquired. 'Will you remain in Texas or make your home here?'

'I'm going to leave that decision to Caroline. I've seen what it's like to have a fretting wife in the house. Ruth's got a good heart, but she just wants to return to her old homeland and my Pappy won't do it. He agreed to come back here for a long vacation but that's as much as he'll do. His life is all about the ranch and that's where he'll stay till his dying day. It's caused a certain coldness in Ruth and I don't want to see that in my wife. I'm not a betting man but I'd put my last dime on us settling in Bloxford.'

I didn't say anything, but entirely agreed with him. 'You realise the Brigadier is in poor health?' I asked him.

'I do. We don't aim to stay long in Texas, we'll be back here right after our honeymoon.'

I nodded, pleased to hear that they had thought about the old man.

'Better be getting back, now,' he said. 'I've got another session with that uppity tailor from London this afternoon and I tell you, Lennox, he sore tries my patience.'

We strolled back, replete and content in each other's company. I must say I was relieved that Hiram was so taken with Caroline. He was a steadfast character and I doubt she'd be able to push him around. And he'd had experience of managing his strong-minded stepmother, which would serve him well when dealing with his determined wife. Fond as I was of my childhood friend, I knew damn well how difficult she could be.

Benson opened the door and we entered the hall to encounter the soprano, Dame Gabriel Forsyth, clutching a damp handkerchief, her eye make-up smudged and rubbed.

'Oh, Major Lennox.' Her voice rose a notch. 'I need your help. I am beside myself with trepidation.' She appeared to be working herself into hysterics. 'It's Count von Graf – he's disappeared, ' she announced through loud sobs. 'I fear the worst!'

CHAPTER 18

Generally, the disappearance of a character such as von Graf would have been excellent news, but as he was our principal suspect, I was decidedly irked.

'Damn,' was the first word to escape my lips.

'You must *find* him,' the lady wailed.

'We most certainly will,' I responded. 'I'll have the police onto it right away.'

'Oh, Major Lennox,' she gasped, handkerchief clutched to her ample bosom, 'how kind you are. To fling yourself into action on my behalf.'

'What?' I looked at her more closely. It occurred to me that she probably didn't realise that I intended to have the bounder arrested on sight. I decided on reticence as the better part of valour, not to mention saving a great deal of tedious explanation. 'Erm, I'll go and telephone the police, Dame Gabriel. Perhaps you should go away.... to lie down, I mean. Wait for news and all that.'

'Please find him. I don't think I can go on without him,' she cried.

'Go on where?' I asked.

She looked at me blankly.

Hiram stepped forward offering his arm. 'Madam, I will escort you to my mother. She is of great help to persons in distress.'

Well, that rather saved the day and should keep both ladies out of my way.

For some unknown reason, the telephone was located in the butler's pantry. It took minutes to get an operator to answer my call.

'Hello, is that you, Mr Dawkins? It's Nellie here.'

'No, it isn't – why do you think it's Dawkins?' I asked.

'Well, he usually rings. Hardly anyone else ever does. Who are you, then?'

'Major Lennox.'

'Ooh, you do speak nice,' she said with exaggerated enunciation.

'Madam, um..Nellie, would you please put me through to the local police station, I need to talk to Chief Inspector Swift.'

'It's Inspector Watson at the station; never heard of no Swift, dear.'

'Look, it's an urgent police matter.' I told her. 'Someone is missing.'

'Well, why didn't you *say*. I'm connecting you now, hold on, dearie.'

Really, rural telephone operators were a law unto themselves and no doubt she'd be listening in on the calls. There was a long pause and it took three more connections until I finally had Swift on the line.

'How do you know he's disappeared?' he demanded.

That gave me pause. Perhaps I should have searched first?

'The soprano told me,' I replied. 'She seemed very certain.'

The line crackled.

'Swift, are you there?' I called into the transmitter cup.

'Yes,' he shouted. 'I was thinking. Look, Lennox, it could be an opportunity to search his rooms. And ascertain if he's actually missing or has fled the country.'

Actually, that seemed to me to be an excellent idea – it was probably why Swift had been made a Chief Inspector of Scotland Yard.

'And it might uncover anything he's been hiding,' I said.

'Possibly. Why is the soprano so concerned about his whereabouts?'

'I suspect there's some sort of romantic connection between her and von Graf.'

'Listen, Lennox. I found a message from Scotland Yard waiting for me. I'd asked them to go to the War Records Office. Jarvis was a charlatan. He joined a Sussex regiment in 1915 as Chaplain, supplying his own credentials. He had all the correct certificates – even had a letter from the local bishop recommending him.'

The line crackled again and I hoped we weren't about to be cut off. 'Swift?'

'Yes, I'll be quick. Geoffrey Jarvis had a brother, Simon, a known thief, whose only talent was art. He was the black sheep of a respectable family. Geoffrey was killed in a bombing raid; Simon took his brother's papers and used his name.'

'Interesting,' I said, being rather impressed by the speed at which Scotland Yard appeared to work. 'Have you contacted the family?'

'The parents are dead. There's a sister somewhere but they haven't tracked her down yet. And Lennox –' he was becoming faint as the line began to break up '– I'm tied up waiting for our experts to arrive, and then we'll dig up what's left of Bartholomew. Won't be with you until the morning. You're on your own, man.'

'Fine.I'll –'

The line crackled and finally failed. I replaced the receiver on its hook, stood up, clapped my hands together and went up to my rooms. I removed the snoozing kitten from my desk, opened the drawer and took out my magnifying glass and tweezers and slipped them into the pocket of my shooting jacket, and shoved two jam jars into the 'poacher's' pocket, for any evidence I might find. I ordered my sleepy dog and kitten to stay where they were, and set off for a spot of sleuthing.

Von Graf's rooms were north-facing, pokey, and verging on the decrepit. From the musty smell in the corridor, I'd say the whole section had been very little used over the past century or so. Whereas the front of the Hall had been maintained to reasonably habitable order, this part of the house revealed how low the family fortunes had fallen. Damp met me on the doorstep, chipped woodwork revealed a labyrinth of woodworm holes bored through the door jamb, the yellowed ceiling plaster was buckled and bowed where it had broken away from lathes, the floor was warped and sagging. I sincerely hoped Hiram's wealth was as substantial as was reputed because an awful lot of it was going to end up buried in the crumbling stones and timbers of this house.

There was a closet and small bedroom with a neatly made bed. A narrow wardrobe stood in the corner, a dressing table under a draughty sash window, a chair pushed against it and an iron-mantled hearth on the opposite wall.

I stood in the centre looking about me. Toiletries were on the dressing table — a hairbrush, comb and shaving items were closely arrayed. These in themselves indicated he was unlikely to have fled. I hope he hadn't just gone to Oxford and was about to reappear during my snoop - perhaps I should have brought Foggy as an early alert. The closet revealed nothing but shirts, trousers and the usual what-have-yous. It wasn't quite as interesting as I'd hoped. I delved about in the dressing table with the same result. His empty suitcases were under the bed along with dust, mouse-droppings and balls of fluff that made me sneeze. I felt around the bed, down the sides, under the mattress and pillows – even sat on it and bounced. It squeaked; I felt rather deflated.

Where would I hide something if I were von Graf? I eyed each nook and cranny, which didn't take long as there were only two, and neither produced a bean. An unlit fire was set in the hearth, I went over and knelt beside it. It smelled of damp soot, meaning it hadn't been lit for a long time. That was peculiar because this room would always have been chilly at any time of year. I removed the sticks first, and then the twists of newspaper, until the grate was exposed. It was very clean, as though someone had carefully brushed it – I could almost imagine Dicks had been in here. I lifted out the grate to reveal the ash-pan. It was empty, so I took that out, too. It was heavy – heavier than it should have been; so I turned it over and finally found a clue. A slim metal box had been attached with small black screws to the underside. I grinned like a cat.

I couldn't open it: there was a brass lock attached and I hadn't any tools to force it. I cocked an ear, listening for sounds of von Graf's return; I didn't want to remain in the place any longer than necessary, and he could be trotting up the stairs even as I paused to eye the box more closely. I replaced the paper and items pretty much as I'd found them – it was a bit hastily done and it wouldn't take long for von Graf to realise that he'd been burgled. I trotted back to my rooms with a jaunty step and the stolen cache under my arm.

I placed the box on my vacant desk and stared at it, rather cock-a-hoop at having uncovered vital evidence. I played my magnifying glass over the screws and lock. I had a toolkit for cleaning my guns in the dressing room, so I fetched it and used the small screwdriver to remove the box from the ash-pan. Then I stared at it again. I didn't know how to pick the lock. I thought I might be able to force it – but would it damage the contents? I shook it – whatever was inside thudded and rattled, which didn't help in the least.

One name came to mind – Greggs. I knew my old butler had a knack with locks: his liking for whiskey had led him to develop unexpected talents. Another name followed, one who was a great deal closer – Dawkins. Benson may be slow and old but he wasn't so decrepit as to leave the keys to the wine cellar lying around, so Dawkins must have picked the lock. I jumped up and went over to tug the bell pull.

'Sir?' Dicks said on entry. 'I brought a pot of coffee.'

'Excellent!' I commended him. 'Where's Dawkins?' I asked as he placed the tray next to my pilfered prize.

'Confined to the kitchen, sir, by Mrs Dawkins. He's on potato-peeling and washing-up. She made him wear an apron and all. Looks a proper Charlie and serves him right.' He was pouring coffee as he said this, and taking a good look at the box.

'You are not to say a word about this, Dicks.'

'No, sir.'

'The box, I mean.'

'Yes, sir.'

'Need to open it.' There were biscuits with the coffee – orange and something, almonds possibly.

'Is that why you're asking after Dawkins, sir?'

'Mm,' I said between mouthfuls. 'Send him up and tell him to come prepared. If he so much as whispers a word of this, he'll be straight in front of the Brigadier and then the beak. Make that clear, Dicks.'

'Certainly, sir.' He went off, grinning.

Dawkins had a black eye, which didn't do anything to improve his lank looks. 'Don't know why ye think I can open locks. I'm not a thief, ye –'

'Dawkins,' I told him, 'not a word. Just open it.' I indicated the lock with my biscuit.

He opened his mouth to whine, noted the expression on my face and closed it again. He withdrew a set of blacksmith-made rods, each curved to form a handle and trimmed to taper down and end in thin hooks or the shape of an 's' or that of a notched tooth. I watched Dawkins carefully: he placed one pick in the lock and twisted it around until I heard a faint click. Then he inserted a shorter one and did the same. On the third click, the lock opened.

'Done it,' he said, and moved to open the box.

'Don't touch it,' I told him sharply. 'And hand over the lock picks.'

That startled him. He grabbed them and stepped backwards. 'Not on your nelly.'

'Your position in this house, or the lock picks. I'll not leave a thief's tool in the pocket of a chap like you. Make up your mind, Dawkins.'

It's rare to see loathing in the eyes of one's fellow man, outside of war, that is, but he really did wish me grievous ill at that moment. A thud at the threshold made us both swing around. The stout figure of Mrs Dawkins filled the doorway, her arms crossed, her apron floured and a look of vengeance in her eyes. Dawkins barely hesitated; he flung the set of picks in my direction and stomped from the room a beaten man.

Tubbs jumped on the prize; they made a pleasant jangly noise. I scooped them off the floor delighted with my booty. I may not have accumulated much evidence during the investigation, but the lock picks were to be added to my detecting kit and I had an underemployed butler at home who could teach me the basics once I returned. I picked Tubbs up, patted him on the head and opened the box.

CHAPTER 19

There were two items within, I picked up the one that most interested me — a pistol. It was a very neat little .25 calibre Walther automatic. I turned it over in my hands, pulled back the slide part way and seeing no round in the chamber, ejected the loaded magazine. I sniffed it, it hadn't been fired in some time and that came as rather a disappointment. I wrapped it carefully in one of my handkerchiefs and pushed it into the back of my desk drawer.

The other item was a ledger. It wasn't very old, nor unusual, being bound with black leather and stamped with gold lettering stating that it was indeed a 'Ledger'.

Book-keeping had never appealed to me but in this instance I was prepared to give it my undivided attention. The book had little to say for itself on the flyleaf, but once opened into the ruled and lined pages of the ledger itself, it revealed all. The first date was over a year ago, the left-hand column was headed 'Item', and next to it was 'Prov', presumably for 'Provenance'. Then 'Own's Price' which I took to be Owner's Price, followed by 'Paid', 'Sold', 'Comm' and finally 'Profit'.

Thankfully it was all in English, presumably to enable Jarvis to share its details. Hiram walked in as I was trying to add up some of the numbers.

'I'm supposed to tell you about your best man duties,' he drawled. 'so here, old man, you take this and hand it over when I tell you.'

I raised my eyes from the book and regarded the handsome box he was holding out to me. He opened it to reveal a finely wrought gold ring.

'Sure you trust me with that, old chap?'

'I sure do. You keep it safe until I place it on the finger of my wedded bride.'

I placed the box carefully in my waistcoat pocket. Thoughts of ball and chain entered my head, but I refrained from mentioning them.

'This calls for a drink.' I rose to ring the bell but he held up a large hand.

He smiled broadly. 'I brought along some good bourbon to mark the occasion.'

He pulled out a hip flask from the pocket of his blue suit and offered it to me. It was raw and strong and numbed the tongue as it went down. I coughed, he laughed.

'You doing your accounts?' he asked, indicating the ledger open on the table.

'No,' I replied, and spilled the beans about my search of von Graf's rooms. He raised his brows and grinned, then leaned in for a closer look.

'This item here,' he said, placing a thick finger on

the page, 'horse and plough, one man, field, trees, artist unknown, framed – it must be a painting.'

'Provenance, B.C., probably being Braeburn Castle,' I said. 'Owner's price £100, sold £220.10s.6d, Comm £10.10s.6d, profit £110.'

'By profit, they mean *their* profit, not the owner's,' Hiram growled.

'My interpretation entirely,' I agreed. 'I assume Comm. to be a commission paid to an individual or a gallery.'

Hiram picked up a chair from beside the fire and came to sit next to me at the desk and we worked through the ledger. There were other items from elsewhere, denoted only by initials, such as C.C., L.M. and F.H.

The descriptions were primarily for paintings although a few items of silver were included. A Goblet, Flagon, Chalice and a Gilt Communion Cup were sold late last year – probably the very items purportedly stolen by Bartholomew. The thought of it made my blood boil. We spent another thirty minutes trawling through the ledger; I made notes in my own book of some of the sums involved.

'I reckon they defrauded the Laird of over ten thousand pounds,' Hiram calculated.

'Agreed – but we may have to ask Florence if she recognises these descriptions, just to be certain the artworks were indeed from the Castle.'

'Yeah,' Hiram drawled. 'But if von Graf comes back, I'll be asking him exactly what these figures mean and I won't be doing it kindly.'

'Looking at the amount of money involved, I doubt he's coming back. A man could live like a king in some countries with the sums they've made,' I remarked.

'And he'll have all the loot to himself now,' Hiram added.

'Damn,' I sighed. 'I hate to think he's got away with this.'

'Are you giving this here ledger to Swift?' Hiram asked.

'Yes, it's vital evidence I'll hand it to him when he arrives.'

'Meanwhile, I'll show it to the gals.' He reached over to pick up the ledger.

I placed my hand on it. 'Not just yet, old chap. Give me some time, would you? Need to think this through. And I'm not sure we should involve them for the moment. As you said, their minds are full of wedding frocks and flowers. We don't want to spoil it for them.'

He stopped, straightened up and shook his head. 'I can only agree with you, Lennox. But you know them thieves have been robbing people blind. Back in Texas I'd be rounding up a posse right now,' he drawled.

I had no idea what a 'posse' was, but it sounded ominous, and if von Graf should show his face in the house again, he would be afforded a very unpleasant welcome.

Hiram left, his jaw tight with anger. I looked around for a suitable hiding place and, lacking imagination, could only think of Fogg's basket, so that's where I put it. Having disturbed the two animals, I decided to take Fogg for a spot of fresh air to blow a breeze through my thoughts. I dropped Tubbs in my pocket as he probably needed an outing too.

The evidence of the thefts excited and perturbed me in equal measure. Seeing fraud laid out in neatly inscribed columns, with the profits from their thievery listed just as any other honest enterprise would be accounted, seemed to make it all the worse. As cold a crime as any I'd heard of, and it had been committed upon trusting, decent people who had given the scoundrels shelter, food and friendship.

Fogg ran through the grass ahead of me as we headed toward the water meadows. Our steps took us in the opposite direction to the chantry and graveyard, where no doubt Swift and his team would be performing their dreadful task. Death was no stranger after four long years of a war which at times had resembled a daily massacre, but that was in a distant land. Here I was at a home I'd known as a child, and the crime had been perpetrated upon people for whom I felt great affection. I was grateful not to be involved in the exhumation.

Spring showers had been scudding across the sky throughout the day but the sun broke through the high clouds during my amble, sending a few warm rays to lift my mood. Fogg ran after rabbits and I stood quietly on a ridge looking down to the broad brook running through a shallow vale between low hills. Cows waded in the water, tugging tussocks of grass from the banks, and watched me, chewing vacantly, with probably not a thought in their heads.

'Major Lennox.'

I heard my name called and turned around unhurriedly, having no wish to be disturbed. It was Miss Busby.

'Major Lennox,' she called again.

'Greetings,' I replied, trying to inject some enthusiasm into the sentiment.

'Oh dear, you do sound rather downcast,' she replied.

I smiled. 'Touch of melancholy, perhaps,' I ventured.

'Any reason?'

'The perfidious nature of Man, I suppose.'

'And that comes as a surprise?' she chivvied me gently.

I laughed.

'They are excavating poor Bartholomew,' she said as she fell in with me. We walked with unhurried steps along an earthen path, well trodden by hooves, upon the ridge. 'I didn't wish to remain nearby. And it is causing tremendous chatter in the village – I find it rather disturbing to my peace of mind,' she said.

'Mm …' I replied.

'Is it causing a ripple at the Hall?' she asked.

I smiled again. 'Lady Ruth has forbidden death and corpses. There are apparently "flowers and flounces" in abundance, but no ripples. And in truth it is better that way.'

She stopped. I turned back to look at her, brows raised in question.

'It is more than the nature of Man troubling you, Major Lennox,' she guessed.

'Hum,' I replied, then let escape a sigh. 'Jarvis was a murderer and a thief,' I said.

'Indeed, and I suspect von Graf is too. They were working together, after all.'

We fell back to walking again, Fogg just ahead of us with his nose to the ground.

'They met during the War,' I told her. 'Von Graf said he was working as a translator, but I suspect he was secretly buying art looted by the troops, and using his contacts in the trade to sell them. You know he owned his own gallery in Paris before the War?'

She smiled and nodded. 'I do, Major Lennox. You told me.'

'Did I?'

'Rather knotty, you said, or something akin,' she replied. 'I take it you are puzzling over the mystery.'

'Yes,' I acknowledged. 'Jarvis wasn't a real chaplain. He'd stolen his brother's identity. He and von Graf must have made the perfect partnership. A talented forger and a handsome art dealer, neither possessing any scruples between them.'

'Yes,' Miss Busby murmured.

'They met Florence's father during the War, and when it was all over they must have decided to go in search of pigeons for the plucking. Once they'd weaselled their way into the Laird's confidence, they purchased his paintings at rock-bottom prices and sold high. Very high. Hiram and I calculated the amount they defrauded from the Braeburns to be over ten thousand pounds.'

'Really? Such a sum would buy every house in Bloxford

village.' Miss Busby looked shocked. 'How do you know the amount?'

'I found their ledger hidden in von Graf's room. Von Graf has vanished. Hiram and I think he's bolted.'

'Does it list where they were selling the works?' she asked.

'No, but they paid commission on some of the sales, which implies that it was a legitimate channel.'

She was silent for a while, digesting the news as we walked. We entered a wood, carpeted in bluebells; Foggy was intent on sniffing out squirrels and bounded through the flowers. The leaves on the trees were unfurling, casting shadows under the boughs, and we wandered through dappled shade and sunshine.

'What about the tenor, Sir Crispin? Where did he fit in?' she asked.

'Another puzzle to pick through, Miss Busby. I'm afraid I don't know yet.'

'It was not a very complex crime, was it?' she commented.

I looked at her quizzically. It had certainly caused tangled knots in my mind.

She smiled. 'The fraud committed by Jarvis and von Graf was really very simple. They befriended the Laird, purchased his paintings and sold them on at a much higher price. Probably found other folk to fleece, too, and no doubt they'd done the same with the officers and troops during the War. But something changed – something drove them to murder Bartholomew, and eventually Sir Crispin, too.'

'The Gainsborough?' I mooted.

'But how did they discover it even existed?' she asked.

'Ruth Chisholm,' I said. 'She encountered them at Braeburn Castle. They helped her translate some of the old archives that are held there. There was mention that one of the Braeburn daughters married a Bloxford and had her portrait painted by Gainsborough.'

'Hum,' Miss Busby replied. 'And Jarvis took the place of Bartholomew, elevating him to a position of trust. I imagine he and von Graf gained the confidence of the Brigadier just as they had gained the trust of the Braeburns and the Chisholms.'

'Exactly,' I said.

'Does Lady Ruth realise she was duped?' she asked.

'I don't know,' I said and added. 'Possibly.'

'Oh dear,' Miss Busby said quietly. 'If she has found out, it would bring consequences.'

'Yes, and that is what has been troubling me. I doubt von Graf killed Jarvis, although I've been trying to convince myself that he did. No,' I sighed, 'I suspect it is someone much closer to home.'

CHAPTER 20

'Ah,' Miss Busby replied. 'What a shame. I'd rather been enjoying our sleuthing, Major Lennox.'

I looked at her sideways. 'What?'

'Well, I am "close to home", you know.'

That gave me pause for thought. We walked on in silence for a while.

'I would be most surprised if it were you, Miss Busby,' I finally replied.

She laughed.

'Why did you find that amusing?' I asked.

'Because you had to think about it,' she answered.

I smiled in turn, but then returned to my troubled thoughts.

Miss Busby remarked. 'Is there someone you fear may be the culprit?'

'No,' I admitted. 'It could be any one of them. Lady Ruth has not only revealed the centuries old secret of the Beauties to two art thieves — she has also introduced them into Bloxford Hall where they have committed murder. She may have been duped, but people have paid with their lives because of her actions.'

'Do you think it may affect the marriage of Caroline and Hiram?'

I considered her suggestion, then shook my head. 'No. A hundred years ago it may have done, but not in this day and age.'

'And yet, this house does not really live in this day and age, does it?'

'You mean the Brigadier?' I smiled. 'He wouldn't stand in the way of Caroline's happiness, whatever the circumstances.'

'But would everybody realise that?' She asked.

That gave my mind a jolt. Miss Busby was indeed very astute, I hadn't considered that at all.

'The motive is the crux of all this,' I mused aloud.

'Indeed, Major,' she replied. 'The evidence may provide signposts along the way but the road is laid by reason. Who ever did this had a very compelling reason.'

'But they all have reason, don't they?' I responded. 'The actions of Jarvis and von Graf has affected all of them one way or another.'

'Oh dear,' she exclaimed.

I stopped and looked down at her, my brows raised in silent query.

'Now I will look at my friends in rather a different light,' she remarked. 'And so will you.'

I let loose a sigh. 'Yes, I'm afraid so.'

The wind had picked up, the sun had vanished

behind grey clouds and the rain began to fall at a resolute rate.

'I think I must dash,' she told me, 'I don't have an umbrella.'

'Nor I, and my dog has a dislike of getting wet.' Tubbs was beginning to fidget in my pocket, too.

We departed in different directions. Fogg became drenched and by the time we reached the front door he had taken on a dejected air.

'Blanket,' I told Benson as we dripped into the hall. Dicks appeared and rustled one up. He wrapped the unhappy hound like a swaddled babe and I shoved him under my arm and carried him up to my rooms. The fire was burning brightly, the oil lamps were lit, the sky had darkened, and it wasn't long before Dicks reappeared with a hot toddy to ward off the chill. Dog and kitten stared into the yellow flames as we dried off, steam rising to mist the inside of the windows. I remembered I'd hidden the ledger in Fogg's basket and retrieved it before it became wet. I had no wish to delve back through it, and tossed it under the bed with Lady Grace.

Once settled into a club chair in front of the blazing hearth I had little desire to move. Tubbs clambered up to sit on my lap and started purring; I think he had discovered his purpose in life, as he had developed the rhythm of a little engine. Dicks had left the stoneware jug of warmed whisky, lemon and honey on the tray beside me and I topped up my glass, sipping it appreciatively. Time was ticking by, I was aware how close we were to the wedding day and my mind turned over all the possibilities.

I stared at the paint on my sleeve again. The Bloxford Beauties were in the Long Gallery and the door would be locked. But I had my confiscated lock picks, and I doubted that anyone would be up there to spot me. I put down my empty glass, removed Tubbs from my lap, told Fogg to stay, and set off with a determined step.

Never having been there before, I wasn't sure how to find it, but by tradition the long galleries in old houses were under the eaves so I trotted up as high as I could and followed a passageway along a meandering course. I ended at the back stairs next to the servants' quarters, and got a ticking off from an exiting maid who wouldn't listen to my well prepared lies.

I ran my fingers through my hair. I could ask the Brigadier, but suspected I would be made to swear on my honour never to set foot in the place. I wandered back to the main staircase and leaned against a window seat. The corridors were swept clean and free of dust. If the Long Gallery was forbidden territory, then no one would be mopping it – so all I had to do was find a grubby corridor. Ha! Reading Sherlock Holmes brought some benefits. Congratulating myself on my fine powers of deduction, I once again set forth. I ended up back at the servants' quarters.

I returned to my perch by the window, inclined to give up and go back to the warmth of my room and join the little duo by the fire. But I told myself that

Holmes would not have retreated, he would have been dogged in his detecting. I looked around. The walls were all wood panelled on this level, honey-coloured rather than dark oak; they must have been replaced sometime in the last century. Perhaps they'd built the door to the gallery into one of the panels. I knocked on a few; they all sounded hollow, so that didn't help. There was a huge tapestry along one lonely corridor, so I scrutinised that. One edge was warped, as though it had been repeatedly gripped. I pushed it aside and there it was, a narrow door, barely visible within the panelling. It had a slim keyhole cut into the woodwork where the lock must be. I grinned like a fool and withdrew the lock picks from my pocket.

Half an hour later my knees hurt and my patience had worn thin. How the devil did an idiot like Dawkins understand the art of picking locks? I'd shoved all of them in one by one and fiddled about waiting to hear the click as something moved, but not a thing happened. I withdrew my flashlight and stared at it, then chose a pick with a large tooth. I listened intently and felt rather than heard the snap of something metal springing back. I pushed the panel, but it wasn't ready to open yet. I shone the torch back into the keyhole.

'Sir?'

That made me jump. I leaped to my feet. 'Benson?'

'Sir, I must tell you that this area is not accessible.'

'I know it isn't, Benson, I've tried my damnedest and I can't get in.'

'I mean, sir, that you are not *supposed* to get in. It is the Brigadier's orders, nobody is allowed here, sir.' Beneath the frizzy white hair and brows he looked quite stern.

'Well, yes. But this is important, Benson. It might even be a matter of life and death.'

'Indeed, sir.' He was short of breath but determined. 'But he would be terribly agitated, sir. I fear I must insist.'

In the face of poor Benson's disquiet I decided to accept defeat. Tomorrow I would choose my time more carefully.

'Benson,' I said as we descended the stairs, 'I know Jarvis was restoring the Beauties – how did he get in there?'

He stopped and looked at me narrowly.

'His Lordship told me about it, Benson,' I explained.

'Very well, sir. The Gurkha, Kalo, unlocked the door for him. The Brigadier keeps the only key with him.' He paused again on a step to catch a breath, then continued. 'He would hand it to Kalo, who would escort the Chaplain to the Long Gallery. The man was permitted to bring his materials and easel with him. He set himself up, I believe, in the room and he would work in there.'

Now that was strange, I thought, because he had Lady Grace at the rectory – so how did he smuggle her out? And why?

'Really?' I replied. 'Did Kalo remain in the Long Gallery with Jarvis?'

'No, sir. Kalo dislikes to be away from the Brigadier's side. He would lock Jarvis in and return to his master.

Then after a time the Brigadier would order him to let the Chaplain out, sir.'

'Hum.' This was food for thought. 'Benson, old chap, you seem to be having a hard time of it,' I told him.

'Rain and damp. I have the rheumatics, sir,' he wheezed.

'Not thought about retiring, old chap?' I asked. 'To a cottage with a warm fireside? I'm sure there are plenty on the estate.'

'I have been with the Brigadier man and boy, sir, in Bengal, Burma and the Boer War. He sent me home during the Great War after I was gassed. He has always ensured I was cared for. I will not leave this house until he does.'

I nodded. Not much more I could say really.

'Drinks will be in the drawing room, sir.'

'Um. Not sure I can stomach much more in the way of opera singers, Benson. Might make it an early night.'

'They will not be attending dinner, sir. They are in rehearsals for tomorrow evening. It is beef stew tonight. And dumplings.'

'Ah, really? Excellent. Then I will put in an appearance. Rather peckish, actually,' I told him.

'Very good, sir.' He gave a short, stiff bow.

We parted at my door and I greeted my little pets, then languished in a hot bath and changed for dinner, emerging just as the first gong sounded.

The drawing room was the family cosy hole, a place of soft sofas filled with feather cushions, and deep chairs with small tables scattered about, where tea cups and brandy glasses found a place to rest. The fire was already burning with crackling yellow flames in the wide hearth.

Hiram and his father had arrived for pre-prandial drinks; they told me the girls were still knee-deep in flounces.

'I told Pa about those scoundrels and the thieving,' Hiram confided as I strolled in.

'Bad news, mighty bad news,' Ford added. 'We'd be looking for a hanging back home.'

Dicks was presiding and offered us sherry but we asked for brandy. We raised our glasses in comradely salute and settled in comfort around the blazing fire.

'We'll keep it under our hats, Pa and I,' Hiram told me. 'About the paintings and Lord Braeburn losing out on all that money.'

'Good,' I said. 'Best to leave it to Scotland Yard.'

'Do you think the police can recover anything? Braeburn's artworks or the money?' Ford asked.

'That's a question best put to Swift,' I said, and switched tack. 'The paintings from the hallway. Don't happen to know anything about them, do you?'

Father and son exchanged glances.

'That was down to my Ruth – she purchased them,' Ford told me, his mouth drawn tight. 'She saw them paintings were missin'. When we was last here, they were up there, but they were gone when we got back. She figured they were bein' cleaned, so she asked von Graf if that were so. He says that the Brigadier had asked for him to sell them – they was to pay for the mending of the theatre, and the wedding. Well, you can imagine what she thought about that! Von Graf said if she wanted to return them to their rightful place, maybe he could buy them back for her. Naturally, she said yes. Cost a pretty penny, as I later found out.' He frowned.

'They're not in the ledger,' I answered. 'I checked.'

'That don't surprise me,' Ford continued, 'because I don't think he ever sold them. I think he was holding onto them to offer them up to my wife, and she walked straight into their trap. Jarvis and von Graf got to know her pretty well, I guess, up in the castle at Braeburn.'

I eyed him. 'How did the paintings arrive back on the wall?'

'I took them back to the Brigadier m'self. I said to him, we're family now. The furnishings in this house is going to our children and grandchildren, I don't want to see nothing sold off for the sake of paying for my wife's fancy ideas. He asked me how I came by them and I came clean, said it was Ruth, and I insisted he tell me the price he received. It took a lot of arguing but eventually he agreed — showed me the papers from the sale to von Graf. There was a mighty big difference between what Ruth paid and what the Brigadier got.'

'When did you discuss this with the Brigadier?' I asked.

'The same day you arrived here. It made me mad. Ruth and I had a big fight about it. I was all for calling the police, but the Brigadier said not to upset Lady Caroline and Hiram. He said we should wait until after the wedding.'

That explained why Ruth was cold toward von Graf that evening at dinner, I mused. I turned to Hiram. 'Did you know about this?'

'Not until today when I told Pa about that ledger you found. Neither he nor ma thought to confide in me.' He gave his father a hard look.

Ford turned to me again. 'Am I right in thinking the police believe von Graf murdered Jarvis?'

'Keeping an open mind, old chap. Nothing determined yet,' I replied.

'You sound kinda doubtful, Lennox,' Hiram said, swilling brandy in his glass. 'And it seems to me, that if you don't reckon von Graf did it, then you think it's someone in this house.'

I didn't have an answer for that and held my tongue. He frowned from under lowered brows and then exchanged glances with his father. A certain froideur was cast in my direction, which made my shoulders slump a touch. I was beginning to understand how Swift felt – this sleuthing came with a certain amount of disapprobation.

The girls arrived at that moment to provide a welcome diversion. We men stood, I offered my seat – Caroline gave me a hug and a bright smile and sat down next to Hiram; Lady Ruth took an upright chair near her husband, and Florence sat on a sofa looking lovely but rather subdued. I moved to sit next to her.

Dicks furnished the ladies with sherry and topped up our snifters as we all settled around the warm flames of the fire, chatter and laughter filling the air. The room formed a comfortable haven as rain pelted against the windowpanes under darkening skies.

'Florence, may I say something?' I started.

She glanced at me, then lowered her eyes and nodded.

'You are not under suspicion. Swift was being hasty – it's a bad habit he has.'

'Lennox …' She smoothed the fabric of her pale pink and blue dress, made of chiffon or some such material. 'It was a terrible thing to say. Just horrid, and he had been so kind. Why did he say such a thing?'

'Um, well.' I sighed and tried to put some suitable sentiments together. 'I think it's because he likes you.'

She laughed coldly and brought her large eyes to meet mine. 'Rather a strange way to show it.'

'I mean,' I stumbled on, 'I think he was frightened to lose you so he over-reacted. His emotions were running high and, well, it's possible he wanted you to reassure him, really.'

'Oh, nonsense,' she replied. 'I don't think he likes me at all.'

She sniffed and took a handkerchief from her purse.

'Truly, old girl. I don't think he meant it as an actual accusation.'

'Can you imagine being unjustly accused of *murder* by the police!' She sniffed some more. 'It's simply dreadful.'

'Well, actually …' I was about to tell her that Swift had done exactly that last Christmas and that the blighter had had every intention of seeing me hang. But then I realised it wouldn't help matters, so I switched tack. 'It's his job, you know. He's supposed to flush out criminals and I think it makes him over-react sometimes. I'm sure he will apologise when he sees you again.'

'He better had, because I'm not speaking to him until he does,' she said with feeling. 'The rapier was useless, you know. He doesn't know anything about fencing.'

'Why?' I asked, not knowing very much either.

'It was unbalanced. The tip must have broken off by at least two inches, probably more. Somebody would have sharpened it afterwards. It's a common problem when fencing, but as soon as I felt the weight I realised it had been damaged.'

'Hum.' Now this was more interesting than tedious lovers' tiffs. 'Would that affect the value of it?'

'Of course. Anybody who collected antique weaponry would reject it instantly: the shortened blade made it worthless.'

'Which could be why it was used as a murder weapon,' I mused. 'May as well bury it in a body if you were only going to throw it away anyway.'

'Quite. And if either you or Swift had simply asked me, I could have told you. Instead, you stood by while he –'

'Yes, yes, I do apologise old thing. And I will explain it to the Inspector,' I told her in my best reassuring tone.

Benson came into the room and spoke quietly to Caroline. She asked a few questions, and then nodded her head.

The old butler shuffled off and Caroline jumped to her feet and clapped.

'Everyone, listen now,' she called out. 'Daddy is eating in his rooms this evening and I think we should have a cosy dinner here, around the reading table. Benson is arranging it. Then we shall play cards and have fun!'

And indeed we did. Florence won a few games and the hurrahs and laughter brought the colour back to her cheeks. Ruth ruled the roost, dishing out advice and enforcing the rules – Ford reined her in with a loving hand. I realised he knew how to handle her, and told myself that I should take note – although bossy women were better avoided, to my mind. Later, Hiram almost forgave me my suspicions, and clapped me on the back as we all parted company on the upper landing before we made our way to our respective rooms. It was a genial and jolly evening, well spent in the company of good people.

CHAPTER 21

My breakfast was taken in early morning sunshine at my reading table with Fogg and the kitten in attendance. We weren't able to enjoy our solitude for long, however, because Swift marched in just as I was tempting Mr Tubbs with a sliver of sausage.

'What did you find in von Graf's rooms?' he asked curtly.

'And a very good morning to you, too,' I replied. 'Ledger and pistol.'

I went to my desk, dug them out and brought them over to the table. He picked up the Walther, turning it over.

'Not the murder weapon — the calibre is too small and it hasn't been fired in a long time,' he concluded.

'My conclusions, too,' I agreed. 'He may have taken it with him, though. Or disposed of it — if he did kill Jarvis, that is.' I didn't really want to voice my doubts to Swift.

'Hum,' he grunted non-committal, then asked, 'has he returned?'

'Not according to Dicks.'

'Did he take anything with him?' Swift pulled the ledger over so that he could more closely peruse it.

'Not as far as I could see,' I told him as I finished my meal and gave the last rasher to Fogg. 'Have you sent out alerts, or whatever you police chaps do?'

'Of course,' he muttered. He was leafing through the ledger, running a finger down the lists of items. 'Sometimes there's no sum entered against commission – they must have sold items directly to a buyer.'

'Yes, I noticed, but there's no indication who it was,' I said, and then changed the subject to something more personal. 'The rapier, the one that was used to kill Bartholomew – I think you'll find it listed.'

'Really. Why?' He looked at me, hawkish as ever, with dark shadows beneath his eyes.

I repeated what Florence had told me about the shortened sword.

Swift flicked back and forth through the pages.

'This must be it: "Rapr, B.C. ins. c1820s. £12.4s.2d." No sale price noted, dated in August last year,' he read out. 'I take it to mean it was never sold. But this is only circumstantial evidence.'

'Nonsense. It's quite clear what it means ... I hope you're going to apologise, Swift. Florence was terribly upset.'

He stopped and looked at me. 'Sent her some flowers this morning, and a note offering my sincere regrets. She'll probably fling them back in my face.' He turned pink about the ears.

'She is most likely having breakfast in the morning room,' I suggested. 'Why not go and see her?'

'We don't have time. We need to go to Oxford today and pay a visit to the Black Cat Club.'

'I've got other things to do, old chap,' I told him, my mind being on the Long Gallery.

'They've started decorating the house for the wedding,' Swift replied.

I looked at him. 'Ah, well …' Images of women in full cry with armfuls of flowers came to mind. 'Very well, I'll come. But not until you've made your peace with Florence. Least you can do, Swift.'

'Very well. I'll go.' He pulled the belt of his trench coat tighter, then hesitated.

'What?'

'Should I give her more time? You know, to calm down.'

'*Go*, Swift.'

He turned and went.

Dicks came in almost on his heels.

'Brought another set of cups, sir. Thought the Inspector would like some tea.' He placed the china on the desk and began setting out the crockery.

'He's on a mission, Dicks.'

'Lady Florence, sir?' He tided the breakfast tray as he spoke.

'How did you know?'

'The maids chatter. They think they make a handsome couple – you know what girls are like, sir.' He had moved to the bed and was smoothing the sheets and shaking the drapes, then tying them back to the bedposts.

'Yes.' I opened my notebook and began jotting down a few thoughts, and then paused to wonder again how I could gain entry to the Long Gallery.

'Dicks,' I said.

'Sir?' He was brushing out the hearth.

'I believe the preparations have started for tomorrow's wedding?'

'Oh, sir, it's going to be marvellous.' He turned to look at me, eyes bright with enthusiasm. 'The ballroom is coming on a treat and the hall is full of flowers. We're starting on the dining room after lunch. Cold collation for the family tonight, sir, before the opera.'

I looked askance at him but he'd returned to setting the fire. 'Is Benson overseeing any of this?'

'He is, sir. He is directing the footmen in the dining room while Lady Ruth is commanding the chapel, and then we all go to the ballroom for the final preparations, sir. It's very exciting to see the house being festooned. Just like the old days, Mr Benson says, when Lady Grace was alive.' Dicks grinned happily at me.

'Hum,' I replied as Swift stepped back across the threshold. It was beginning to feel like a railway station in here. I gave up trying to write and returned my pen and notebook to the drawer.

'Ready?' Swift said, almost chirpy. I took it to be a good sign and followed him out. We made rapid steps across the hall, which was indeed decked with flowers, and more were being carried in by flustered maids and footmen as we escaped the commotion.

I have a great fondness for my Bentley, and after taking one look at Swift's police-issue Austin Seven I insisted we go in my car. Admittedly it was rather draughty, and it wasn't my fault Swift didn't have goggles and gloves. Fortunately I couldn't hear his complaints above the wind rushing past our ears.

We didn't find the Black Cat Club; with hindsight, I probably should have asked Andrew Dundale where it was. We drove around the city and eventually, as we nosed down a gentrified back street, we came across a place named the Black Cat Art Gallery. I drew up outside.

'Didn't you ask your police chaps where it was?' I asked Swift as we made our way up the front steps of the handsome Georgian house.

'Said they'd never heard of it,' he muttered. 'Thought you knew.'

A limp specimen greeted us at the door. Swift whipped out his police badge and shoved it under his nose.

'Oh, I say. Is this a raid?' The lad wore a pink cravat – what is it about these arty types that they feel they must sport the strangest get-ups?

'Need to ask a few questions,' Swift told him, and kept on walking forward, causing the fop to retreat backwards ahead of him. 'Are you the owner?'

'No, I'm Nigel,' the fop replied. 'Are you going to arrest me? Really, I'm quite innocent, you know. Wouldn't harm a fly, ask anyone. I can call one of my friends. Sir Crispin Gibbons, he's very top drawer, he would tell you –'

'Sit down,' Swift interrupted as he backed Nigel into a cramped office behind a stately staircase.

Nigel slid into a chair behind a small antique desk, rather a handsome one actually – somebody had good taste – and I glanced around. The back wall had files stuffed into fitted shelves, but my eye was drawn to a large painting on the wall beside the window, a pleasing landscape of sheep, trees and meadows. There were more framed canvases leaning haphazardly below it. Swift and I took a chair each and drew them up opposite Nigel as he watched us, wide-eyed in a pale face under a fringe of blond hair hanging languidly over his brow.

'Who owns this building?' Swift demanded again.

'Sir Crispin Gibbons,' Nigel replied. 'Such an absolute darling, you know. Doesn't come here often, but he doesn't need to because he has *moi*,' he pointed a limp hand toward himself. 'Trusts me absolutely. "Nigel," he says, "you are my right hand. Run the place as I would, that's all I ask." And of course he knows my taste. "Just buy the best and the sales will follow."'

Not only was he a fop, he was a garrulous fop and a fidget, too – he brushed aside his hair and smoothed his trousers, crossed and uncrossed his legs and waved his hands about as he prattled. 'And, I must tell you –'

Swift cut him short. 'He's dead,' he said expressionlessly.

Nigel's jaw dropped; at least he stopped talking.

'Dead? You mean … Crispin? No, it can't be true!' His hand rose to his cheek. He seemed genuinely shocked. 'How could he be dead?' he spluttered. 'I saw him only a fortnight ago, and he was perfect, as always; how could –'

'Squashed,' I told him. 'By a soprano.'

He stared incredulously. Swift frowned at me.

'A bad fall caused by a collapsing trap-door. He fell first and the leading lady landed on top of him,' Swift explained.

Nigel's eyes widened. 'Not that dreadful woman Dame Gabriel Forsyth? She'd be the death of anyone! Oh, this is too much. I have to go and lie down.' He rose to his feet and put his hand to his brow. 'I need to mourn,' he wailed.

'Sit down,' Swift told him rather unsympathetically to my mind. 'Did Crispin supply the artworks here? The stuff you have for sale?'

Nigel pulled a pink polka-dot handkerchief from his pocket and sniffed into it. 'No, not at all. Crispin never actually *did* anything. He was awfully rich, I mean quite hideously wealthy, and generous to a fault … Oh, I can't believe it. I'm developing one of my headaches …' He trailed off and blew his nose loudly.

'So where did all this come from?' I asked, indicating the paintings in the room and then toward the rest of the gallery, which was hung with some very fine pieces in proper frames, not one of which had a price ticket attached.

'Well,' Nigel sniffled, 'when we first opened two years ago, the local landowners would send a man in with something they had to sell off. Repairs, taxes and these horrendous death duties, you know. It absolutely kills the poor souls, although I must say it has rather opened the market up. Anyway –' he crossed his legs '– when Crispin started the Noble House of Opera he would leave his card with the patrons and they would telephone me and I'd go and take a look around, give them advice about what would sell and what was more valuable. The art market is awfully good now that the Americans have developed a taste for it. We pack most of our stuff off to the United States, it's positively booming.' He gave a watery grin.

'You imply that something changed,' Swift said.

'Dame Gabriel elbowed her way in. No class at all, no refinement.' Nigel expanded with a wave of the hand. 'She began to take along Count von Graf, a self styled "expert", and she introduced him to the opera patrons. Well, it wasn't long before they were cutting in on our business. And she had the nerve to come in here asking me to sell their stuff. Naturally I complained to Crispin, but he really didn't care. "Nigel, darling," he would say, "we will prevail. Nobody will stomach these parvenus for long." And he was quite right. These last few months all our old clients have come back, and I have not had to suffer that woman or the pompous Prussian since Christmas.'

I suspected Jarvis and von Graf had found bigger fish to fry by then, but I didn't say anything because there was something else I had on my mind.

'If Crispin was so wealthy, he must have had another reason other than profit, for opening this gallery,' I asked of Nigel. 'What was it?'

He dabbed his handkerchief across his eyes. 'Well, he wanted first choice on the goodies,' he admitted. 'He would say, "Nigel, if anything special comes up, I have first dibs, dear boy. Save the very best for me." Crispin was a collector, you see, he had such exquisite taste – well, we both have you know, although it's rather immodest to admit it. Naturally I held the choicest pieces for him to peruse before they went up in the gallery.'

'Anything recent?' Swift demanded.

'Not from me,' Nigel said. 'But last time he was here he was very excited about something. He said it was probably one of the most extraordinary works of art that had ever been offered to him.'

'What was it?' Swift had his notebook on his lap and was jotting this down.

Nigel suddenly became coy. 'Am I *required* to speak? Because I'm not sure what my rights are. I mean, really, this is still a free country, I can remain silent, can't I?

'No,' Swift snapped.

Nigel's face fell. 'Oh, very well. It was an "off-market" piece. Risqué, you know; and lacking provenance; so it couldn't be sold in public. That meant it would go at a knock-down price. It's the way certain connoisseurs acquire a first-class work of art for very little actual money.'

'Is this quite normal? In the art world, I mean?' I asked.

'Oh yes, there has always been a very healthy black market. It's probably bigger than the real one,' Nigel admitted.

'What was this painting? The one Sir Crispin was after?' Swift asked.

'Are you sure I have to tell you, because –'

'Yes,' Swift snapped.

'Oh, really, you are quite the brute,' Nigel complained. 'Well, he said it was an early Gainsborough. Commissioned when the artist was just starting out and was something out of his ordinary line. Crispin wouldn't tell me any more, but he said he would show it to me once he got his hands on it.'

'Did you see it?' I asked.

'No,'

'Who was he buying it from?' Swift snapped.

'I have no idea, he was going to tell me all about it,' Nigel began to wail. 'That was the last conversation we had. Oh, I shall never be able to look at another Gainsborough again now.' He howled and started sobbing into his handkerchief.

Swift and I exchanged looks. The Gainsborough was almost certainly the one from the Bloxford Beauties – something must have gone wrong with the transaction and led to Crispin's murder.

'Where are your books?' Swift cut across Nigel's loud lamenting.

Nigel wiped his eyes and turned mulish, crossing and recrossing his legs. 'Well, I suppose I have no choice but to show you. But I must protest. And I'm in shock. Now I'll be left all alone to run this place without Crispin's guiding hand …' He broke off to blow his nose loudly again.

'Think I'll go and take a look around,' I told Swift, and stood up.

'Lennox,' the Inspector called after me, but he was too late – I'd made my escape.

It was a very nice art gallery, I must say. The rooms were painted white, the floors were highly polished wooden boards. The paintings were quite excellent, being mostly country scenes with cows and whatnots, and there were portraits of horses and dogs – nothing boring at all. I strolled around, hands behind my back, peering at this and that, and then went to stand at the bottom of the staircase. A small note stating that it was private was propped on the first step. No doubt it was the fop's quarters, and I really didn't want to go up there, but, I reasoned, Holmes wouldn't have held back.

I took the stairs two at a time. It wasn't so much a bedroom as a boudoir, all modern furniture, pale silks and mirrors. At least it was tidy and everything was put away neatly. It didn't take long to uncover a couple of paintings squirrelled away in the back of a cupboard, but they were both ghastly modern stuff, with heavy lines and dark colours. I could barely make out the artist's name – Picasso, or something. I tossed them back into the wardrobe. If *that* was an example of Nigel's taste he wouldn't get very far.

I returned to the gallery and could hear Swift remonstrating with Nigel, who was still sniffling. There was a cellar door near the rear of the building, behind a small kitchen; it was locked. I had my new lock picks in my pocket and jangled them thoughtfully. I ran my hand over the lintel first and was almost disappointed to discover that the key was there.

It was well oiled, as were the hinges, and I opened it silently. Broad stone steps descended, and I followed them down into a dark corridor. I fumbled a bit, not being able to find any sort of light switch, then bumped into another door. It was unlocked; I pulled it open and stepped into light. Or rather lights – lots of them, of the electric sort, which were arrayed about the room. Some were in crystal chandeliers and others in table lamps, and there was a long row of them lining a stage at the far end of the very large room.

Behind the long bar was a picture of a lounging black cat wearing a red ribbon, and below it, painted in red, were the words 'The Black Cat Club'.

CHAPTER 22

'Hello?' A lady was mopping the floors. I may not have heard her straightaway, as I was staring around at what was undoubtedly a genuine den of iniquity.

Circular wooden tables with four chairs each filled the area facing the stage, which was a simple raised platform with red curtains draped each side. The rear wall was gaily painted with a fresco of ladies doing the can-can – I recognised it from a boisterous visit I'd once made to Paris – which, despite it being abroad, had been a thoroughly enjoyable experience. It all looked rather jolly, actually.

'Excuse me, old chap. But we're closed, you know.'

The lady with the mop had come closer and was now attracting my attention. I eyed her warily. It was a man, in a curly blond wig.

'What?' I replied.

'Closed.' He came up to me. 'I say – Heathcliff Lennox! It's you! How marvellous to see you again. Made it through the War then?'

'Um …yes … Awfully sorry, but you couldn't refresh my memory, old chap, um, old girl …?'

'Mildew,' he replied, then grabbed his hair and yanked off the wig revealing an entirely bald head. 'I was the rowing cox at college. Don't you remember?'

'Chap with a bit of a hair issue?'

'That's it. Used to be ribbed mercilessly when I tried that oil on it. Didn't work, by the way.'

'No.' I regarded his pate shining in the overhead lights. 'Never quite caught your actual name? Can't be *Mildew*.'

'No, well, it's Rupert really, but I'm Mildred here. We've all got exotic names, you know. Comes with the job.'

'Right.' I was thoroughly confused now. 'You work here, then?'

'I'm the manager – I work the bar, too. Lulu isn't in today so I'm having to do the mopping. Would you like a drink? We have some super wines here, absolutely top-notch.'

'I think a brandy would be a good idea,' I told him, her, whoever it was. I sat on a bar stool as Mildew tugged the wig back onto his head and poured some amber liquid into a goblet.

'Cheers,' he raised his own glass and I echoed the sentiment.

Actually, it was very fine brandy indeed and by the bottom of the glass I felt decidedly improved.

'I assume you know Crispin Gibbons and Andrew Dundale?' I asked leaning on the long mahogany bar.

'Oh, yes. They were our star act – the Darling Sisters. A great loss, we were all devastated.'

'You know he's dead, then. Crispin, I mean.'

'Andrew came and broke the news. Shocking. I had to completely change the acts around. Fortunately there's no shortage of talent in this town. Plenty of chaps willing to put on a song and dance.'

'In frocks?' I replied.

'Oh yes, it's very poplar. The members are all from the Oxford colleges. They love dressing up. But we're very discreet, you know. Private club and all that. Just boys being boys, ha-ha. Letting our hair down and having a fine time together.'

'Mm.' Well, he wouldn't be letting much hair down, I mused. Must say this shone an entirely new and unexpected light on the Oxford colleges. 'But Crispin owned this place and the gallery upstairs?' I asked as Mildew poured another tot of brandy into my glass.

'Yes, he did. It was one of his pet projects. I run the club and Nigel has upstairs. Always kept them separate, though. There's a discreet entrance into here from the rear of the building. Different clientele, you know – well, mostly. By the by, I haven't had the heart to tell young Nigel about Crispin. Perhaps the police might do it, they have training in that sort of thing. Sensitive – Nigel, I mean. Thought I'd better let the professionals break it to him gently.'

Obviously he hadn't met Swift.

We spent a comfortable half hour over a couple more brandies, reminiscing about our rowing and rugger days at college when Mildew suddenly jumped up.

'I must the put the music on,' he announced.

'On what?'

'Gramophone! We've just acquired one — they're all the rage, you know.' He went to a rather handsome cabinet in the corner of the bar area and opened it up to reveal a mechanism with a round turntable and a large trumpet type thing. I went over to take a better look. I'd heard about these contraptions and was keen to see it in action.

'Right,' he said, frantically turning the handle, 'here we go!'

We watched in fascination as the sound-disc slowly revolved. I observed carefully as the needle followed grooves on the disc to produce the music. It was the can-can and a very merry rendition it was. As it crackled slowly to a halt a door slammed at the rear of the building and I looked up to see a rare sight. A group of chaps wobbled in on high heels, sporting unlikely wigs and dressed in assorted frocks — one of bright green, a couple of reds, a dashing yellow, a turquoise blue and a rather ghastly orange. Some of the dresses were sewn with sequins and they glittered in the bright lights.

'Mildred, darling,' one of them called out. 'You're playing our song.'

'Oh, hello, girls,' Mildew greeted them, his voice warmed by the brandy.

There was general laughter and loud chatter as they made their way onto the stage.

A few more chaps trickled in through the door, followed by a small crowd. They all sported frocks in the feminine style, with differing degrees of success.

I raised my brows at Mildew in enquiry.

'Dress rehearsals, we always get some of our regulars, and it's free!' he said while frantically pouring pints of beer for the new arrivals.

'Rather brave of them, to wander the streets in that get-up. It's broad daylight out there.' I didn't like to say that I was surprised they hadn't been arrested.

'Oh, we have a large dressing room on the way in,' Mildew explained. 'It's all part of the fun, you know.'

Cigarettes had been lit, beer sipped and friends greeted as the audience settled in. It didn't take long for the club to develop a warm smokey fug.

One of the 'ladies' on stage called out to Mildew. 'Play it again, sunshine, we're lined up, ready and waiting!'

I looked over and indeed they were all linked arm in arm and making a very colourful spectacle.

Mildew rapidly wound up the gramophone, I turned in my seat to watch from the bar as the other 'chaps' in the audience assembled around the circular tables. We were given a rollicking performance of a very loud can-can, complete with whoops, synchronised stomping and some very high kicks. It was marvellous!

I stood up along with the rest of the audience and was giving my loudest applause with a few rousing 'bravos' when Swift appeared. He walked into the place and just stood and stared at the dancers, then me and then the empty glasses on the bar.

'Have you found anything?' Swift snapped.

'No, nothing to declare,' I told him, and introduced

him to Mildew, Mildred, or whoever he was. A number of other chaps called out merry greetings too.

Swift refused a drink; he got a bit stuffy, actually. I could tell it wasn't quite his thing so I decided we'd better push off back to the house.

We had a jolly drive through the countryside; I opened up the Bentley to give her a bit of a blast, roaring through the lanes, cutting across the corners – it was splendid fun. Swift rather spoiled it by turning curmudgeonly – I couldn't hear his exact words, but I could spot he was in a sour mood.

I trotted off to my rooms to greet Fogg and Tubbs and rang Dicks for some strong black coffee. I was on my third cup when Swift returned to disturb my peace.

'The Bloxford Beauties,' he said without preamble.

'Ah, yes. The Gainsborough,' I replied.

'We need to see them,' he rejoined.

'Ah, yes, yes, good idea, old chap. Follow me,' I said, and made for the door. I must admit I was not feeling entirely up to par, but I put on a game front.

His temper had improved and he was almost civil by the time we reached the top floor. I assumed he'd been to visit the lovely Florence and that all was now going swimmingly. He told me he'd found a considerable number of items in Nigel's books that corresponded to von Graf's ledger, proving that many of the artworks had indeed been sold through the gallery.

We rounded the corner to the hidden door and were met with an unpleasant surprise in the form of Dawkins.

He was leaning against an oak coffer on the far wall, picking his nails. He scowled when he spied us.

'Dawkins, clear off,' I ordered him.

'Can't. Got me orders. Mr Benson says I'm to stay 'ere and not let no one up. You've got to go back down.'

'You are relieved of your duties, Dawkins,' I warned him.

Swift took my arm. 'Lennox ...' He shook his head and turned to descend the stairs.

'Why the retreat, Swift?'

'It'll cause trouble if we barge in there. That idiot will alert the whole house, not to mention the murderer,' he said as we reached my rooms. 'You said one of the paintings was at the rectory, that means it must have been smuggled out. There has to be another entrance.'

He was right – the brandy was fuddling my brain. I looked at him, trying to think it through. 'Nursery,' I said at last.

'Yes?'

'The Long Gallery was originally intended as a place for the children to play. There's probably a staircase connecting the two, so the governesses wouldn't have to drag the little blighters through the house.'

'Right. That makes sense. Bring the painting,' he ordered.

'Why?'

'Because we should return it,' he said.

'Ah. Yes. Very well.' I fetched Lady Grace from under my bed and stuffed her, still wrapped, under my arm.

The nursery rooms hadn't been used since Caroline was a child, and the furnishings were draped in dull Holland cloth. My heart rather sank. I recalled the place being full of toys and games played before blazing fires while maids ran in and out with trays laden with hot milk and dainties for our afternoon tea. The gaily coloured wallpaper, decorated with depictions of ribbons, dolls and toys, was faded and streaked with damp. I could make out the shape of the old rocking horse under one of the covers, and the fort and dolls-house below others. I hoped Caroline and Hiram would pack the place with children and bring it back to life again.

'Where would it be?' Swift broke into my thoughts.

I went over to the large windows and looked around the room, my hand to my chin. We'd never found a secret door when Caroline and I had played here all those years ago, but then we'd never thought to look. I recalled the maids coming and going and realised they hadn't always used the main door. They had sometimes come from the direction of the day room where there were French beds for afternoon snoozes. I strode in that direction and found a dusty door part way down the corridor which opened onto a narrow staircase. It led downwards and had an air of mouldering redundancy. The back was closed off with a double panel that looked as though it was once an opening.

I pushed my fingers into a gap at the side where the dark wood butted up to the rough plastered wall. It came away easily: it had simply been wedged in place.

'This looks like it,' Swift said as we tugged the second board away. A set of worn stone steps rose upwards. They were covered in a light layer of dust that showed signs of boots having been up and down fairly recently.

I drew my flashlight from my pocket, lit it, and led the way up.

The door at the top opened easily and silently, as though someone had oiled it. We walked into the room, staring around us. We were under the eaves of the roof, but there were tall mullioned windows built into the length of the outer wall. It gave onto a magnificent view – from this height we could see for miles across green fields and beyond the hills and woods to the villages in the vales. There was evidence that one of the windows had blown in because it had been crudely covered with a square of plain wood nailed across the broken panes. No doubt it was caused by the storm that the Brigadier had described.

The room was rightly named the Long Gallery because it was indeed very long, and a good fifteen or sixteen feet wide. The walls were mainly panelled in simple yellow pine squares – it must have made a marvellous playroom and skittle alley; it was a shame Caroline and I hadn't known about it, we'd have made this our childhood headquarters.

Swift and I advanced into the centre where a large fire-place was filled with dusty pine cones. On the far side, the sun shone in dust-filled rays onto the gilt-framed portraits of the Bloxford Beauties. We approached into the light, suddenly aware of the jewel-like colours reflecting from the paintings. It was breathtaking; we paused for an instant and stood in silent admiration. There is nothing like an exquisitely painted lady in a state of near undress to bring a smile to one's face.

They were, for the most part, quite alluring; a few were truly beautiful; and a couple were fulsome, if a little plain.

'Artful,' Swift remarked.

'That's one way of putting it,' I replied, standing with my arms crossed, taking in the dazzling array.

'They've been cleaned,' he said. 'No dust or mould on the canvases.'

'Hum,' I bent to take a closer look at a buxom brunette. 'Miss Jayne Spencer,' I read out. 'Must have been an early bride. The fan she's holding in front of her, um, nether regions, looks like Regency period.' It wasn't a large picture, none of them were, the biggest being around three feet by two or thereabouts.

'Yes,' Swift mumbled, and bent closer to another painting.

'This one is even older,' he said. 'That's a King Charles Spaniel held to her chest. They were the height of fashion during the Restoration.'

We made our way slowly along the line – and I must say that it was quite the most pleasant afternoon I've spent in many a long day. I didn't even mind missing lunch.

'This is Miss Busby – look.' I said.

Swift looked, then looked again. 'She was beautiful, wasn't she.'

'Indeed,' I agreed. A young Miss Busby was smiling joyfully from the canvas, a gauze scarf tossed over one shoulder and draped across her strategic points. 'Terrific figure, too,' I remarked in admiration.

'Which one is the Gainsborough?' Swift asked.

'This one, probably.' I returned to a lady wearing an elaborate white wig and not much else. 'Think they all wore wigs at the time, about seventeen forty or fifty – before the French revolution, anyway.'

'Can't see a signature,' he said as we scrutinised the canvas closely.

'There's a name, though,' I added as I peered at the frame. 'Lady Eleanor Braeburn. It must be this one.' I took a step back to admire her.

'Hum.' Swift came closer and studied her face. 'She has a resemblance to Florence, doesn't she,' he remarked.

'Yes,' I agreed, and there was a touch of Ruth about her, too, but I thought it politic not to mention it.

'Clegg said something about a harp, didn't he?' Swift added.

'He did,' I said, still gazing at the lady, who was smiling gaily, her chin resting on her crossed arms, leaning on the top shaft of a gilded harp. Her body was hazily indistinct behind the strings. I regarded her face: it really was quite astonishing the way the artist had caught her expression with a few simple brush strokes. I knew very little about painting but it seemed terribly clever the way the whole portrait had been devised in light and shade. The face and harp were in bright colour, but the body and background melded together into suggestive shadows rather than precise forms.

'It's good, isn't it,' Swift observed.

'And it's *here*,' I commented.

'Yes, assuming it is the Gainsborough,' he replied, 'it hasn't been stolen.'

'Mm,' I agreed, thinking that it rather destroyed our theories about von Graf and Jarvis's motives.

'They're…' Swift started to say something then fell silent.

'They're what?' I asked.

'They're having fun, aren't they?' Swift spoke thoughtfully. 'As though it's all done in jest. And I suppose their new husbands must have felt the same way.'

'Yes, what of it,' I replied.

'Well,' he started and stopped again. 'It's not how people see them. I don't mean literally, like this, I mean just in general. They're usually seem so remote and stuck up.'

'Toffs are people too, Swift,' I told him. 'It just that the circumstances are different. Try not to see us through blinkered eyes.' I nearly added that he should stop being so judgemental, but suspected the comment wouldn't be well received.

He walked up and down the gallery again, stopping here and there to observe the finer details of the portraits. None of the ladies were actually naked. They were draped in fabric or holding fans and whatnots in strategic places. It was all mere suggestion, but it did forever capture them in the beauty of their youth.

'This one looks like Lady Caroline, but it's not her, is it?' Swift stopped in front of another painting. I moved to join him.

'No, it's Lady Grace,' I replied, 'which is most remarkable because I have another one here.' I unwrapped the picture I had been carrying under my arm and placed it on the floor.

We stood and stared at them both; they were virtually identical. It felt rather surreal to see them together.

'One of them is a copy,' Swift said, stating the obvious.

'And a damn good one,' I agreed.

'That's what he did, didn't he,' Swift mused.

We moved back to the Gainsborough.

'Yes,' I said with my hand to my chin. 'So – is this a copy? And if so, where's the real one?'

CHAPTER 23

'We'll try the theatre first. Clegg may be there,' Swift said as we jammed the boards back into place across the hidden staircase.

'I think we need some lunch first, old chap,' I reminded him. 'Rather peckish, you know.'

'No, Lennox, time is passing, we need to nail this.' Swift strode off down the stairs.

I had brought Lady Grace back with me. Leaving her there would have been too peculiar, and besides, she was evidence.

'I'm going to leave the painting in my rooms, Swift,' I told him, and went off in that direction. He followed, though I could hear him grumbling.

Dicks had left a tray of cold cuts, including some excellent ham, two large pieces of pork pie, sliced apples, cheese of three varieties, Cook's best pickle and some bottles of beer. Dicks may have his idiosyncrasies, I thought, but he was a sound chap. I placed the painting on my desk and we both tucked in with Fogg and Mr Tubbs in attendance. Despite Swift's griping at the delay, we both set off with a more energetic step.

The theatre was bursting with theatricals. The whole troupe was present and most of them were prancing about in full costume. Some were being sewn into their garments by the wardrobe master, others were adjusting straps and stockings. Lizzie, dressed as Carmen in her scanty scarlet frock, spotted us first.

'Yoo-hoo,' she called. 'I say, darlings, are you sleuthing – ha-ha!' she trilled. Heads turned in our direction.

'Police business,' Swift growled, and stalked onto the stage to continue straight down the wooden side-stairs behind the curtains to the area below without saying another word. I hastily followed suit as Lizzie advanced with a gleam in her eye.

Clegg was indeed there, shifting props under the eye of the moustachioed baritone, attired for his role as a toreador.

Swift butted in: 'Need to question this man,' he snapped at the toreador.

'Well, how rude. We are preparing for the performance, you know,' the toreador grumbled. 'It is tonight and I don't see –'

'Out,' Swift ordered him, pointing toward the stairs.

That got rid of him, leaving only poor Clegg looking nervously from behind round spectacles at the Inspector.

'Don't worry, Clegg,' I reassured him. 'We know it wasn't your fault.'

'Oh, sir,' he smiled beneath the beard. 'I'm that relieved to hear it. Been worrying myself to death, I have.'

'Lady on a harp,' Swift said.

'Ay? What of it?' Clegg replied warily.

'What did you mean, Clegg?' I asked him.

He sighed and looked at his feet. 'It were that painting – the one I found. Beautiful, she is. Like an angel from heaven.'

'Where is it?' Swift snapped.

'In my work shop. She makes for pleasing company while I'm making and mending.'

'I think you'd better show us the way, Clegg,' I told him.

He led us to the small, arched door set into the walls, paused to extract a large key from his waistcoat pocket, unlocked the door, then pulled it open. A worn track wove through bright spring grass to a low barn between tall trees. The building was ancient, made of honey-coloured stones, its roof dipping almost to the ground. It was probably a tithe barn once, I thought, some time in the past when the monks tilled the land and sang softly in the chantry for the souls of the dead.

'Come through here, mind ye heads,' Clegg called as he led us into the dark interior where rough-hewn planks were stacked each side of a narrow walkway. It smelled of freshly cut wood, sawdust, mice and old birds' nests in the rafters. He kept going until we came to a smaller room, filled with light from two large windows cut into one wall. The other walls were hung with tools of every sort — chisels and chippers, hammers and punches, pincers and hand-drills and more. I would have spent happy hours looking around, had my eyes not been drawn to the canvas propped up in the corner on a makeshift easel. It was the Gainsborough – or an exact copy of it.

We stopped and stared. The image seemed to fill the small space with vibrant colours and the pure beauty of the subject. It was a plain canvas without a frame, but the same lovely lady smiled out at us.

'Where exactly did you find her?' Swift asked.

'Behind the Tosca painting,' Clegg replied.

'Not sure what you mean, old chap,' I told him. None of us had taken our eyes off the Gainsborough.

'But you know the story of *Tosca* – don't you?' Clegg said as he noticed our blank looks.

'No,' I replied.

He turned to eye me closely. I suppose he thought people from the house would have accumulated some culture in their time, but most of it had entirely passed me by.

'*Tosca* is by Puccini – he was a clever chap, he was. Romanic it is, but tragic,' he began with enthusiasm. 'The leading man – that being Sir Crispin – was playing an artist called Cavaradossi. In the first scene, Cavaradossi is in a church painting a picture of the Mary Magdalene – you know who *she* is, don't you?'

He looked at me as though I were some dim-witted schoolboy.

'Yes, Clegg, of course I do,' I said. 'Go on.'

'Well, an old friend of Cavaradossi's comes in – he's called Angelotti – and he's on the run from the police so Cavaradossi has to hide him. Then Tosca comes in, she's the leading lady – that's who Dame Gabriel was playing. Anyway, Tosca sees the painting and realises Cavaradossi hasn't used her as the model for Mary Magdalen, he's painted another lady – a much prettier one. Now, Tosca's the jealous sort, so she gets herself in a bit of a lather …'

'Wait.' I held my hand up. 'We only need to know about the painting, not the whole opera.

'But it's a wonderful story. You'd be right glad if ye heard it, Major Lennox.'

'No, I wouldn't, Clegg.'

'How did you find this painting?' Swift demanded, indicating the Gainsborough.

Clegg sighed heavily, causing sawdust to drift from his beard. 'That Chaplain, Jarvis, he painted the backdrops and the picture for the opening scene. Had a talent for it, never seen no one so good as what he did. Anyhow, he brought the Mary Magdalene here a few days before the show so they could use it for rehearsals. He told me to put together an easel cos he didn't have one to spare, so I said I would. And I did. But I wanted to make sure the picture wouldn't be falling off, so I was tryin' to make some stays to fix it in place. While I was moving the painting on and off, the back came loose – it were only held on with tape and a few staples, which weren't right to my mind. So I prised it away and that's where she was –' he nodded towards the Gainsborough '– wedged into the back of the frame.'

'You stole her,' Swift accused him.

Clegg reddened and lowered his head. 'Ay, I did, and I know it were wrong, but that Chaplain, Jarvis, he was a nasty piece. Fine as could be to your face, then laughin' and making things up behind your back. He called me a wooden-top and a dwarf, among other things. He did it to me and he did it to a few others that I know of. And he took stuff, things that weren't his – some of my tools, for a start. I didn't think this painting was his, and I reckoned that sooner or later the right person would come and claim it back.'

'Has anyone else seen it?' I asked.

'No, they haven't. You're the only ones who know about it, aside from me.' Clegg replied.

'What happened to the other picture, the one of Mary Magdalene?' Swift asked.

'Taken away by that German bloke the night after Sir Crispin was killed. I were working till late and he came in, didn't say a word, just tossed a cloth over the painting and walked off with it, bold as you like.'

'Don't happen to recognise this paint colour do you?' I showed him my sleeve. I hadn't been able to match it to any of the other paintings we'd seen.

'Could be from that Tosca painting that he did, looks about right,' Clegg replied.

'We're taking this with us,' Swift announced, and shrugged off his trench coat to wrap around the painting. 'You should have told us about it before,' he snapped as he tucked it under his arm.

'Ay, well, if you'd asked I would ha' done.' Clegg turned to me. 'Who does she belong to?'

'The house,' I answered. 'This lady is a member of the Bloxford family.'

His brows rose in surprise.

'You'll keep this to yourself, won't you Clegg,' I told him.

'Ay. I will that, though I'm right sorry to see her go,' he sighed.

We left him looking forlorn and took her back to my rooms and unwrapped her on the reading table. Tubbs came over and placed a playful paw on a piece of cord hanging from the back. Not having examined it properly, I turned her over.

'Cobwebs,' Swift remarked. 'Or the remains of them, anyway.' He ran a finger down the dusty inside of the wood stretching the canvas. It left a pale streak behind and he rubbed the grime from his hand with his handkerchief.

'I'd say this was the original,' I offered.

He nodded in agreement, then reached for Lady Grace. The woodwork was spotless, not a speck of dust; it looked brand new.

'And this is a copy,' he replied as he tugged his trench coat back on.

'Why would he copy Lady Grace?' I mused.

'No idea,' Swift said thoughtfully, then switched tack. 'Are you going to the performance?'

'What?'

'Tonight. It's *Carmen*. Florence asked me, and, erm, I agreed to go.' He was wrapping the paintings up together in the cloth as he talked, and avoided looking me in the eye.

'I thought you said "time is of the essence", or some such thing, and we had to get this nailed?'

'Yes, and we will, but …' He ran a hand over his hair while running out of words.

I laughed.

'What's so amusing?' he retorted.

'Nothing,' I replied. 'Have a nice evening.'

'Humph,' he said, placed both paintings under my bed and walked out. Amusing though I found it to observe Swift's Socialist principles vanishing in the face of tender emotions, I really did want to sit down with my notebook and think about the strange events of the day. Fogg was in need of a walk, too, and he came to tell me with a wag of the tail and a limpid look in his chocolate brown eyes. I put my pen down, slipped Mr Tubbs in my pocket, and set off with my dog at my heels.

Mist was rising over the meadows as I wandered the grassy pathways down to the brook. There was nothing to be heard other than birdsong in the hedgerows and the low of cattle in the distance. Fogg trotted ahead, nose to the ground, unhurried in the serenity of descending dusk. We halted at the brook, a broad, shallow stream where swans would sometimes glide by, barely causing a ripple on the still waters. I woke Tubbs and set him on the grass, and sat down beside him. Fogg came to join us and we stared into the distance until the kitten spotted a small frog and jumped on it. He trapped it under a paw, then didn't know what to do. I distracted him with a piece of long grass, waggling it under his nose until the frog escaped. I listened to the toll of church bells ringing the hour as I unravelled the mystery of murders in my mind. Then I gathered up my little family and returned to the house with a heavy tread and a heavier heart. I deduced what had happened and what was yet to happen. And I realised that I would have to act soon if I was going to prevent another murder.

Dicks had been in my rooms and left a fresh saucer of milk for Tubbs and a bowl of choice cuts for Fogg. I picked out some liver for the kitten as he was growing by the day, then gave them each their respective meals. I rang the bell for my own dinner and sat at my desk before my notebook. By the time I'd run out of ink, Dicks had still not appeared. I rang the bell again and read back over my jottings. Most of it made sense although there were a few questions that remained unanswered. I underlined the name of the murderer. Perhaps I should use the word assassin rather than murderer? I mused. Or executioner?

'Lennox.' Caroline walked in without so much as a by-your-leave and addressed my back. 'Are you coming?'

'No,' I replied as I blotted my page. 'Things to do.'

'Nonsense. Supper is on the table, it's all ready for us. Do come along,' she ordered me.

'Where's Dicks?'

'Busy. Everyone is busy. I'm not going unless you come with me, Lennox.' She sounded just as she had as a girl – bossy and annoying.

'Look, old stick …' I turned to face her and she

suddenly smiled, her eyes shining. She looked radiant and terribly happy.

'I'm getting married tomorrow, Lennox.'

I closed my book, rose to my feet and walked over to her, then caught her up and twirled her around in my arms. 'And I think it's marvellous.'

'Come on,' she took my hand. 'Be happy *with* me – with all of us. Enough skulking in your room, you old crum-dudgeon.'

I laughed at the name she used to call me when we were children.

We went downstairs, her arm tucked in mine.

'I'm sorry if I've been cross with you about the detecting, Lennox,' she said.

I looked at her, surprised to hear her apologise, as it wasn't in her nature. 'Couldn't leave murder unaccounted for, old thing,' I told her. 'Done my best to keep it out of the house, you know.'

'Daddy was pleased you dug up Bartholomew, he told me so. Miss Busby, too. She took him under her wing when he was a child. He was an awkward sort, always being teased by the other children.'

I stopped on a step and stared at her. 'Miss Busby knew Bartholomew as a child?'

'Yes, didn't she tell you? His father was Chaplain here before the War – quite a while before, actually. He brought Jeremy with him, sent him to the local school. Miss Busby taught him until they left a few years later.'

She tugged me on downstairs, she with a light step

and I in deep thought. We passed through the flower-festooned hallway and then the open French windows and onto the long, broad terrace behind the house.

Small jars of flickering candles had been placed along the table, which had been laid with care and fine cloth and bore platters of delicately cut sandwiches, slices of cold cuts, piled bowls of fruits, pastries, fresh-baked bread rolls, champagne on ice and all the delicacies the house could muster.

Everyone was present: the Brigadier sat in an upright chair from the house, Kalo at his side; Swift was self-consciously holding Florence's hand; Ford was smiling at Ruth, who looked prim as usual. Hiram grinned broadly when he saw us arrive.

'I've winkled him out of his hole,' Caroline called out.

They greeted me warmly, with pecks on the cheek and glad hands shaken.

Damn it, I thought, I didn't want to spoil all this.

CHAPTER 24

Cyril Fletcher was right about opera – it was ear-shattering stuff. In such a small theatre *Carmen* could give the eardrums a serious rattling. Lizzie threw herself into the role of the gypsy femme fatale, a part for which she seemed entirely suited. Andrew was the hapless suitor and Dame Gabriel had been demoted to Second Maiden or something because she was only a soprano and Carmen was a mezzo-soprano. I assumed it to be an operatic conceit, as they both sounded the same to me.

Four hours in a hard chair surrounded by fidgeting farmers and friends was an experience I sincerely hoped never to repeat. Miss Busby invited me to sit with her; she arrived with the crowd of attendees just as we finished our cold collation on the terrace. She did try to explain the plot, but I can't say I took in much of it, as it was rather complicated and my mind was elsewhere.

I looked around the full house and spotted Clegg on his three-legged stool at the back, a beatific beam on his face. The best bit was the 'March Of The Toreadors', which was pretty rousing stuff. I was still humming the tune to myself after I'd escaped the throng. I was planning to retreat to the peace and quiet of my rooms, when I was waylaid by Hiram and Ford, with Swift in tow.

'It's my last night of freedom, Lennox, and I think we men should take a drink together,' he drawled.

'Erm, right o, old chap. Best make it a quick one, though – your bride will have my hide if I don't get you to the altar in good fettle tomorrow.'

'She sure will,' Hiram laughed as he put his arm around my shoulders and led us back to the drawing room. A fire was lit and burning brightly, decanters and glasses were set on a low table surrounded by sofas and deep wing chairs. One brandy led to another – Ford and Hiram soaked the stuff up without, apparently, much effect. Swift and I, on the other hand, became merrily and completely soused. I staggered to my bed some time later and slept very soundly indeed.

Dicks woke me with eager cheerfulness the next morning. He placed my breakfast tray on the reading table and pulled the curtains wide.

'Isn't it wonderful, sir. The whole house is brimful with excitement – can't wait to see Lady Caroline, sir. We're all going to line up as she goes through to the chapel with the bridesmaids and the Brigadier. Then, when the ceremony is done and the bride and groom come back through the hall, we've got rose petals to throw over their heads from up on the stairs. Lady Ruth has organised it – baskets full of them, there are. It's going to be truly memorable, sir.'

'Dicks?'

'Yes, sir?' he said as he clattered and banged cups and whatnots about. 'Where are the headache powders?' I asked, pulling on my dressing gown.

'Top drawer of your bedside cabinet, sir … And the chapel is draped with garlands. There's swathes of silk and lace woven with pink and white roses along the walls. And the ballroom looks like it's straight out of a fairytale, sir. There are real cherry-blossom trees in pots, and Lady Ruth has had huge flower arrangements specially made –'

'Dicks,' I cut in, 'if you don't be quiet I'm going to have to shoot you,' I told him as I rummaged in the drawer. 'Or myself.'

He shut up, eyed me with a wry grin, then proceeded to quietly feed Fogg and Mr Tubbs and finally went off to join the bustle below.

Bacon, egg, sausages and copious amounts of fried bread, plus the powders, improved my hangover but not my enthusiasm for the day's events. Fogg demanded a quick dash to the front lawn, and as we raced down and then back up the stairs, I pondered the question uppermost in my mind: *How long before the next death?* I didn't think the murderer would kill before the wedding, but I doubted they'd let the day pass before the final execution took place. I had to act before they did.

Swift walked in as I was shrugging on my shooting jacket. Fogg greeted him with a woof and a wag of the tail; I managed a grunt.

'No news on von Graf?' he asked.

'Not in the house,' I replied. 'Your chaps heard anything?'

'No sign of him. Um, don't have anything for a *headache*, do you, Lennox? They've invited me to the wedding and I'm not ...'

I tossed him the powders and pointed towards the water jug. He helped himself as I eyed him.

'Swift ...'

'What?'

'I think I know where he is.'

'Von Graf?'

'Yes.'

'Where?'

'I'll show you,' I said, and led the way toward the door.

Swift finished his powders, placed the glass on the table, tightened the belt on his trench coat and followed me out. Fogg was at our heels but I explained to him that he wouldn't like it and sent him back to join Tubbs in his basket.

We strode up the hill, the fresh air clearing our heads. A thin sun was emerging through wispy clouds; pale mist lay wreathed in the hollows. Crows squawked from treetops and a blackbird suddenly trilled a song from the roof of the mausoleum as we passed the chantry graveyard. The rectory was shuttered up, probably by the police after they'd searched it on the day of Jarvis's murder. But the key was still under the upturned flowerpot and I retrieved it, Swift watching me closely as I did.

Despite my best efforts, the door squeaked as I pushed it open and we halted on the threshold to listen for signs of life. Swift shook his head. Hearing nothing, we trod quietly into the messy kitchen and then the stink hit us. It wasn't as bad as the stench from poor Bartholomew, but it was still pretty putrid.

'Tells its own story,' Swift remarked, all efforts to remain silent rendered redundant.

Von Graf was slumped in a chair near the empty easel in the far corner of the room. We walked over and looked down at him.

'Been here a few days,' Swift said.

'Mm,' I replied. 'He's wearing the same clothes I last saw him in.'

'When was that?'

'The day Jarvis was murdered. He cornered me at lunch so I told him about the killing. He seemed shocked.'

'Looks shocked now,' Swift remarked, leaning in to scrutinise the corpse more closely.

Von Graf's skin had taken on a sickly grey hue. His eyes were blue glazed and slightly protruding, his gaping mouth showing a few gold fillings and a lolling, bluish-grey tongue. Death did not become him, although in my view he damn well deserved it.

'Shot,' Swift remarked, carefully examining the expanse of blackened blood around a large hole made in von Graf's expensive shirt.

Another sword had been left beside the corpse. It had been driven, point first, into the bare wooden floorboards.

'I'd say the sword is identical to the rapier left next to Jarvis,' I remarked, eyeing the Bloxford insignia on the hilt.

'Yes,' Swift replied. 'Probably the other half of the duelling pair.'

'The bullet went right through his heart, by the looks of it.'

'And out the other side,' Swift added as he peered around the back.

'Must have come up here after your Bobbies had searched the place,' I said. 'And the killer followed him.'

Swift used his pen to lift aside the flap of von Graf's jacket. Flakes of dried blood fell off and spun away as he exposed the lining. There was nothing to see so he tried the other side, and in the inside pocket found a small, robust-looking key.

'It's from a safe deposit,' Swift observed.

'Mm.' I recognised it as such. 'Need the box number and bank.'

'I do know that, Lennox,' Swift remarked dryly.

He continued searching but nothing more came to light. He stuffed the key in his pocket, his brow furrowed.

I pulled out my fob watch and noted the time. 'Must be going, old chap. And you'll have to be quick, too, if you want to make the ceremony.'

'Give my regrets if I'm not there, will you. It's going to take a while to explain this to Watson and his crew. They're becoming irritatingly enthusiastic about murder enquiries.'

'Swift …' I began.

He turned to look at me.

'I could do with you at the house,' I continued. 'I

know who did this and I'm going to expose the murderer today.'

'Lennox, you can't. They're getting married, for God's sake.'

'No choice, Swift,' I said. 'Look, I need the evidence. Those letters and the rapiers – not the plank, it's a bit of a heavy handful. But I do need the rest. Please, old man.'

He stared at me, consternation in his eyes under a heavy frown, and then asked, 'Tell me who you think did it!'

I stopped in the doorway, paused in thought, then said. 'Very well, I will, but only if you will keep the name to yourself until afterwards.'

Swift continued to stare at me. 'What about this?'

I nodded. 'Including this — don't report it to Watson – not yet. Wait until this day's over, would you?'

He thought about it for a moment more, then reluctantly gave his agreement. 'But not a minute longer,' he warned me.

'Fine,' I replied, and told him who did it, watched his face fall, then turned on my heel and strode down the hill as he gazed after me.

I barely had ten minutes to change and present myself for duty. Dicks was on tenterhooks as I gained my rooms.

'Sir, sir, you have to hurry.'

'Quickly now, hand me the rig, will you.'

He had my best formal morning suit ready, including grey tails, white waistcoat, notch collar and white bow-tie. He helped me into it, then grabbed the topper off the shelf.

'It's got mould on it, sir.' He frowned in consternation as he turned it around in his hands.

'Give it a quick dusting, then, there's a good chap,' I told him, and he grinned, briskly brushed it down and handed it to me with a wide smile.

Hiram strode in. 'Ready?' he asked. He was looking rather serious, probably had a touch of nerves.

'Greeting, old chap,' I replied as I pulled on white gloves. 'As you can see.'

'The ring?' he asked.

'Damn – just a minute.' I found the box he'd given me in the desk drawer. Tubbs jumped in as I tried to close it and started flipping out the pens.

'Dicks.' I turned to him. 'He's all yours.'

Hiram and I took the stairs at a smart pace and looked down to see a crowd assembling in the hall. Apart from the servants, many of the guests were arriving and were being directed through to the chapel. Ruth must have been lying in wait, she came straight over to us as we stepped onto the black and white chequered tiles of the hall.

'Hiram,' she uttered, and stopped. I'd swear she had a tear in her eye. She broke into a smile and reached up to embrace him. 'Hiram, you look simply glorious.'

'Gee, thanks, Ma,' he returned.

Ford found us, too, and shook my hand vigorously before turning to his son and dragging him into a bear hug.

We extracted ourselves and made our way through the crowd to the chapel, which, as Dicks had described, was liberally garlanded with wreaths and whatnots, and looking really rather splendid.

Candles had been lit in the sconces and the scent of beeswax mingled with the fragrance of abundant roses. Sunlight shone through the vibrantly coloured glass and the gilded frescos on the ceiling glinted in iridescent hues. More people crowded in, chattering quietly as they shuffled into the pews.

Hiram stood squarely facing the altar as the vicar from the village offered a muted greeting. He whispered a few words to the groom while I looked around at the congregation. Ruth and Ford took their places behind us, he wearing much the same get up as Hiram and myself, and she very smart in a tailored purple frock with a large diamond brooch in the form of a thistle and crown. Miss Busby arrived looking altogether prettier and a lot less expensive in lavender blue. She gave me a bright smile and a cheery wave, which I returned, provoking a frown from Ruth.

The assembled were generally colourful, some highly polished in the latest glitzy fashions while the locals wore their Sunday-best tweeds and moleskin, and gazed around in wonder. I recognised a few faces from my and Caroline's past, mostly from our fox hunting days. Couldn't recall any names, but I suspected that if they each mounted their horse I'd have placed them all instantly.

A note was struck on the organ, catching everyone's attention, and the crowd fell into a hush, peering around toward the doors. Hiram remained stock-still at the altar and the vicar cleared his throat.

Suddenly the chapel bells rang out a tuneful clamour and more organ music struck up. The low hum of whispering suddenly became a gasp as the bride finally appeared, veiled in white, a coronet of pale pink roses on her head and a matching bouquet in hand. She glided down the aisle, her arm supported by the Brigadier, smartly turned out in full dress uniform — upright, stern, and very proud beside her. Florence and the other two bridesmaids followed wearing the palest pink silk, their hair woven with ribbons and roses. They made a truly beautiful procession, marred only slightly by a mulish-looking pageboy who sulked along behind the girls, scowling at the guests.

Hiram turned to face Caroline as she arrived at his side. The Brigadier formally placed her hand in her groom's, and then she lifted her veil to gaze up at him. She smiled a dazzling smile as he grinned down at her, the light of love in both their eyes. A sigh echoed around the room as everyone watched the young couple, then drew their collective handkerchiefs and settled down to enjoy the spectacle.

Can't say I'm much of a judge of the like, but by the sniffles, sighs and smiles I'd say it went off rather well. I handed the ring over when asked and was thereafter redundant, so it didn't seem particularly onerous. Can't imagine what was in the two pages of tasks Ruth had given me – really, some people do make a fuss about nothing. The whole caboodle drew to an end, the music played and we followed the happy couple through the hall, where rose petals were tossed in gay abandon upon our heads, a shower of fragrant delicacy and very prettily done.

Swift found me on the terrace sipping champagne.

'Lennox.'

'Swift?'

'What are you going to do?'

'Finish my drink.'

'Then what?'

'Tell Hiram to gather the family in the drawing room in half an hour.'

'Is that all?' He shook his head at a proffered glass of bubbly.

'No. You need to find Dame Gabriel and Andrew Dundale, too. Did you bring the pieces of evidence?'

'Yes, left them in the drawing room. I'm really not sure about this, Lennox. You could at least tell me what you intend doing.' He scowled at me.

'It's a *fishing* expedition, Swift. I can't be sure what will come of it. But we can't stand by and risk another murder. Surely you can see that.'

He nodded but looked as doubtful as I felt.

Florence came over and slipped her arm through Swift's as I went to drop the news into Hiram's ear that we needed a family gathering rather urgently. He took some persuading: only the words 'life and death' finally swung the matter.

I left it to him to tell the guests whatever convenient excuse he could think of, and no doubt he'd have to calm his new bride, too, who would be livid. I went off with a heavy heart to retrieve the two Beauties from under my bed.

CHAPTER 25

It took an hour to get them all gathered in the drawing room. Caroline had given me some very choice words as she stalked in, still decked in her white wedding finery and looking quite delightful despite the fury in her eyes.

'Lennox,' she stormed. 'What do you think you are *doing*?'

Ruth came over to join her in battle. 'How dare you, young man. Do you know how long all this has taken to arrange? There are over a hundred people downstairs.'

'Yes, yes,' I replied between barrages. 'Don't worry, old stick. I've given instructions to Dicks and he's quite capable of rounding them up. He's going to send them off to eat, shortly.'

Swift arrived with Florence; he looked red-faced, and she had a very high colour, too. I assumed they'd had a tiff.

The Brigadier was the last to arrive, Kalo at his side.

'Major,' he snapped, 'this is a court-marshalling offence. I'll have your wings for this.'

'It won't take long, sir,' I lied, and turned to the old butler. 'Benson, would you ensure that the doors are closed, please.'

Swift came over. He indicated the items of evidence on the reading table – the sheaf of faked papers, the black-bound ledger, two wrapped canvases and the three shining swords – all illuminated by bright sunshine slanting through mullioned windows. 'Everything's there. You'd better know what you're doing, Lennox,' he warned. There wasn't much I could say in reply, because I wasn't sure that I knew either.

I'd had the sofas and chairs arranged in a semi-circle facing me, and the fire lit, despite the sun falling into the room, because I'd no idea how long we'd be here. The Brigadier, impeccable in his Army uniform, sat alone on a small, upright sofa in the centre; Kalo stood behind him. Miss Busby was closest to me. She looked bright and inquisitive and excited by the drama – she was the only one who was. Ford and Ruth Chisholm, frowning and angry, were seated next to her on the large, comfortable couch, then Hiram and Caroline on the smaller sofa, Caroline's white bridal gown billowing about her.

On the opposite side, nearest the doors, were the two opera singers. Andrew Dundale looked like a dyspeptic cherub in a dark red velvet jacket and black corduroys. Dame Gabriel was beside him, rather more subdued in a muted green outfit that had seen better days. They both looked as though they were dressed for travelling, which no doubt they were, now that their operatic duties were done.

Swift and Florence sat together. He reached for her hand and she allowed him to take it, reconciled, although they were both looking daggers at me. Actually, they all were. Benson remained behind me so I couldn't see his expression but I imagined he was as surprised as everyone else to be here.

'Ladies and gentlemen,' I began. 'I do apologise for this interruption to the day. I will not keep you any longer than is necessary.' I reached for the old rapier, the one from Braeburn Castle, and picked it up, turning it over in my hands, and then placed it down again. 'The reason we are here is because there is a murderer in this room and before this day is ended they have every intention of killing again. I will not stand by and allow that to happen.' Shocked murmurs rose among them and I held my hand up for silence, looking at each of them as I did so.

'Innocent blood has been shed and murder has followed upon murder.' I paused momentarily, then continued. 'This story begins during the War with the meeting of two men, neither of whom held a scruple between them. Jarvis and Count Gustav von Graf met while they were both attached to a Scottish Highlanders regiment. Geoffrey Jarvis had indeed been a priest, but he was killed in a bombing raid. His brother, Simon, stole his dead brother's papers, and his identity with them. What better position to establish false trust and respectability than as a chaplain. Jarvis used this fraudulent identity for the rest of his life for exactly that purpose.' The eyes of everyone in the room were now fixed firmly upon me.

'He and von Graf built a lucrative trade in looted art. The soldiers supplied it, Jarvis made any necessary repairs, and von Graf sold it. Jarvis was an excellent artist and restorer; von Graf had owned galleries in Paris and London. For two crooked scoundrels, it was a perfect partnership.'

'No!' Dame Gabriel shouted. 'You know nothing about him. Count von Graf is an honourable man, he is not –'

'Quiet,' I cut in. 'Madam, you will wait until I am finished,' I told her briskly, then picked up again.

'The armistice brought their business to an end and they searched for fresh pigeons to pluck. They had encountered the Laird of Braeburn during the War and used this connection to inveigle themselves into Braeburn Castle, did they not, Florence?'

She regarded me warily, probably wondering where I was leading.

'Your father had returned from the War to find the Castle falling about his ears. Actually, many of us found that our properties had suffered while we were away fighting. He'd met both Jarvis and von Graf, knew their talents – though almost certainly not their methods – and invited them to help him sell off some of the family artworks to shore the place up. He was duped to the tune of thousands of pounds. We found proof of it.' I stopped to hold up the ledger.

'Can I see that, young man?' Ruth cut in.

'No,' I said, and placed it back on the sunlit table and continued.

'Did he eventually realise what they were doing, Florence?' I focused on her, beautiful in her rose pink bridesmaid's dress, sitting with Swift.

She gave a slight nod of the head, looking a little flustered. She spoke quietly. 'He wasn't sure. When Hiram voiced concerns about the derisory amounts from the sales, I think he began to wonder if they had tricked him. But he found it terribly difficult to believe that two men in whom he had placed his trust and had invited into our home would have stolen from him – and one of them was a chaplain. When they left with the Chisholms he asked me if he should write to them, perhaps warn them.'

'But he didn't, did he?' I remarked.

'No.' She shook her head, a delicate flush to her cheeks. 'I told him he shouldn't. Nobody had believed Hiram. We were entirely ignorant of the art world and we thought it would sound like sour grapes if we made accusations we couldn't support. Ruth had been utterly convinced by them. She was far more sophisticated and knowledgeable than we were, so I'm afraid we said nothing.' Florence sniffed, holding back tears. Swift pulled out a handkerchief and offered it to her.

'Count von Graf was an expert in the rarefied world of art dealing,' I stated. 'Indeed, the Count was not only knowledgeable about the Great Masters, he was also highly cultured in other areas, being a connoisseur of the theatre, the classics and opera. And he knew how to charm – he was remarkably good at turning the heads of susceptible ladies. Wasn't he Ruth?' I stared directly at her.

'Now you look here, Lennox,' Ford growled. I waved him down with a calming hand.

'Von Graf beguiled you, didn't he, Ruth?'

She glowered at me but didn't speak.

'He was a European aristocrat, steeped in the culture you so craved back in the hot, dry desert of Texas. And you met him at your ancestral home, Braeburn Castle, didn't you. He and Jarvis were guests of Lord Braeburn – a more respectable endorsement could not have existed in your eyes. And so they used you for their own ends.'

'Are you saying my wife colluded with these crooks?' Ford leapt to his feet, fists bunched.

'No, I am not, Mr Chisholm, please sit down.' He wasn't inclined to do so, but I carried on anyway.

'You didn't realise they were using you. You were on your own quest, to discover the mysteries of your ancestry. The Laird gave you the keys to the muniments room, the very place where all the archives and manuscripts of the Castle were held, including titles, wills and inventories. Jarvis and von Graf offered their help, and as a consequence they were able to rifle through those papers to discover exactly what was held in the Castle and where it was, making their duplicity so much easier. And you also uncovered a secret of great value, didn't you Ruth?' Her colour became high and her jaw taut.

'Lady Eleanor Braeburn had married a Bloxford. In the tradition of the Bloxford family she had her portrait painted by one of the foremost artists of the day, none other than Thomas Gainsborough himself. I've no doubt you were thrilled, Lady Ruth, to find a link joining your family to the Earl of Bloxford and, of course, to Lady Caroline.' She watched me with ice in her eyes.

'And through you, they uncovered the nature of the portrait and the secret of the Bloxford Beauties. And Jarvis and von Graf must then have devised a plan. They knew that by hanging onto your tailcoats they could worm their way into Bloxford Hall. And once in situ, they had the chance to lay their hands on a work of art of enormous value: an early Gainsborough, unknown in the art world.'

'You are twisting the truth, Major Lennox,' Lady Ruth asserted with tightly controlled venom.

'I think not, my lady,' I replied. Ford moved forward in his seat again, but I frowned a warning and he sat back, then took his wife's hand in his and squeezed it.

'Von Graf met you, didn't he, Dame Gabriel?' I now turned toward her and she straightened up in her seat, ready to do battle. 'He charmed you with his knowledge of opera and his handsome looks. I doubt it took him long to extract the secret of Crispin's rather ingenious method of acquiring art through his opera company. By all accounts, Crispin was a dilettante and a collector. He had set up the Black Cat Art Gallery, which allowed the great and the good of the district to sell pieces discreetly.

Crispin made sure he had first choice of the offerings and took a cut of the sales. He was actually doing much the same as Jarvis and von Graf, but he was doing it legitimately and honestly. Von Graf seduced you, didn't he, Dame Gabriel? You became lovers.' My eyes remained upon her. 'That's why you conspired with him.'

'Really,' Ruth Chisholm snapped frostily. 'How vulgar.'

'I – we … Major Lennox, you are *indiscreet*,' Dame Gabriel stammered.

'Quiet, woman,' the Brigadier suddenly bellowed. 'You are a brazen hussy, madam.'

Dame Gabriel's chins wobbled, and then she burst into tears.

'Oh do shut up, Gabby,' Andrew Dundale snapped. 'Pull yourself together.'

'Quiet!' Swift stood up and yelled. 'Let's get this over with, shall we.'

'Yes,' Caroline interrupted, 'because it's my wedding day and I don't see why it should be spoiled by that dreadful old bat. Why don't you just arrest her and let us all leave?' She was fuming, but I could hear the tremble of anxiety in her voice.

'Silence!' I yelled. Good Lord, it was turning into mayhem. 'Sit down, *now*.'

They sat down and mostly shut up. I tried again.

'Von Graf saw opportunity in abundance. The Cotswolds are awash with old mansions, virtual treasure houses, and many of them are owned by people with diminishing incomes. Control of the Noble Opera would garner an entrée to those houses, many of them ripe for exploitation. And of course, there was the greatest prize of all – the Gainsborough. For that, von Graf needed access to *this* house. He already had Ruth's trust, but gaining the Brigadier's trust would take more than charm alone. Jarvis was already masquerading as a man of God, and how better to wheedle his way into the family's confidence than as their Chaplain.'

I paused for a glass of water and stared around me. Up to now, little of this had come as news to anyone, except possibly Benson. The poor old chap was standing by the door, sleeves falling over his wrists, bent of back and knee. I wished he'd sit down. I let loose a sigh and turned back to the assembled throng.

'Von Graf and Jarvis devised a plan, as sickening as it was simple. Murder Bartholomew and step into his shoes. And having murdered once, the second time becomes so much easier, and so eventually Crispin's death followed.'

A gasp rippled around the room as the weight of the words fell.

'That's not true! It isn't true, you dreadful man,' Dame Gabriel shrieked.

'Yes, it is,' Andrew Dundale got up and moved to another seat. 'I can't think why I didn't see it before, you wicked harpy. Poor Crispin. You're as bad as they are,' he shouted at her from a safe distance.

She blanched beneath the heavy make-up, lips trembling. 'What do you mean by that?' she stammered. 'I hope you aren't implying that I am involved.' She waved a beringed hand about.

'Madam, you are the reason we are here today,' I snapped. 'You are involved up to your damn neck and beyond.'

'This is nonsense. You must speak to the Count, he will explain. I am leaving. I will not be subjected to such vile lies.' She clambered to her feet, grabbing her handbag. Voices were raised as she rose.

'Stay where you are, madam,' Swift stood up and shouted. 'Or I will place you in handcuffs.'

That quietened them down. I waited until they were once more silent and the only sound in the room was the crackling of logs in the grate.

'Jeremy Bartholomew was killed in cold blood, buried in an occupied grave and his good name sullied by falsehoods. This was the blade used to kill him.' I held the Scottish sword high, its blade glinting in the light, then carefully placed it to one side of the table. 'A rapier carrying the insignia of Braeburn Castle. In this instance, Jarvis and von Graf had actually paid over and above its value, not realising it was badly damaged and worthless. I assume your father sold it to them, Florence?' I looked at her but she didn't raise her eyes, just fingered the roses in the delicate bouquet that she held in her lap. 'That was another reason you didn't want to make accusations, wasn't it, because I doubt your father had mentioned the damage done to it?' She looked away, toward the windows, Swift sighed and took her hand again. I felt a bit of a churl to suggest that the Laird of Braeburn hadn't been entirely honest.

'Jarvis concocted a plausible reason for Bartholomew's disappearance.' I held up the sheaves of cheap notepaper that Miss Busby had brought to me a couple of days ago, now supplied by Swift as evidence. 'These are entirely fake, manufactured to imply that Bartholomew had a lady friend with whom he was planning to run away. But he did not run away, nor did he steal any silver from this house. As we know, the poor man was run through and buried in a grave behind the chantry. If it weren't for the absence of bluebells and the keen observational eye of Miss Busby, we may never have unearthed him.' I turned to look at her, and she smiled back at me.

'You knew him, didn't you, Miss Busby?'

'I did. He was a shy young man and rather troubled,' she replied.

'Yes. But you'd known him as a child, too, hadn't you? You taught him,' I said.

'Ah,' she said. 'Who told you that?'

I glanced at Caroline, but she was smoothing the fabric of her pristine white gown and didn't look at me.

'Major Lennox. Are you suggesting I am a murderer?' Miss Busby demanded with a hint of amusement in her voice.

'Unlikely,' I replied, 'but let me continue, dear lady. Jarvis killed Sir Crispin Gibbons. I'm not sure if it was solely to gain access to the lucrative art world he'd opened up, or perhaps it was because of the Gainsborough. You could enlighten us, Dame Gabriel? I know Crispin discovered news of the portrait – did he realise it was being stolen? Did he threaten to tell all?' I fixed my gaze upon her.

'I am remaining silent.' She sniffed into a handkerchief, dabbing her mascara. Contemptuous eyes fell upon her and she shrank before them.

I continued. 'It was an unlikely and rather ingenious murder, made easier by the unfortunate Crispin suffering from haemophilia. Any sort of bad fall would probably have led to his death. Jarvis swapped the plank below the trap-door with the old rotten one, causing it to give way beneath Crispin during the last act of *Tosca*. I expect it caused Jarvis some amusement to devise such a dramatic exit for the leading light of the opera company. But things didn't go to plan on the night of Crispin's murder. As you know, Dame Gabriel, the trap-door should have collapsed before you arrived at his side. The plank must not have been quite as rotten as it seemed because it held up until you set foot on it. I imagine you were rather surprised to tumble down on top of Crispin, although it certainly ensured he died.'

'Oh, oh,' she cried, blowing her nose. 'It's not true,' she mumbled behind the handkerchief.

I turned my gaze away from the damn woman and toward the Brigadier. 'It must have taken some time for you to agree to allow Jarvis access to the Long Gallery and the Bloxford Beauties, sir?'

He didn't reply, just stared through me. 'You have already told me that you wanted to put the house in order for your daughter and new son-in-law. I imagine Jarvis played on that wish in order to persuade you to let him repair the damage caused to the Beauties by the storm. Jarvis did indeed restore the pictures, and he surreptitiously copied the Gainsborough and eventually smuggled the true portrait out. I don't know if you realised there was another entrance to the Long Gallery, sir, but he found it and made use of it.'

A tic flickered in the Brigadier's jaw but otherwise he remained utterly motionless.

I paused to unwrap the canvases and held up Lady Eleanor Braeburn for all to see. 'This is the true Gainsborough.' Another gasp went up as they saw the vivid painting, many of them for the first time. 'It was the perfect plot – make a copy of the painting, leave it in the Long Gallery where it would hang undisturbed, and sell the original for a fortune on the black market. No one would ever come looking for it because no one would know it was missing. It was as simple as it was lucrative.' I paused to look at each one of them, their faces fascinated and distressed at the same time.

'But unease was growing. Jarvis wasn't a pleasant character, and people began to see through him. Crispin died in strange circumstances, and despite your silence, Dame Gabriel, I'm convinced he spoke out. And the bluebells came into season, but there was a gap, a vacant space that shouldn't have been there. Suspicions and evidence began to mount and rage grew in the breast of one person, a rage that finally turned murderous. I'm convinced this person was then told by Crispin that the ancestor of both the houses of Bloxford and Braeburn was being touted for sale before the eyes of a corrupt market. It was the last straw – a defilement of family honour. And they realised they had not only allowed it to happen, but had inadvertently *colluded* in it. You had already guessed some of it, hadn't you Hiram?' I turned to regard him; he gazed back steadily.

'You told everyone. You did your very best to warn them. But nobody would listen. Actually, that's not quite correct: *somebody* had listened, and now they acted.' I turned away from him and took up both rapiers, each blazoned with the Bloxford insignia. 'They left their signature.' I held one blade high. 'This sword was left next to Jarvis –' I placed it back on the table '– and this one –'

'No, no, do not tell me,' Dame Gabriel shrieked, both hands held to her bosom.

'– was left beside the body of Von Graf,' I finished, and she burst into loud sobs.

'He is dead, then?' Ruth asked above the racket.

'He is. Probably killed the same day as Jarvis, although we didn't find him until this morning.'

'Good,' she replied coldly. 'He deserved it.'

'When did you realise you had been deceived? I asked her.

'My husband informed me the day you arrived.' She regarded me haughtily. 'He discovered I had purchased the three missing paintings from the hall. I was embarrassed that my designs for the wedding ceremony had caused the Brigadier to sell some of the family treasures. I believe you are aware of this, there is no reason to bring it up now.'

I held her gaze for a moment, then turned to address her husband.

'You discussed this with the Brigadier, didn't you, Ford. And he said he would deal with it, didn't he?' I asked.

His regard was cool in return. 'Yeah, and you know that, too, Lennox.'

I turned to address the impassive face of the Brigadier. 'And you did deal with it, didn't you, sir.'

CHAPTER 26

'Lennox, you've gone far enough,' Hiram growled at me. 'I will not sit by and allow you to make accusations against my bride's father.' He stood up, creating a looming shadow.

'Silence,' the Brigadier snapped suddenly.' Sit down, young man.'

Hiram sat down, eyes dark under glowering brows.

'Daddy.' Caroline reached a hand out toward her father. 'Don't say anything.'

I picked up the portrait of Lady Grace. 'Did you know Jarvis had made this copy?' I asked him.

His eyes flashed in fury, then he snapped at Kalo in Nepalese. The Gurkha came on silent feet, snatched the picture from my hands and tossed it into the fire. It burst into brightly vivid flames and burned to ashes as Kalo returned to his master's side.

'Did he intend to blackmail you, I wonder?' I mooted, but received no reply.

Swift extracted his hand from Florence's and came to join me, turning his hawkish gaze on the people in the room.

'You knew, didn't you?' Swift said. 'All of you. You knew what was happening'

'I didn't,' Andrew Dundale called out.

'Shut up, Andrew,' I told him.

Swift continued. 'The Brigadier told you he'd take care of von Graf and Jarvis, didn't he, Ford? And the very next day, Jarvis was found shot and a Bloxford sword was left next to the body. You knew who had done it,' he shouted, and then he turned to Ruth. 'And so did you – you must have.'

They stared back impassively.

'And you knew him better than anyone, Caroline.' Swift's voice faltered as he saw tears begin to course down her face. He turned to Florence but she wouldn't return his gaze.

Hiram slipped his arm around his bride's shoulders; Miss Busby glanced at me, and then back at the Brigadier.

Swift's face had fallen and his shoulders had slumped. Now he pulled himself together and straightened up.

'Did you kill them yourself, Brigadier?' he asked. 'Or did you instruct Kalo to do it for you?'

'Those blackguards lied their way into our home and then stole from us. They were going to expose the ladies of this house to the gaze of degenerates. They took our honour to hawk to the highest bidder. Of course I killed them.'

A hush fell as his words echoed around the room.

'Did Crispin tell you about the Gainsborough?' I asked.

'Yes,' the Earl snapped, ice and fury in his voice.

'You were going to kill Dame Gabriel too, weren't you? You wouldn't allow her to leave this place alive, not after what she has done.'

He glared at me without expression. Dame Gabriel let out a squeal of fear and cowered in her chair, her eyes wide with terror.

Swift stepped forward, feeling in his pocket for the handcuffs he always carried, and drew them out. 'Lord Neville, Earl of Bloxford,' he began as he approached the Brigadier. 'I am arresting you –'

'No!' Caroline screamed, and sprang to her feet, closely followed by Hiram and the rest of the family, all shouting at once.

'Yarrrghhhh …' A scream broke across the hullaballoo. Kalo pulled an evil-looking knife from inside the back of his loose tunic. Wielding it above his head, he leapt onto the back of the sofa from behind the Brigadier and from that height threw himself at Swift like a panther springing from a tree. Quick as a cat, Ford pulled his pistol from his boot and shot him twice in quick-fire succession, but Kalo kept on coming, propelled by his leap, and landed full bodied on top of Swift. They crashed, tangled together, to the floor as shouts and screams of horror erupted. Bright red blood spurted across the rug, Dame Gabriel fainted, and I, being the closest, yanked Kalo away from the Inspector. It was too late: the bullets had killed the Gurkha; his deadly knife, the kukri, fell from his hand as I turned him over. Swift was winded but unharmed; he struggled to his feet breathing heavily. Florence rushed to his side, tears streaming down her lovely face.

'Daddy, Daddy …' Caroline was crying out and holding onto her father. The Brigadier had collapsed and was now leaning back in his seat, ashen-faced and barely breathing. Hiram was on the other side of him, holding him up, preventing him from slipping to the floor.

'Benson,' I shouted to the shocked butler, 'go and call a doctor.'

Poor Benson stared at me round-eyed, then staggered to a chair and collapsed into it. I yanked the bell sharply. We needed Dicks, he came in after a short delay and stood on the threshold staring at the general chaos and, in the centre, at the dead body of the Gurkha and the blood seeping into the carpet.

'Major Lennox, sir! What have you done?' he asked, incredulous.

'Doctor. Get him now, Dicks.'

He dragged his eyes away from the bleeding corpse and nodded, turned, and ran toward the stairs.

Miss Busby came to my side. 'I think the Brigadier should be carried up to his bedroom, don't you, Major Lennox?'

I turned gratefully toward her. 'Yes, yes, of course. Hiram, Ford, Swift,' I called to them, snapping them out of their daze.

Between us we conveyed the old man up to his rooms and manoeuvred him gently onto his bed. Ruth and Miss Busby took over and ordered the rest of us out.

They undressed him and put him in pyjamas, made him comfortable on propped-up pillows, and called us into his room while drawing the heavy curtains to shut out the day. Caroline sat beside him holding his hand while Florence lit candles against the gloom. Ruth held a taper in a flickering flame, then put it to the papers screwed up in the hearth, already set for the evening fire. A blaze blew up as the kindling took hold and spat fire into the silence.

Swift came to me quietly. 'I'm going to telephone the police, Lennox. We need to deal with the Gurkha.'

'No, Swift. No police, not yet.' I looked over to the scene at the ancient four-poster bed where the Brigadier gasped for breath, grey-faced and gaunt. Caroline was sitting on the edge of the bed in her bridal gown, pale pink flowers in her hair. Graceful and distraught, she held his hand firmly clasped between hers. Miss Busby, Ruth and Florence gathered around her in support.

'We cannot let this become public, Swift. He doesn't deserve to leave a dishonoured name. He was a great man, a great soldier. I'm asking you, on behalf of all of us, to withhold this. Please Swift. Let it play out.'

Swift turned to view the scene at the bed, catching Florence's eye as he did so, then swung back to face Hiram, Ford and me. I could see the turmoil in his face, the dilemma between his sworn duty and his desire to support this family and the girl he loved. He went to one of the high-backed carved chairs by the fire and sat heavily. We men followed him and waited.

'I don't blame you for wanting to call in the law, Swift, but I don't think it's right,' Hiram told him.

'Neither do I,' Ford echoed.

Swift sighed deeply and dropped his head between his hands. He remained in that position for some time, no doubt fighting with his conscience. Florence came over and knelt at his side. He looked at her, then slowly placed a hand on her tear damp cheek and finally nodded. They went to join the group by the bed and we followed.

Dicks came in, supporting Benson by the arm. The poor fellow was almost as grey as the Brigadier, I fetched a chair to set amongst us and we settled him into it to await the end.

The room fell silent but for the gasping breath of the Brigadier and the crackle of flames from the fire. We clasped each other's hands and crowded close together as the old man's heart gradually gave way.

Brigadier Neville Bloxford, eighth Earl of Bloxford Hall, took his last breath on this earth one hour later, surrounded by his family and the people who loved him.

We remained at his side, saying quiet prayers and murmuring our last goodbyes. Eventually Hiram led Caroline, both in their wedding finery, slowly from the room as Benson closed the old man's eyes. The rest of us filed out to leave the doctor to make the final arrangements.

We retired to the morning room, still bright with late-afternoon sunshine. Sounds of laughter and merriment came from the distant ballroom where the wedding guests were celebrating Caroline and Hiram's marriage.

We closed the door to shut out the noise, gathering ourselves in window seats and on small sofas in the sun.

Andrew Dundale had departed, as had Dame Gabriel. In order to protect the Brigadier's name, she would have to be allowed to go free. But she had been a party to Crispin's death and we would ensure that her reputation was ruined one way or another. And should she ever murmur a word about this family to the wider world, I myself would see to it that she was brought to justice and hanged for her misdeeds.

I watched Hiram carry a glass of brandy to Caroline, trying to put some colour in her cheeks. He sat next to her and pulled her to his chest as she broke into fresh sobs.

'They will recover, you know.' Miss Busby came and sat next to me. Dicks brought her a glass of sherry and handed me a snifter. 'They will go away, visit Texas, and, if I know Caroline, return here and start turning this house around. It will become a happy home once more – they will bring it back to life.'

I nodded. 'Yes,' I said, though with little enthusiasm. 'Miss Busby,' I began.

She sipped her sherry and regarded me over the brim.

'They did know, didn't they. They all knew who killed Jarvis,' I said.

'Not at first, no. But I think after the incident with the hall paintings, Ruth suspected what the Brigadier intended. That's why she was trying to put a halt to your sleuthing. I doubt that Hiram had even an inkling. And

Caroline's thoughts were entirely on the wedding. No Lennox, I don't believe they all knew.'

'Hum.'

'Nothing you, or anyone else could have done, would have stopped him.'

'No,' I sighed. 'But you guessed though didn't you.' I looked at her. 'Did you tell him where Bartholomew was buried?'

She shook her head. 'Lennox, I am not the only one who lights candles for the dead. The Brigadier used to visit the chantry, too – Grace is buried up there. And he wasn't ignorant, he would have understood the meaning of the missing bluebells.' She looked at me appraisingly. 'Was that how you realised it was him?'

'The bluebells?' I returned her gaze. 'Yes. Stupid of me to take so long really. Who else could have understood their significance. Ford and Hiram, and probably even Ruth, would know nothing of our wild flowers. Florence does, and she had good reason to shoot Jarvis and von Graf, but she'd never met Bartholomew. That left only you, Caroline and the Brigadier. Caroline had an alibi for the time Jarvis was shot.' I smiled. 'I suppose you may have done it, Miss Busby, but the Brigadier had the greater motive.'

She managed a weak smile in return. 'He had a great sense of honour,' she said. 'He would have considered it his sworn duty to protect the Beauties.'

'And I was quite aware of that,' I said.

She sighed. 'He will join Grace now. He was never the same after she died, you know.'

I nodded in silence.

She continued. 'They're going to inter Kalo in the mausoleum, along with the Brigadier. I discussed it with Caroline and Hiram.'

'Good,' I replied. The brandy was warming my blood; I raised my glass. 'Kalo Biralo. May he rest in peace.'

'Black Cat,' she said.

'What?'

'That's what it means – *Kalo Biralo* is Nepalese for Black Cat. The Brigadier told me once. They found him, lost and wounded; he was a young man and he didn't even know his own name, or perhaps he wouldn't tell them. But he was a killer, silent and stealthy as a cat in the night. So they called him Kalo Biralo.'

'Ah,' I said softly. That would explain it.'

EPILOGUE

Around midnight I went down to the ballroom and stopped the orchestra, which brought the merry dancing to a halt, and addressed the audience with a few chosen words. I informed them that the Brigadier had fallen ill and the bride, her groom and attendant family would remain at his side. This gave them the cue to end the celebrations and wend their way home. I should have told them the old man had died, but I didn't have the heart to speak the words out loud.

The rectory containing the rancorous corpse of von Graf burned down in the night. I don't know who did it. It wasn't me, but I thought it was a damn good conclusion.

The next day we gathered in the morning room. It was a poor wedding breakfast but it brought us comfort as tears were shed and soft words uttered. Benson was utterly confused. Miss Busby took matters in hand and had him put to bed while a cottage in the grounds was prepared for his future retirement. Hiram quietly gave an order for Dicks to be fitted for a new butlering uniform.

Mr Tubbs and Foggy seemed to sense my grief and sat on me whenever they had the opportunity. Must say, there isn't really enough room on a chap's lap for both dog and cat however small, but they were a warm consolation during a bleak time.

Swift went doggo – none of us saw him for three days. I assume he was battling with his conscience. There was not much we could do other than console a forlorn Florence.

Two coffins were ordered. The undertaker quibbled at this, but Lady Ruth dealt with them at her haughty aristocratic best and they delivered them as demanded.

'Have you seen him?' I asked Hiram, dressed for the funeral, as we all were.

He shook his head and drawled in a low voice. 'No sir, and nor has Florence. Guess he's hurting.'

We were walking down the stairs as we spoke. The festoons of flowers had been taken away and the house swept clean of the wedding bunting. The coffin was placed on a long refectory table in the middle of the hall. We men, being myself, Hiram and Ford plus a group of old friends and neighbours from the locality, assembled quietly around it. The ladies came slowly down from the drawing room to join us. They wore their mourning weeds with dignity, backs straight and veils falling across their faces.

Just as we were preparing to heave the simple oak coffin onto our shoulders, Swift arrived. He too was in mourning garb, and walked quietly and slowly to the coffin and stopped in front of it. He made a short bow, then stood and paused for a few moments as though in silent prayer before turning toward the ladies. He presented himself to each one and kissed their hands.

'Swift,' Hiram called to him as he made to stand at the rear. 'We'll be needing your help, my friend.'

We carried the Brigadier on our shoulders up the hill to the chantry and the old graveyard. The ladies followed holding handkerchiefs crumpled in their gloved hands. Behind them, the servants formed a procession in spruced uniforms; Benson was heavily supported by Dicks; Dawkins mooched along at the rear. As we approached the chantry a large crowd fell silent as a single bell tolled a plaintive note.

Many of the villagers had seen military service, following the Brigadier to war as part of his regiment. They had dug out their uniforms, brushed them off, buffed up leather and brass and now formed a guard along the pathway. They lowered their heads and held their caps in their hands as the Brigadier's coffin passed by.

After a sad and solemn service, a trumpeter played the 'Last Post'. We men once again took the old soldier on our shoulders and carried him to the mausoleum. We laid him to rest next to the mouldering coffin of Lady Grace. The Gurkha, Kalo, had been deposited in his own coffin the evening before, and Hiram, Ford and myself had already placed him in the mausoleum in the quiet of the night. He now lay at the Brigadier's feet and there he would remain until time rendered them to dust.

Miss Busby told me that Inspector Watson and the rest of the country's constabulary were apparently in hot pursuit of Von Graf. There was quite a large price on his head, which was understandable, as he was believed to have murdered two chaplains and Sir Crispin Gibbons, a respected patron of the arts, who was tragically missed by the local operatic community.

We waved the Chisholm family off in an open-topped car to catch the White Star ocean liner the morning after the funeral. Swift disappeared again, and with considerable regret, I dropped Florence off to catch the train north to the Highlands of Scotland.

I hadn't had a chance to ask Swift about the safe deposit box, but I had searched through the ledger and found no mention of where it might be located. I doubted he'd discovered its whereabouts either as I'm sure he'd have made it known to us.

I returned to my quiet home at the Manor, Ashton Steeple, with my dog at my side and my kitten in a wicker basket. In those peaceful surroundings, the days and weeks turned softly from spring to summer.

'Sir, sir,' Tommy Jenkins shouted as he raced into my library.

'What?' I said as I put down the tangled fly lure I'd been trying to tease apart with my pliers.

'Telegram, sir. Might be urgent, sir. The telegraphy boy delivered it just this minute.' He held out a yellow card with closely typed lettering as he whipped off his cap; the late summer sun was tumbling through the windows, catching his tousled brown hair. 'Mr Fogg chased him, sir.'

I grinned a wry smile. 'Very good, Jenkins. Did he come back in?'

'Yes, sir. Sneaked in under your desk. Pongs a bit, sir. Rolled in somethin' smelly.'

I peered into the shadows beneath my feet and caught sight of two chocolate brown eyes looking back at me. Caught a whiff of him, too.

'Uhum,' I muttered, and read the telegram out:

Major Lennox. The Manor. STOP. We're home! STOP. Texas simply marvellous. STOP. Hiram says Howdy. He's starting on the Library. STOP. Then the roof. STOP. See you at the wedding. STOP. Much to tell you. STOP. Caroline Chisholm. STOP.

'You going to another wedding, sir?' Jenkins said as I placed the card on my desk.

'No, Jenkins, I am not. They've already had one wedding ceremony and that was complicated enough. I have no idea what she's talking about,' I replied tersely, although I was pleased to hear they'd returned home to Bloxford Hall.

'I thought Cook said Mr Tubbs wasn't supposed to drink milk, sir,' Jenkins said. Tubbs stopped to look at us, wide blue eyes in a sooty black face, with ears too big for his small, rotund form.

'What? Ah, yes.' I scooped the kitten from my tea

tray where he'd been dipping his paw into the milk jug and licking it clean – a habit he'd acquired of late. 'Well, Cook will have to explain it to him because he doesn't listen to a word I say.'

'Yes, sir,' Jenkins grinned.

'Bathe Fogg, will you, Jenkins. I don't want him coming down to dinner smelling like that.'

The smile faded from his face. He sighed, dug Fogg out from under my desk, and despite the dog's pleading eyes and drooping ears, carried him off in his arms.

There wasn't much peace that afternoon as Greggs came in shortly afterwards and fussed about, tidying up the tea tray and rattling cups. He was poised to carry it out when he turned to me.

'You found the invitation, sir?' he asked.

'What invitation?'

His eyes slid in the direction of the mantelpiece, where a gilded envelope stood propped against the old clock.

'Greggs …' I objected as I rose to fetch it. 'How many times do I have to tell you …?'

I slit it open with my letter knife and scanned through it.

'Hector Gordon MacDonald Braeburn, Laird of Braeburn Castle requests the presence of Major Heathcliff Lennox on the occasion of the marriage of his only daughter, Lady Florence Braeburn to Mr Jonathan Swift. The ceremony will take place at Braeburn Castle …'

I stopped with a sigh and dropped the card on my desk. 'Another wedding shindig, Greggs. Really – what are they thinking?'

'I couldn't say, sir. I believe there is more on the back, sir.'

I frowned at him: he'd obviously steamed it open and read it. There was a neatly written message in dark ink: 'Lennox, Need a best man, appreciate it if you would accommodate, Swift.'

'Your friend, sir?' Greggs intoned.

'No. He's a detective.' I stopped. 'Actually, he *was* a detective, with Scotland Yard. But he resigned a couple of months ago, after Lady Caroline's wedding.'

'Really, sir?' Greggs asked with the hint of a hope that I might mention something of the mysteries of Bloxford Hall; but he was to be disappointed – that subject was a deeply buried secret. Greggs hadn't even managed to extract a word from his nephew, young Dicks, now butler of the stately pile.

'Hum,' I replied without enthusiasm.

'Will you be attending, sir?'

'What?'

'The nuptials, sir?'

'Erm ...' I ran my hand through my hair. 'Suppose I'll have to. Greggs ...?' I began.

'Sir?'

'Don't happen to have any of that Jameson's left, do you?'

He adopted an air of innocence. 'There may be a smidgen, sir.'

'Couldn't have a snifter, could I?'

He looked at the ceiling as though he'd become suddenly very deaf.

'I will replace it, Greggs,' I added.

'Very well, sir.'

I do hope you enjoyed this book. Would you like to take a look at the karenmenuhin.com website?

As a member of the Readers Club, you'll receive your FREE short story, 'Heathcliff Lennox – France 1918' and you can also LISTEN to the complete audio book entirely FREE. If you haven't heard narrator, Sam Dewhurst-Phillips, you're in for a treat. With his rich deep voice and perfect accent you'll hear Lennox as he really sounds.

Put the kettle on and drift away to a bygone age with Lennox, Greggs, Swift, Foggy and all your favourite characters.

You'll find your free book and audio book on the 'World of Lennox' page at karenmenuhin.com where you can also view portraits of Lennox, Swift, Greggs, Foggy, Tubbs, Persi and Tommy Jenkins. And there are 'inspirations' for the books, plus occasional newsletters with updates and free giveaways.

* * *

Here's the full Heathcliff Lennox series list. You can find each book on Amazon.

Book 1: Murder at Melrose Court
Book 2: The Black Cat Murders
Book 3: The Curse of Braeburn Castle

Book 4: Death in Damascus
Book 5: The Monks Hood Murders
Book 6: The Tomb of the Chatelaine
Book 7: The Mystery of Montague Morgan
Book 8: The Birdcage Murders
Book 9: A Wreath of Red Roses
Book 10: Murder at Ashton Steeple – available for pre-order. Previewed date of publication, Summer 2023 (or earlier

All the series can be found on Amazon and all good book stores.

And there are Audible versions read by Sam Dewhurst-Phillips, who is amazing, it's just like listening to a radio play. All of these can be found on Amazon, Audible and Apple Books.

A little about Karen Baugh Menuhin

1920s, Cozy crime, Traditional Detectives, Downton Abbey – I love them! Along with my family, my dog and my cat.

At 60 I decided to write, I don't know why but suddenly the stories came pouring out, along with the characters. Eccentric Uncles, stalwart butlers, idiosyncratic servants, machinating Countesses, and the hapless Major Heathcliff Lennox. A whole world built itself upon the page and I just followed along...

An itinerate traveller all my life. I grew up in the military, often on RAF bases but preferring to be in the countryside when we could. I adore whodunnits.

I have two amazing sons – Jonathan and Sam Baugh, and his wife, Wendy, and five grandchildren, Charlie, Joshua, Isabella-Rose, Scarlett and Hugo.

I am married to Krov, my wonderful husband, who is a retired film maker and eldest son of the violinist, Lord Yehudi Menuhin. We live in the Cotswolds.

For more information my address is:
karenmenuhinauthor@littledogpublishing.com

Karen Baugh Menuhin is a member of
The Crime Writers Association

Printed in Great Britain
by Amazon

28355347R00175